OUTSTANDING PRAISE FOR CONOR DALY AND
LOCAL KNOWLEDGE

"A fast-paced mystery. The lawyer-turned-golf-pro just putted a three-footer to a sudden-death victory in the Metropolitan Golf Championship. A dream come true."

—*The New York Times*

"LOCAL KNOWLEDGE is a punchy page-turner chock-full of colorful characters and snappy language."

—*Golf Magazine*

"Conor Daly has done what no other man has been able to do—get me interested in golf. LOCAL KNOWLEDGE is fun, well-written, and extremely interesting."

—Marissa J. Piesman
Author of *Personal Effects* and *Unorthodox Practices*

"[Daly] scores a birdie with this spirited first mystery, set in the world of pro-am golf. . . . Even non-golfers will delight in Lenahan's love of the game and the fairway world."

—*Publishers Weekly*

"Like all good mysteries, LOCAL KNOWLEDGE is full of colorful characters with motive and opportunity. . . . Daly is superb at pacing and building suspense."

—*The New York Journal*

ALSO THIS MONTH FROM CONOR DALY!

BURIED LIES　　　　　　　　　(1-57566-033-4, $18.95)
It looks like lawyer-turned-golf pro Kieran Lenahan finally has a shot at the PGA tour, but a week before he is supposed to play at Winged Foot in Westchester County, his pro shop goes up in flames. The fire marshal is calling it arson. When Kieran's caddie falls in front of an oncoming train and his former girlfriend insists he was pushed, can Kieran find a connection between his caddie's death and the fire?

DON'T MISS THESE OTHER GREAT WHO-DUNITS!

ROYAL CAT:
A BIG MIKE MYSTERY　　　　　(1-57566-045-8, $4.99)
by Garrison Allen

More than mischief is afoot when the less-than-popular retired teacher playing The Virgin Queen in the annual Elizabethan Spring Faire is executed in the dark of night. Her crown passes to Penelope Warren, bookstore owner and amateur sleuth extraordinaire. Then the murderer takes an encore, and it's up to Penelope and her awesome Abyssinian cat, "Big Mike," to take their sleuthing behind the scenes . . . where death treads the boards and a cunning killer refuses to be upstaged.

DEAD IN THE DIRT:
AN AMANDA HAZARD MYSTERY (1-57566-046-6, $4.99)
by Connie Feddersen

Amanda arrives too late to talk taxes with her near-destitute client, Wilbur Bloom, who turns up dead in a bullpen surrounded by livestock. A search of the Bloom's dilapidated farm soon uncovers a wealth of luxuries and a small fortune in antiques. It seems the odd duck was living high on the hog. Convinced that Bloom's death was no accident, Amanda—with the help of sexy cop Nick Thorn—has to rustle up a suspect, a motive . . . and the dirty little secret Bloom took with him to his grave.

Available wherever paperbacks are sold, or order direct from the Publisher. Send cover price plus 50¢ per copy for mailing and handling to Penguin USA, P.O. Box 999, c/o Dept. 17109, Bergenfield, NJ 07621. Residents of New York and Tennessee must include sales tax. DO NOT SEND CASH.

LOCAL KNOWLEDGE

CONOR DALY

KENSINGTON BOOKS
KENSINGTON PUBLISHING CORP.

KENSINGTON BOOKS are published by

Kensington Publishing Corp.
850 Third Avenue
New York, NY 10022

First Kensington Hardcover Printing: May, 1995
First Kensington Paperback Printing: May, 1996
10 9 8 7 6 5 4 3 2 1

Printed in the United States of America

For Emily and Gregory,
And for my Father,
Who gave me the germ of this story.

LOCAL KNOWLEDGE

The useful knowledge acquired by a golfer based on the experience he has gained of the best way to play a particular hole or a particular course.

—from *The Encyclopaedia of Golf*
compiled by Webster Evans
St. Martin's Press, 1974

CHAPTER
1

Mike Onizaka winced as his fifteen footer burned the cup and spun dead on the lip. He stood motionless, the anguish of another defeat setting in. Then he whipped his putter in a furious swing of frustration and stomped toward the ball. The air crackled, the green quaked. The crowd rustled nervously behind me. We all had heard the rumors of blind drunks, violent temper tantrums, fealty to a sponsor who demanded success at any cost. I'd always ascribed these stories to xenophobia. But watching my opponent subtly change from a golf pro to a downsized sumo wrestler with powerfully rounded shoulders and a paunch as soft as iron, I felt a twinge of chauvinism.

Onizaka glared at his ball for a long moment before tapping it in. The crowd held its collective breath as he walked stiffly to the fringe. My caddie plopped my freshly buffed golf ball into my hand.

I cleared my mind, crouched at my coin and aimed the label of my golf ball straight at the cup. Three feet of close-cropped bluegrass separated me from a sudden-death win in the Metropolitan Golf Championship. I glanced around, freezing the scene in a mental diorama. Wykagyl Country Club, New Rochelle, New York. Present day. Onizaka strangling his golf glove, local sportswriters scribbling on notepads, police auxiliary raising hands for silence, golf nuts in all shapes and sizes jockeying for a view. I wanted to remember every detail. This putt meant far more to me than a title and a fat paycheck. The Met winner also earned an automatic berth in the Classic, the local stop on the PGA Tour. I had screwed my one chance at becoming a touring pro. This three-footer was my backdoor to a dream.

I rammed it home.

The gallery exploded in applause. My caddie danced the samba with the flagstick. The sportswriters barked for comments. The police joined hands to prevent a wholesale stampede across the green. I waded through the crush to offer my hand to Onizaka. Shreds of his glove littered the fringe, and I wondered if devotion to good sportsmanship might cost me a working set of knuckles. Luckily, someone grabbed my shoulder.

"Please come with me, Mr. Lenahan."

The county trooper stood a full head above me. Black, articulate, with a ranger hat strapped tightly to his jaw and forearms the size of Popeye's, he radiated a calm detachment in the floodtide of bodies roiling around us. Sometimes the most minor detail reinforces the reality of a situation. I became the Met champ the instant my putt clicked against the bottom of the cup. But the idea of this gladiator steering me safely to a blue and white cruiser parked on a macadam cart path drove my accomplishment home. My stomach fluttered pleasantly. All hail the conqueror.

But when the trooper opened the rear door I sensed something strange. And when he gunned the cruiser clear through the clubhouse parking lot I knew this wasn't a victory procession.

"Where the hell are we going?" I said, my fingers entwined in the cage separating the front and back seats.

"Milton," he said. "You are wanted for questioning."

My chest collapsed against a thumping heart. Minor detail, hell. I was in trouble. Sudden, severe, indefinable trouble. A minute ago I had climbed to the top my own little world. Now I felt like a poor slob who'd been flattened by an air conditioner from twenty stories and stood before St. Peter wondering what the hell happened.

I resisted the normal inclination to jabber my way into deeper hot water. I'd been a golf pro for five years, more than half the length of time I spent as a practicing attorney. A *bete noire* from my previous life was the client who tried to buddy up to his arresting officer. Cops aren't your buddies. They are paid to arrest people, and a good part of the job involves bending what you say into something they want to hear. I wasn't strictly under arrest. *Questioning* was the last word the trooper said before retreating into authoritarian silence. So I settled onto the seat and watched the suddenly unfamiliar scenery whip past while searching my memory for the last crime I may have committed. An ignominious start to my reign as Met champ.

I expected Milton to mean the Milton Police Station, but we skirted the village and turned into the grounds of my employer, the Milton Country Club. The cruiser's suspension bucked down a service road that dipped and curved through wooded hills until it smoothed out at the wide treeless expanse known as the linksland. I pulled myself up to the cage. Two hundred yards beyond the windshield, several Milton squad cars gathered alongside a pond. Their gumball lights flicked bright blue against the hazy July sky.

A siren whooped behind us and an ambulance whisked past, its tires kicking up clouds of grass and sand. The trooper parked behind the squad cars and ordered me out of the back seat. Several cops huddled on a rocky island that supported the twin spans of a wooden footbridge linking the eighth green with the ninth tee.

"Yo, DiRienzo!" the trooper yelled across the water.

DiRienzo straightened up, a hulk in white shirtsleeves towering above the huddled uniforms. His eyes locked onto mine, and he lumbered across the bridge.

"Lenahan," he growled at me, then turned to the trooper. "Thanks, bud. You want to stick around and see how we work?"

A hint of a smirk crossed the trooper's face. "I'll pass," he said. He flicked the brim of his hat in a curt salute and marched to his cruiser.

"What the hell's going on here, Chicky?" I said. DiRienzo's given name was Charles, and he hated the diminutive nickname. I didn't like being hauled away from a tournament, so we were even.

"I'm asking the questions, okay?" DiRienzo's head was about three sizes too small for the rest of him, like a football player minus a helmet. The hairless red arms poking out of his shirtsleeves looked like boiled hot dogs. "You hired Tony La Salle to dive in this pond, right?"

Another Milton patrol car crunched to a stop behind us. A police diver in full scuba gear bounced out. His partner lifted the trunk and began pounding stakes into the hardpan and stringing bright orange tape.

"What happened to Tony?" I said.

"Nothing. Now did you hire him? It's a very specific question."

I noticed Tony now. He knelt on the far side of the island and stared very intently at the water.

"Yeah," I said.

"Want to tell me what the hell a golf pro needs with a frogman?"

"I hire Tony twice a year to dredge golf balls out of the ponds," I said. "Technically, any ball lost in a water hazard becomes property of the club pro."

DiRienzo closed one eye and considered my explanation. I'd

known Chicky since his days as a rookie patrolman pounding along Merchant Street. He wasn't very smart, and compensated by casting suspicion on everyone and everything around him. He owed his detective shield to tenacity and departmental politics rather than any talent for detection.

He thumped my chest with the back of his hand. I followed him across the bridge and instantly saw the object of everyone's interest: several sausage links floating on the dark water about three yards off the island. A dragonfly danced around them, then spun off into the marshes.

A few sausages seemed like a strange reason for the commotion. Maybe I had missed the point. Then the sausages seemed to leap right out of the water at me, and I realized with a sharp jab to the solar plexus the sausages were fingers. Human fingers. Swollen, coated with pond scum, their flesh a garish purple.

I hunkered down beside Tony La Salle, who crouched on a rock with his toes curled into the water. Tony was an ex-Navy frogman who billed himself as an underwater salvage expert when he wasn't shucking clams.

"I was pickin' along when I felt somethin', sorta like a dead fish maybe wedged between two rocks," he said. Dried pond water crusted his hair and mustache. A fresh coat of sunburn raged on his brow. "I pushed and grabbed, and then it popped up like a goddam Jack-in-the-box."

"Any idea who it is?"

"I wasn't using a mask. I was rootin' around in the shallows with my hand. Probably can't see anything in this soup anyhow. I'da had to raise him, and I wasn't gonna do that. I ran down to the call box at the end of the service road. Called the cops from there. DiRienzo ask about me?"

"He wanted to know why I hired a diver. I told him."

"So did I. He didn't believe me."

"Suspicion is his civic duty."

The police diver eased into the water with a nylon net strung between inflatable yellow bladders. His wake rolled lazily across the pond as he submerged. The hand sank out of sight. Draughts of bubbles spiraled in the water.

The diver surfaced and gave a thumbs up. A moment later, two yellow floats popped into view. Slung between them was the body of Sylvester Miles. The left side of his head lay flat against his left shoulder.

Any body in a water hazard is a shock, but Sylvester Miles' grinning death mask shook everyone. He was one of Milton's leading citizens, a man who had parlayed hard work and a war hero's reputation into a chain of clothing stores in Westchester and Fairfield counties. He also was a founder and one-third owner of Milton Country Club. I could say, without sounding maudlin, that he had rescued my golf career from the ash heap.

The diver pushed the float against the island and two cops lifted the body. Water streamed out of collar and cuffs. Heavy objects dangled in the back of Miles' dark windbreaker. The cops laid out the body, and a doctor from the county coroner's office took over. DiRienzo didn't bother us again until the ambulance attendants zipped up the body bag.

"How much of the pond did you cover before you shook hands with Miles?" he said to Tony.

"Three-quarters, maybe a little more."

"Find anything other than golf balls?"

"A few clubs, a rake, a garden hose."

DiRienzo's eyes, already a shade too close together, narrowed into dark slits. "Where are they?"

Tony led us across the bridge to his staging area on the bank of the ninth tee. Three golf clubs leaned against a wire basket brimming with muddy golf balls. Layers of dark brown rust darkened the heads and shafts. The wood handle of the rake ended in splinters dulled by months beneath the water. Algae coated the garden hose, transforming it at first glance into an Amazon snake.

"I'm impounding all this stuff and anything else my men find," said DiRienzo. His tone carried a challenge, but I didn't snap. He could sell the junk for all I cared.

Tony explained where he covered and where he hadn't, and DiRienzo sketched a crude map of the pond in a notepad. Then he focused on me.

"You knew him, right? Miles was a honcho around here."

"Everyone referred to him as the owner, but he's actually one of three." The newness of Miles' death confused my verb tenses.

"Who are the others?"

"William St. Clare and Dr. Frank Gabriel," I said. DiRienzo dutifully scribbled the names. All of Milton knew this triumvirate, but DiRienzo obviously planned to examine the most basic facts.

"Did he play much golf?"

"Not as much as you would think. A round on weekends, maybe another midweek. What he enjoyed best was walking the course in the evenings. His house is right on the golf course." I pointed down the eighth fairway. Behind the tee, the linksland ended at a wooded hill. The gables of a Tudor mansion rose above the treeline. "I ran into him whenever I practiced. Most times he'd be carrying one club and hitting three or four golf balls in front of him. Other times he'd inspect the course. If he noticed anything amiss, he'd tell the greenskeeper."

"Was he out here yesterday evening?"

"I don't know. I played thirty-six holes at Wykagyl and only stopped back here after dark."

"What about you?" DiRienzo said to Tony. "What time you get out here this morning?"

"Seven A.M. I didn't see nothing."

"Do you think someone killed Miles while he was practicing?" I said.

The linksland was forty odd acres of flat terrain dotted by greens, tees, ponds, and tide pools. The only cover was a belt of brush growing along the harbor inlet and a wall of reeds marking the boundary between the club and the Marshlands Nature Conservancy. Not the place where you could commit a crime unnoticed, especially since there always was a foursome or two somewhere on the linksland at any given time of daylight.

DiRienzo ignored the question. He walked back to the island and detailed a rookie to chauffeur me back to Wykagyl. The rookie seemed peeved at being banished from a murder scene, but at least he let me sit in front. And at least I knew where I was going and why.

I gladly avoided Wykagyl's post-Met festivities. I loved the game, loved competition, but hated all the glad-handing and backslapping that followed a tournament. Sylvester Miles' death afforded me the perfect excuse for a quick exit, though the news caused barely a ripple of sobriety as it coursed through the crowd. Besides, the sight of those sausage fingers spoiled my appetite for the hot-cold buffet.

I discreetly pocketed my winner's check and headed toward the parking lot where caddie and clubs leaned against a fence. Concern over my sudden disappearance went only so far as securing payment for three days' not so hard labor.

"You weren't the only one dragged away by the cops," said my caddie. "Onizaka downed a few Scotches in the clubhouse bar, then started ranting about how the tournament was fixed."

"Fixed? I birdied the last three holes to tie him, then the playoff hole to beat him. We didn't even need any rulings from the officials."

"Hey, this is what he was shouting, okay? The barman tried to shut him up, but Onizaka slugged him. Someone called the cops, and they carted him away. Hope they book the bastard. He ain't back yet, see?"

Ten yards down the fence, a set of hi-tech Japanese clubs sparkled in a blue golf bag. Onizaka had built a reputation as a perennial also-ran. He often led in the early stages of our local tournaments, only to self-destruct in the final round. Rumor mongers blamed a Scotch bottle buried deep within the folds of his golf bag. But he'd been stone-cold sober today as his six shot lead dwindled to nothing. I simply blew him away with my late birdie barrage.

I collected my own clubs, and drove back to Milton Country Club. A ton of work awaited me in my shop. Now that I needed a week off for the Classic, I decided to set about doing it.

An unmarked police car hogged my usual space, so I parked near the caddie yard. A group of caddies interrupted debate on the murder barely long enough to congratulate me on winning the Met. My greatest victory upstaged by violence. Christ, what a world.

I heard the shouting even before I opened the pro shop door. DiRienzo demanded access to the bag room and Pete O'Meara, my seventeen year old shop assistant and sociology experiment, refused at the same decibel level. These were confirmed adversaries, DiRienzo having arrested Pete at least a dozen times. Pete locked both hands on the doorjamb and seemed willing to sacrifice his scrawny frame to defend the shop commandment that no one but staff and members may enter the bag room. Great to see a kid thinking independently.

"Shut up!" I yelled.

DiRienzo smoothed the front of his shirt. His suit jacket lay crumpled on the floor, a sure sign I'd just saved Pete from something unfortunate.

"Let me guess, Detective," I said. "You want to see the clubs Sylvester Miles stored in the bag room."

"Yeah. That's exactly what I was trying to explain to this wiseass."

"Pete, you could have let him in."

"But—"

"Pete."

Pete flung himself from the door and plopped onto a stool behind the cash register counter.

"He should have a warrant," he said.

DiRienzo folded his suit jacket over his forearm. "Stop acting like a Legal Aid lawyer, kid. You'll live longer that way."

The bag room was a large storage area behind my repair shop. The members paid me a yearly fee to keep their clubs cleaned and the caddies' fingers out of their golf bags. I explained this to DiRienzo as I led him to Miles' clubs.

"And you leave that wiseass in charge when you're not around? Isn't that like the fox guarding the henhouse?"

"We haven't had one complaint of theft since I hired Pete. That was almost two years ago."

"I know when that was," said DiRienzo. "I was Youth Officer, remember?"

The Youth Officer was Milton's idea of a liaison between the police department and the town's wayward adolescents. The YO theoretically combined a sympathetic ear with the mantle of authority. Talk about foxes and henhouses. DiRienzo as Youth Officer was like the blind leading the insane.

I yanked Miles' golf bag down from the rack. His set was intact, the same fourteen clubs he'd stored since I took over as golf pro two and a half seasons earlier. DiRienzo noted the make of the clubs in his pad. I explained that Miles didn't use these clubs when he practiced. He most likely kept another set at home for his evening jaunts. DiRienzo rifled through the pockets and made more notes about the balls and tees.

"The O'Meara kid minded your shop for you yesterday?"

"As usual."

Back out in the shop, Pete still sat at the register with his elbows on the counter and his hands on his temples. His face was the crescent moon personified. A turned up nose and lots of forehead and chin. DiRienzo placed both hands beside Pete's elbows and lowered himself until his nose was inches from the boy's.

"Did you see Sylvester Miles yesterday?" he said.

"Was I supposed to?" Pete said without flinching.

DiRienzo gripped the countertop, trying to maintain his composure. His knuckles went white.

"Do you keep a record of who plays?"

"Caddymaster does. I don't."

"But you see most people before they go out to play."

"Look, you want to know if anyone played, ask the caddymaster. I didn't see nobody after four in the afternoon. The weather was bad, so nobody played."

"What time did you leave?"

"Seven, quarter after maybe."

"How did you get home?"

Pete stuck out his thumb.

"You didn't cut across the golf course into Harbor Terrace."

"I just told you," said Pete. "I hitched."

"What are you driving at?" I said to DiRienzo.

"Just want to see if maybe he saw Miles on his way home." DiRienzo turned back to Pete. "What'd you do until seven?"

"Things. Cleaned clubs. Changed a few grips. Kieran taught me things."

"He's a big help," I chimed.

DiRienzo looked at me doubtfully.

"I would have left earlier," said Pete. "But Dr. Gabriel needed a golf cart."

"I thought you said nobody played," said DiRienzo.

"He didn't. He said he had to check something out. Kept the cart about a half hour. Otherwise I would have left earlier. He tipped me two bucks, though."

Pete rode home with me, as he often did on evenings I didn't practice until sundown. I expected a deluge of adolescent questions about the murder, but Pete fooled me by asking about the Met. At least someone was interested. I recounted how I birdied the last three holes to tie Miko Onizaka at the end of regulation play, then added a fourth birdie on the first hole of sudden death. Pete wasn't familiar with the Wykagyl lay-out, so I spared him a blow-by-blow and described only the high points. The entire account ended well before we reached home, which then left time for the adolescent questions.

"Do they know like how he got killed?"

"DiRienzo didn't brief me."

"Did he just get dumped in the pond? There were like rocks in his jacket, I heard."

"DiRienzo didn't like say."

"Damn. Sylvester Miles, deader'n hell. Ain't that a bitch?"

Pete and I both lived in Limerick, upscale Milton's only bona fide working class neighborhood. The name derived from the Irish immigrants who settled in this community of converted summer cottages in the early 1900s. The men found jobs with the railroad, and the women worked as domestics in mansions along the Sound. The neighborhood was mixed now, each decade of the century folding in another nationality: Italians in the '20s, Hungarians in the '50s, Bolivians and Brazilians in the '70s and '80s. Two-family houses sprouted among the cottages like flowers in a weed patch. But the neighborhood kept its name; institutions like Toner's Pub endured. And Limerick's original bloodline still worked on the railroad, which was electric rather than diesel and boasted solid-state cars that passed through town with a whisper. The few remaining domestics worked for successful Limerick boys like Brendan Collins.

Pete hailed from what our therapy-obsessed society vapidly labels a dysfunctional family. His father, Tom O'Meara, was a Metro North electrician who nearly lost a leg in a railyard accident. He settled his claim for peanuts rather than tough out a trial, and spent every penny on transforming his front porch into a private den and buying a secondhand motorboat he moored in the public marina. Mangled and sullen, he collected monthly disability checks, contracted small electrical jobs on the sly, and occasionally used his wife for a punching bag. Gina was a mousy Bolivian immigrant who oozed guilt from every pore. She blamed herself for Tom's accident, blamed herself for his unpredictable blasts of temper, and absorbed his body blows with incantations to *Jesu Christi*. Neither parent paid Pete any mind. Tom couldn't manage his own life, let alone another human being's. And Gina harbored the idiotic notion that if she pleased her perpetually dissatisfied husband, they all three would return to familial bliss. If ever they'd been there.

Small wonder Pete had a police record as long as his proverbial arm before his sixteenth birthday. Vandalism, shoplifting, public intoxication, possession of a joint. Minor offenses in the grand scheme of the criminal justice system, but enough to earn a gangster's reputation in a town like Milton.

I knew Pete's history because I almost became his uncle. I'd lived with his Aunt Deirdre—Tom's younger sister—on and off for five years before the road to marriage permanently forked. Deirdre gave Pete his only sense of direction in an otherwise rudderless existence. She bought him clothes, sheltered him from temptation, and generally tried to instill a sense of values. She even took him into her apartment for six months when Tom and Gina went through a bad stretch and Family Protection Services wanted Pete placed in a foster home.

But even Deirdre was no match for Pete's last run-in with the law two summers earlier. Youth Officer DiRienzo had convinced the town judge to sentence Pete to six months at an upstate youth farm for a relatively minor vandalism incident. Tom O'Meara didn't raise a fuss; he probably liked the idea of one less mouth to feed. So Deirdre turned to the Honorable James Inglisi, my former law partner and our mutual friend.

Judge Inglisi blew into Town Court in typical gruff fashion. He intimidated the town judge, insulted a social worker, and pissed off DiRienzo, but eventually hammered out a deal. Instead of the youth farm, Pete accepted two years probation conditioned on finding part-time employment during the school year and full-time employment during the summers. I volunteered to hire him as my shop assistant. I'd always liked Pete. And having grown up in Limerick as a shanty Irish kid myself, I felt an affinity for whatever drove his recklessness.

Pete wasn't exactly the shop assistant from central casting. He had terminally bad posture and a habit of leaning against any inanimate object within reach. His black hair straggled to his shoulders. He wore ragged football jerseys and faded jeans. His manners made a grease monkey look sophisticated. But he developed into a damn good shop assistant. He played a decent golf game, showed a talent for club repair, and, despite DiRienzo's insinuations, was impeccably honest. I couldn't shake the vague suspicion Pete always teetered on the verge of backsliding. But so far my fears had been unfounded.

I wheeled my car into the O'Meara driveway. Like most Limerick houses, Pete's was a pastiche of architectural styles: the dormers of a Cape, the stucco of a Tudor, and the curlicued woodwork of a Victorian. Tom's enclosed porch protruded from one side like a goiter. The blue light of a TV flickered through the screened windows, throwing Tom's head into a wavering silhouette.

"There he is," said Pete. "Just my luck he ain't fishing tonight. All he'll do is sit on that porch and watch war movies on the VCR and bitch. At least he doesn't hit Mom anymore. I guess he figures I'm big enough to pop him back."

Pete yanked open the door and loped down the driveway to the back of the house. Must be comforting to know you're keeping your father in line.

CHAPTER
2

The next day the club was lively as a dirge. The sun glowed weakly behind persistent clouds. A harsh breeze tossed the red, white, and blue bunting left over from the Fourth of July. Golfers tiptoed past the pro shop and spoke in whispers. Even the caddies refrained from their usual spats. The ambience hardly improved when Randall Fisk popped into the shop just before noon.

Fisk covered the metropolitan golfing scene for a local newspaper chain. Despite his relatively unimportant beat, he fancied himself an investigative journalist and informed his columns with all manner of "serious" topics. One story, devoted to women's restricted starting times at a particular country club, exploded into a tirade on the Equal Rights Amendment. Another, intended as a paean to a toothless septuagenarian caddie, explicated Fisk's bubble-headed theories on redistribution of wealth. Crazier still, Fisk professed never to have played the game. "If I play it, I can't criticize it," he once told me. "Someone must seize the role of watchdog." As if golf were a bureaucracy worthy of a Cabinet post.

My personal introduction to Randall Fisk's journalism was a column about my troubles with the PGA Tour brass. The facts were basically true, but the insinuations bordered on libel.

"Quite an exit you made yesterday," he said. "Or was that an exit at all? Was someone, or some local golfing body perhaps, interested in a urine sample?"

Fisk pulled a wrinkled handkerchief from his pants pocket and dabbed at a single bead of sweat meandering down the curving ridge of his nose. His interviewing technique featured a symphony of twitches, tics, and grunts calculated to annoy his victim into submission. I took a deep breath.

"I was needed here. Someone had an accident."

"That's not what I heard. A blow to the collarbone, another to the occipital lobe of the skull." Fisk shivered. "Stones shoved into pockets and shirt to weigh down the body. These aren't accidents. I understand you identified the body."

"There were several of us. Everyone knew him."

"And this diver." Fisk looked up at the ceiling and seemed to snatch the name physically out of the air. "This Tony La Salle. You hired him."

"To pull golf balls out of the ponds. So I could sell them and donate the proceeds to the caddie scholarship fund." Where was this going, I wondered.

"Such an odd turn of events." He plucked an iron from a display rack and pressed the clubhead to his chin. "You with the well documented, ah, troubles, finally winning yourself a spot on the Tour, however fleeting it may be, only to be whisked away from your triumph by the state police."

"County trooper," I said. "Let's get our law enforcement authorities straight."

Fisk nodded playfully, noting this fact for the record.

"You missed the action yesterday," he said.

"I don't like post-tournament parties."

"I'm referring to your chief rival's tirade."

"I didn't know I had a rival."

"Ah, Kieran, still confusing your public and private selves. You and Miko Onizaka have been knocking heads in these tournaments ever since the Tour banished you to this patch. Therefore, you are rivals."

I wiped my thumb on the glass top of my display counter. Fisk had manufactured this "rivalry" during my first year at Milton Country Club after Onizaka and I battled to a second place tie in the Connecticut Open.

"Why the rivalry?" I had asked him at the time.

"The golfing public needs a focal point for the inexorable Japanese take-over of American golf," he had replied in all his stilted splendor. "I have chosen you and Miko as the standard bearers."

In fact, Onizaka played the stereotypically inscrutable Asian as well as he played golf. We barely traded a word during our several competitive rounds. Strip away the rumors, and I didn't know a damn thing about him other than he worked as a staff pro for a Japanese golf equipment company with a large outlet in southern Connecticut.

"The funny part," said Fisk, "is that your rivalry is bent toward an ironic denouement."

"What the hell do you mean?"

"A little rumor a little birdie told me. Or was it a bogey?" Fisk smirked the kind of smirk I wanted to drive a fist through. "A Japanese concern plans to buy Milton Country Club. And when they do, guess who will be installed as head pro? Miko Onizaka."

"Get the hell out of here!" I winged a set of leather head covers, but Fisk ducked out of the way.

"Ta ta, Mr. Met," he chortled.

The phone rang not long after lunch. A male voice identified himself as Roger Twomby—pronounced Toomby—then fired off a rapid succession of WASP names ending with his own. I recognized the law firm as an estate administration heavyweight, with offices in Manhattan, Palm Beach, and several other communities where the rich went to die.

"We drafted the last will and testament of Sylvester Miles and are counsel to the executor in the probate proceeding. The reason I am calling is that a clause in the will directly involves you."

"I inherited money?"

"Not exactly," said Twomby. "The clause is quite unique. I believe a face to face is necessary. In, perhaps, ten minutes. At the deceased's home."

I left the shop in Pete's hands and drove across the golf course in an electric cart. Sylvester Miles had been my boss, and a damn good one. But we never became friends, never hoisted drinks at the clubhouse bar, never grilled burgers on his backyard patio, never even played a round of golf. I spent the entire ride searching my memory for any hint why he would name me in his will. I found none.

The Miles house stood on a ridge that descended from the posh neighborhood of Harbor Terrace, crossed the seventh hole like the spine of a subterranean monster, and flattened out onto the dun-colored fairways of the linksland. I parked my cart where the stone fence marking the club property line humped over the ridge. The view was impressive, even by Harbor Terrace standards. With one sweep of the eye you could take in the marina, the linksland, the golden reeds of the Marshlands Nature Conservancy, and, at the mouth of the inlet, two rocky islands forming a gateway to the Long Island Sound.

The driveway was crowded. A Milton squad car and an official-looking Plymouth pinned a pair of Mercedes to the garage door. Behind them, a dusty Volvo hissed with recent exertion.

The same rookie who had driven me back to Wykagyl the previous day answered the door. They weren't ready for me, he said, and showed me into a parlor. At the far end of the room, framed by a window bay, Adrienne Miles stretched to tip the spout of a watering can into the hanging pot of a lush spider plant. A sleeveless gold tunic reaching to mid-thigh matched her wiry blonde hair. A black body stocking hugged the rest of her.

Adrienne lowered her watering can, and our eyes locked in that provocative way where you feel you're rushing toward each other on dollies.

"I'm terrible sorry about Sylvester," I said, and the twenty feet of parlor between us telescoped back to normal proportions. She smiled wanly and returned to her plants. After a final long draught into a ficus, she glided past me, eyes averted, and left the room. Musky perfume floated in her wake.

Everyone in town knew Adrienne's story, or thought they did. Fifteen years earlier, Sylvester Miles flew to a fashion convention in Chicago and flew back with a bride. Adrienne was thirty years his junior, so words like *gold digger* and *sugar daddy* rattled behind them like empty cans on string. The club women treated her like a pariah. The older ones saw her as a threat to their husbands; the younger ones criticized her obvious lack of education and breeding. Small wonder she rarely appeared at the club. My only previous contact with her had been idle chatter at the annual Awards Night dinners. She always seemed pleasant, but plainly couldn't wait for those nights to end.

I wandered into the hallway. The rookie stood with his ear cocked against a closed door. Behind it, a male voice thundered unintelligibly.

The door suddenly flew open, and a tall, gangly man collided with the rookie.

"Damn you, too," the man said with a snort. He adjusted a small brown package under his arm and lurched toward the front door with a gait as knock-kneed as a giraffe's.

"We want Mr. Lenahan next," a voice I recognized as Twomby's called from inside the room. "And Mrs. Miles, too."

The room undoubtedly was Sylvester Miles' den. A large mahogany desk angled across one corner. Along the entire back wall, silver cups and pewter plates from Syl's many golf victories twinkled in pools of light. Across a thick burgundy carpet the size of a putting green stood a fully stocked bar. Chicky DiRienzo sat heavily on a barstool, his suit jacket draped across his lap and his omnipresent notebook on his knee. He nodded with a dopey *we meet again* grin on his face.

Roger Twomby stood behind the desk with his hands stuffed into the open mouth of a briefcase. He was a gaunt man with bloodless lips and spindly arms like the forelimbs of a Tyrannosaurus Rex. He lay a single sheet of legal-sized paper on the blotter and offered me a dead fish handshake.

"I presume you know Mr. St. Clare," he said. "He is the executor of Mr. Miles' will."

William St. Clare rose from one of two matching leather recliners. He was a former mayor of Milton, a co-founder of MCC, and Sylvester Miles' closest friend. His body bulged like a brandy snifter. Ambrose Burnside sideburns brushed against earlobes the size of quarters.

"And of course you know Detective DiRienzo," continued Twomby. "He requested to attend these proceedings as an observer, and of course the estate is cooperating, just as the Milton police department is cooperating with us."

"How does a police department cooperate with estate proceedings?" I said.

"Just an expression of good will," said Twomby. "We are all cooperating with each other."

St. Clare opened a closet and trotted out a black and white kangaroo golf bag containing a set of irons. Then he poured himself a drink and lay back in the recliner.

"Please sit, Mr. Lenahan," said Twomby, indicating a wing chair to his right. Adrienne Miles slipped silently into its mate at the opposite end of the desk. Her skin looked smooth as butterscotch, and her hard, strong features promised to age well. She pointedly avoided meeting my eye. Her fingernails held far more interest.

Twomby cleared his throat. "Here is the clause, Mr. Lenahan. Listen carefully. 'I direct my executor to sell at auction my set of *Blitzklub* golf clubs for the highest possible price. In this regard, my executor shall retain the services of Kieran Lenahan, the golf professional at the Milton Country Club, to lend his expertise in obtaining the highest possible auction price for said clubs.' "

"That's it?" I said when it became obvious that the clause had ended.

"The remainder of the clause does not concern you," said Twomby. "Do you understand the direction?"

"I've never heard of a *Blitzklub*, and I've never attended a golf club auction. Otherwise, it's perfectly clear."

"I confess I am mystified as well. I questioned Mr. Miles quite severely when drafting this clause, and he assured me that you would cooperate. Oh well, the clause speaks for itself, and Mr. Miles was extremely adamant.

"Now, although the will has not yet been admitted to probate, we, that is the executor and myself, believe the best interests of the estate dictate an expeditious marshalling of all assets, and since the arranging of an auction requires substantial preparation—"

"You want me to get the ball rolling."

"Exactly, Mr. Lenahan. Now, since the nature of these assets will require—"

"Are these the clubs?"

No one answered, probably because they weren't experts. I reached for the golf bag.

The *Blitzklubs* were the oddest set of irons I'd ever seen. Their design was pure 1990s golf technology: angular heads with the weight distributed in the heels and toes; metal with the dull finish of cast iron and the density of forged steel; a gooseneck hosel slightly offsetting the heads from the shafts. But the decorative features harked back to the Third Reich: *Blitzklub* lettered in Gothic typeface and underscored by a lightning bolt; tiny swastikas encircling the iron numbers; a Maltese cross inlaid on the clubface.

I thumbed each of the irons. The heads bore the nicks and scratches of moderate use. Bits of dirt and grass clung to the grooves. But the sole markings were deep and crisp and highlighted by goldleaf paint.

I pulled the five-iron from the bag. Tiny swastikas ribbed the black leather grip. The shaft was a smooth, shiny gray. An old fiberglass dinosaur, I thought. But when I waggled the club the shaft felt more like graphite than fiberglass.

I stole a glance at Adrienne. She had one palm open and trailed a finger of her other hand along the life line and up the mound of Venus. She seemed less like a grieving widow than a petulant child forced to sit through a boring dinner. She sure didn't give a damn about these clubs.

I emptied the bag and leaned the clubs in size order against the desk.

"The pitching wedge is missing," I said, pointing to the gap between the nine iron and sand wedge. "Can any of you explain that?"

"As I said, Mr. Lenahan," said Twomby. "I questioned Mr. Miles quite severely—"

"You told me. A set of irons with a matched sand wedge should include a matched pitching wedge."

My expert opinion thudded about the room. St. Clare mumbled into his drink. Adrienne played palmist. DiRienzo scratched a pencil across his pad.

"Doesn't matter. I'll do my best to follow the will's directions." I gathered the clubs together. "I assume I may take these with me."

"Of course," said Twomby. "You'll need them in order to arrange the auction, I presume."

"I will."

"Fine," said Twomby. "I can tell you without reading the remainder of the clause that you will receive a commission for your services."

"Who gets the rest of the money?"

"None of your damn business," snapped St. Clare.

I knew that would get a rise out of someone; I didn't expect it to be the ex-Mayor. Everyone bid me good day except for Adrienne. The rookie showed me to the door. As I walked to my cart I noticed the dusty Volvo idling in front of the house. The knock-kneed man stared at me through the window. Then he punched the car into gear and shot off down Harbor Terrace Drive.

Back at the shop, play had dwindled to its late afternoon trickle. I sent Pete home at six and saddled up an electric cart. Despite all the hubbub, I still had a tournament to prepare for.

I loved the golf course in the evening. A hush descended over the landscape. Water hazards smoothed to glass. Shadows ribbed the fairways. And for one magical moment, if you watched very carefully, the grass shifted from green to blue before tumbling into darkness.

The Milton Country Club layout was a unique blend of parkland and linksland. The original holes were built in the 1890s by a man named Tilford, who dreamed of carving a golf course out of a rolling forest of oak and ash. Unfortunately, Tilford routed only twelve holes before running out of room. He offered to buy additional acreage from his neighbor, a man named Caleb Park. But Park resented Tilford's plan for bringing this newfangled game to Milton. He not only refused to sell Tilford one square inch of property, he also forbade his only son Josiah from ever doing the same.

The golf course remained the private playground of the Tilford family until the 1960s, when three leading Milton businessmen—Sylvester Miles, William St. Clare, and Dr. Frank Gabriel—bought the estate and fashioned six more holes out of wasteland obviously ignored by Tilford. Set hard between Milton Harbor and the Marshlands Nature Conservancy, deeded to the town by Caleb Park's son, this terrain so closely resembled a Scottish seaside links that the architect did little more than cultivate greens and tees.

The three owners retained title for themselves rather than spread ownership among the members. It wasn't the normal method of country club management, but the owners realized Milton was a jewel of a golf course. The twelve parkland holes were lush, deceptive, and precisely manicured, and the six linksland holes gave you the feeling of St. Andrews. The club sold annual playing privileges like term life insurance. The members renewed year after year, and the waiting list numbered in the hundreds.

I played the first few holes in decent form, but my swing soon fell out of kilter. By the time I drew even with the Miles house I decided my heart wasn't in golf. A single Mercedes was all that remained of the cars that had jammed the driveway earlier in the day. Despite the thick green lawn, the razor-sharp shrubbery, and the newly painted stucco, the house seemed desolate, as if the death of its owner somehow had extinguished its soul.

I tooled through a flock of Canadian geese scraping for food on the linksland's skimpy fairways. At the pond, the orange tape snapped in the breeze. Tire marks left by police cars tattooed the hardpan. I walked along the tape, not expecting to see anything the cops hadn't noted. Several craters gaped in the pond bank. A swath of divots scarred the fairway where someone had practiced hitting pitch shots across the water to the eighth green. The water was murky as ever.

I crossed the footbridge and parted a screen of reeds behind the green. The tide was out, and a long shelf of mud stretched toward the buoys that guided boaters along the harbor inlet. The previous week's constant sunshine had baked a tiny patch of sand into a flat hardpan broken only by a gash from the keel of a small boat. Below a wash of mussel shells, the sand darkened to mud.

When I was young, the caddies would steal down on hot summer afternoons and skinny dip in the inlet. Not being a swimmer—in fact, being petrified of water—I stood on the sand and watched for the Harbor Patrol speedboat. No one dared swim here now. Silt choked the inlet, and motor oil slimed the water. But I still visited this beach whenever I wanted to think deep thoughts.

Milton Country Club always had seemed as safe and as sheltered as the harbor. For twenty years, no matter how far I ranged, I felt tethered to its fairways. Its parochial concerns of pars and birdies, of matches won and putts missed, of greens fertilized and tees clipped provided a brief respite from the realities outside the stone fence. Now the club had seen a murder.

I wondered about Adrienne. Will readings weren't lively affairs. But she had seemed curiously detached, if not downright uninterested. Or maybe helpless was a better description—a woman suddenly sitting on a fortune and surrounded by jackals ready to tear off hunks of cash with their jaws. Oh well, I had my role. Arrange the auction of those *Blitzklubs*, whatever the hell they were. For a fee. Maybe I was a jackal myself.

A boat engine sputtered, and a familiar looking motorboat festooned with fishing rods drifted past. Tom O'Meara fiddled with the outboard engine. I stepped into the reeds. Tom was the last person I wanted to spot me in a contemplative mood.

People think the job of a club professional is constant amusement. Hell, they see the pro while they're playing a game. *Ergo*, the pro must be having fun, too. In fact, the workday of a club pro is as tedious, and as unglamourous, as a coal miner's. It's just not as dirty or dangerous.

My contract with Milton Country Club requires me to run a pro shop with normal business hours (basically, dawn to dusk), maintain a fleet of electric golf carts (about as durable as five dollar watches), officiate the weekly club tournaments (featuring arguments as childish as kindergarten spats), and teach golf lessons. Unofficially, I am a headshrinker to golf nuts, a father confessor to unhappy spouses, a registrar of sundry complaints, and, not often enough, the object of female desire.

Playing the game doesn't appear in the job description. That's because the Professional Golfer's Association, the umbrella group to which every club professional must belong, cares more about its members' ability to read a balance sheet than read a putt. We're businessmen in sports togs. But uncage me and I can play a mean game. And with a bit of luck, as happened at the Met Championship, I can show my wares on a grander stage.

Another of my unofficial functions was to attend the wakes of deceased members. Most were quiet affairs. The women sat in the viewing parlor while the men, dressed in muted golf shirts and blue MCC blazers, stood in the foyer swapping golf stories about the departed. The memorial service hastily organized by the local VFW post resembled a testimonial dinner, minus the food.

Miles wasn't just a big man at the club; he was a bona fide war hero, WWII vintage. You wouldn't have guessed it to see him decorating display windows in his flagship store on Merchant Street or lowering himself on rickety knees to line up a putt. But if you knew about his past you'd have seen a hawk in the bent nose, darting eyes, and raked back silver hair. On damp days you'd have noticed a slight hitch in his stride, the result of an ankle wound. And that constant twisted smile? Nerve damage from hand to hand combat, or so the story went. Miles gained such notoriety that the Town Council erected a permanent tribute in the lobby of Town Hall: a helmet, a Springfield grenade rifle, shell casings, and a laminated copy of a *Milton Weekly Chronicle* story about his war exploits.

I shouldered my way through several knots of elderly men clogging the front steps of the funeral home. From all the strange faces and the blue and gold piping, I took them for VFW members from other towns. The air inside reeked of lilies and cheap cologne. A VFW banner hung from the ceiling of the main parlor. Beneath it, an elderly vet stood at a podium draped in black. Between whines of microphone feedback, he railed about how Syl Miles should have been awarded the Congressional Medal of Honor for single-handedly capturing a German mortar nest near Anzio.

Smack in the middle of the audience sat the knock-kneed man who had stormed out of the Miles' house that afternoon. His puffy cheeks and a tousled mass of salt and pepper hair loomed over the bent gray heads of the old vets. Unlike the others, he met each heap of praise with a faint but unmistakable scowl. I certainly never saw him before today, but a strange sense of familiarity, perhaps an intimation of someone I once knew, tugged at my memory.

I backed away from the speeches and joined the usual gaggle of club men congregated in the foyer. No golf stories circulated tonight, just wild speculation about the murder. The police had been unusually stingy with details, and these men, who fancied themselves town elders, were miffed at the lack of info. I listened long enough to fulfill my pro-

fessional duty, then drifted toward the door. As I passed the main parlor, I noticed the knock-kneed man was gone.

Out on the sidewalk a group of vets surrounded a Milton cop who
had ticketed a car with Pennsylvania plates for parking in a prohibited
zone directly in front of the funeral home. The owner, a bandy-legged
gent wearing a powder blue leisure suit and an olive drab army cap,
shook his fist in the cop's face.

"Go after the real criminals," he shouted. "Not innocent people
paying their respects to the dead."

Judge Inglisi and I went back twenty years, when his brief fling with golf
brought him to Milton Country Club. I was a caddie; he was a portly
beginner who showed no sign of ever mastering a full shoulder turn. His
caustic exterior never quite fit in with the staid elements of the membership. But his penchant for generous tips made him a darling among
the caddies. To us he was Big Jim, and a pisser of a loop.

I was a champion golfer in high school and college, but, being
practical-minded, pursued a career in law instead of golf. When I finished law school, Big Jim hired me as his associate. The practice hauled
in the usual small town staples: oldsters needing wills, families buying
houses, punks grinding through the criminal courts, accident victims
dreaming of lottery-sized verdicts. Inglisi & Lenahan lasted seven years
without fistcuffs. Then Big Jim fooled enough voters to become county
judge, and I headed south for a long delayed golf apprenticeship.

Since my unexpected return to Milton, our friendship trailed off to
rare beer-filled evenings. The schedules of a golf pro and a judge
meshed very poorly. Still, he was my court of first resort whenever I
needed advice or oddball information. He'd bitch and moan and yell at
me like a *de facto* stepfather. But he'd always churn out some imagina-
tive ploy or dig up the dope. Though he wouldn't dare admit it, he ad-
mired me for casting off a sober profession to pursue a dream. Catch him

at a candid moment, and he'd confess he'd rather have been a test pilot.

Most summer evenings, Judge Inglisi drove directly from the courthouse to the Westchester County Airport. After terrorizing the skies in a Cessna, he would eat dinner in the quonset hut that masqueraded as a terminal, then wander over to the Air National Guard hangar and trade flying stories with pilots, technicians, whoever might be around. I found the Judge standing beneath the cowling of a turboprop while two mechanics scurried over the wing assembly. Clad in a leather bombardier jacket, he looked like a medicine ball with feet. He chattered on, oblivious to the thick smell of jet fuel or the staccato bursts of pneumatic ratchets. I crooked my arm around his neck in typical greeting. Surprisingly agile despite his weight, he spun out of the hold.

"I'm having a conversation here," he said, pressing tufts of springy white hair behind his ears. A generous nose dove into a walrus mustache sprouting from his upper lip. His nostrils flared whenever he was angry, and right now they opened full throttle.

"These guys aren't listening to you."

"Of course they are. I'm a judge."

I dragged him out onto the tarmac.

"You knew Sylvester Miles, right?" I said.

"Bastard conned me into joining that damn club of his all those years ago. Ridiculous, me trying to play golf."

"I meant he was a client before you hired me. I remember seeing the files."

The Judge cocked his head and narrowed his eyes as if listening to the wail of a distant air raid siren. His bushy eyebrows had kept the blackness of his younger days and added intensity to his steel-gray eyes.

"What are you up to?" he said.

"A lawyer named Roger Twomby called me to the Miles house this afternoon. Miles named me in his will to sell a set of golf clubs at auction. But something about the will strikes me as odd. I want to read your draft to get a feel for this one."

"What the hell does an old will that's been revoked twenty times matter?" That siren in his head wailed louder.

"Twomby only read me the clause that named me. He didn't even finish it."

"Maybe the rest isn't any of your damn business."

"He did the same thing to Adrienne, only read her parts of the will."

"Maybe it's none of her goddam business either."

"She's the surviving spouse. And she doesn't seem to have a clue to what's going on. Twomby and St. Clare controlled the whole show. And DiRienzo was there, too. Observing, he said."

The added cast brightened the Judge a bit. "St. Clare must be executor, huh? And the only things DiRienzo observes are what jump up and bite him in the ass. But what the hell do you care?"

"I want to know what I'm getting myself into."

"I'll tell you what you're getting into. Hot water. Now you just won the Met—and by the way, congratulations—and you're about to play in the Classic. Sell the damn clubs and be done with it. Don't get any more involved than you have to. Remember Florida."

"This isn't Florida."

"Neither was Florida when it started. You were doing someone a favor. But the truth is if you minded your own business down there you'd be on the Tour right now, and we wouldn't be having this conversation, or any of the other ones we've had in the past two years."

"I'm not planning anything stupid. Nothing will keep me out of the Classic."

"But you can't contain your curiosity."

I nodded as humbly as I knew how. Some of the steel melted out of his eyes.

"I'd be divulging the secrets of a former client," he said.

"A dead former client. And we were partners, so that rule doesn't apply between us."

I knew I just cleared the last hurdle. The Judge stared back into the hangar, shook his head, and motioned me toward a chain link fence separating the tarmac from a parking lot. The sun hung low over the distant tree line and sprayed pink through the evening sky.

"I didn't do much work for Miles," said the Judge, inserting a thick elbow between the spines of the fence and relaxing his bulk. "He liked to spread his legal work around. He had one lawyer for his business dealings in New York, another in Connecticut. A different one handled his real estate. I was his will man.

"The first one was a typical wealthy bachelor will. Most of the estate went to charity, some to a brother, a few token bequests to trusted employees and former lady friends.

"Then one day Miles contacted me about an incident at a convention in Chicago. He saw a fight in the hotel bar. Older man, younger woman. A real donnybrook. He tried to break it up and ended up clocking the man in the mouth. Loosened four of the guy's teeth. Miles was worried about possible criminal charges. I told him that if he hadn't been arrested immediately, the other guy probably wouldn't swear out a complaint. Especially if the woman wasn't the guy's wife, and the wife didn't know about the woman. Miles was relieved. Then he told me he spent the rest of the convention with her. She was a secretary from Cleveland, and the guy with the dental problem was her boss. They were attending the same convention as Miles."

"Adrienne?" I said.

The Judge nodded. "Miles was nuts about her. Right from my office, he called an airline and reserved three tickets, one going out to Cleveland and two coming back to New York. Flew out there the next day and talked her into marrying him. She jumped at the chance. Hell, she'd been fired before her boss hit the deck."

"Everyone thinks she seduced Miles."

"Hey, everyone thinks lots of things that aren't true. I don't know exactly what happened in Chicago. If anything, it was the other way around.

"The upshot was that Miles wanted his will redrafted from typical bachelor to typical married sap. Everything to the wife, no conditions. No life estate, no trust, nothing. And all to a girl thirty years his junior he met at some damned convention. I told him, as diplomatically as I could, that he should have a prenuptial agreement. May save your life, I told him, kidding around. He didn't laugh. He was so crazy about the broad he wouldn't listen. Wanted no part of a prenup, just wanted that new will. So I drew up the bastard. For the measly fifty bucks I charged in those days, it wasn't worth the argument. I'd land the probate work no matter who the beneficiaries were.

"Things rocked along for a few months. Then Miles came into the office and announced he wanted to cut Adrienne out of the will. I told him you couldn't cut a spouse out of a will in New York. It never would get through probate. So he said okay, let's make things tough for her. So I cut her down to the bone, stuck his brother back in for a song, and left the bulk to charity.

"That started the merry-go-round. Miles came back every month, cutting Adrienne's share, adding to it, writing the brother in, writing him out, changing charities on a whim. Didn't take a genius to figure out they weren't getting along. But he never wanted a prenup, so this was his only choice. I must have done fifteen codicils before I said, Why don't you just divorce her and save us both the heartache. He got pissed off, told me at his age a divorce was worse than a bad marriage. Financially, that is. That was the last I saw of his business."

"What were the codicils like?"

"Aw, Kieran, I don't remember every little detail. They were stupid. Like they might direct Adrienne to buy particular stocks on certain dates and sell them on certain dates regardless of value. Dumb things, because no matter how I wrote the codicils Adrienne always ended up with a fortune. Sometimes it just didn't come as easy as others. From what you told me, old Syl never changed a bit."

CHAPTER
3

Andy Anderson's golf repair shop sat amid the squalor of a half vacant industrial park astride the Metro North Railroad tracks. Despite the early morning hour, Andy already had company. A sports car with baroque fins and numerous spiny antennae butted up against the front door. Double-tinted window glass perfectly matched the deep purple body paint.

I nudged my heap into the adjoining space and squeezed out carefully since the slightest nick probably would activate a modern defense system. As I gathered the loose *Blitzklubs* out of the trunk, the shop door squealed open. I slammed the lid and found Miko Onizaka staring at me.

Black hair bristled above his broad flat forehead, then splayed in a ragged tail over his shirt collar. Wrinkles etched his shirt and pants, the same outfit he wore the last day of the Met. He cocked his head as if measuring me. But despite the hard stare, he reeled just slightly off balance.

I shouldered the *Blitzklubs* and walked toward him, my right hand extended for the bittersweet mix of condolence and congratulations I should have offered immediately after the playoff. The booze smell hit me at five feet. I muttered something vapid about competition. Onizaka sneered, ignoring my outstretched hand, running his dull eyes from head to foot and back again. My fingers twitched, ready to tighten into a fist at the first wrong move. But Onizaka only screwed his mouth into an odd grin, then staggered to the sports car. After grinding gears, he shot away in a cloud of rubber and gravel.

I used foot, hand, and shoulder to loosen the shop's front door. The building was little more than a shack with exposed plumbing, a splintery wood floor, and a potbellied stove. The equipment was just as seedy—scarred workbenches, rusted vises, worn out lathes, carbon crusted etnas, and all manner of screws, nails, wood inserts, and grip plugs arranged in warped cigar boxes. But with Andy's wizardry, this collection of ancient junk took on magical properties.

Andy had come to America to add a dash of international flavor to the professional staff of the renowned Winged Foot Country Club. Never enamored with the country club life, he spent every free hour honing the clubmaking skills he had learned from his father and his grandfather in Scotland. Eventually, he quit his job and set up his own shop. He manufactured one set of clubs per month ("only for the connoisseur") and subcontracted oddball repair jobs from local pros ("most canna even change a grip without buggering up the club").

Andy's knowledge of golf lore was phenomenal. He could regale you for hours about the windswept links of Jacobean Scotland or discuss the evolution of the mashie in language worthy of a physicist. But his real joy came from gadding about the countryside in his minivan and conning valuable golf clubs from unsuspecting antiques dealers.

"Cheerio, Kieran," he said as he steered a rack of newly refinished woods toward a drying room.

Looking at Andy was like looking in a mirror, if I didn't examine the image too closely. We were both reed thin through the hips and squarely wide in the shoulders, as if we wore shirts without removing the hangers. Andy had the hands of a blacksmith and sinews like thick telephone cables coiling down his forearms. Mine were cut from the same die, though an arm-wrestling match would be Andy's without contest. The main physical difference was in our hair. Andy's mop was tawny brown while mine ran to premature gray. Of course, Andy never had practiced law.

The rack caught a seam in the floorboards and nearly toppled.

"Damn!" said Andy, scrambling to save his handiwork from ruin. He steadied the rack and jumped it into the drying room.

"You just missed your rival," he called from inside. "He's had a bit of the barleycorn, I'd say."

"Started right after the Met."

"Aye, and congratulations, laddy. Your fast finish must have had quite an impact on the man."

"I can see that."

"But you didna see this."

Andy's hand reached out brandishing a broken golf club. I recognized the bright blue pistol-shaped grip. Two days ago, it had been Onizaka's mallet-head putter. Today it looked like an elongated barbecue fork.

"He vaporized the bugger," said Andy. "Along with several others. He wants them all repaired right away. And don't you want to know why?"

I didn't answer.

"He thinks he'll play in the Classic," said Andy. "Well, he hopes to, anyway."

"He's expecting me to step aside?"

"You have to understand, Kieran, the man is desperate. Pitiful, too. I arrived here at six this morning and found him sleeping in his car. Talked to me for over an hour, which was bloody torture between his English and the barleycorn. He said his sponsor's pulled his backing and he needed the Met, and the Classic berth, to remain in the U.S. Otherwise, it's back to some triple-decker driving range in Tokyo for him."

"What about his job?"

"Apparently that canna keep him here."

"Forgive me if I'm not touched."

"You donna want to give up the Classic, eh?" Andy said with a laugh.

"No way," I said. "Did he mention anything about my job?"

"At MCC? Are ye not solid there?"

"Far as I know. But I heard it was up for sale to a Japanese company and Onizaka was in line to be club pro."

"He said nothing to me. But he was very clear about the Classic. He wants to play."

I whaled several violent swings with a *Blitzklub*. Fisk, the Judge, the PGA Tour brass, now Onizaka and Andy. I was tired of people picking at the few things I did right in life.

Andy returned, wiping his hands on a greasy rag.

"What do you have there, another replating job—holy shit!"

He snatched the club from my hand and carried it under a light.

"No, yes, no, yes," he debated with himself as he spun the iron to take in every surface and angle. "Bring the rest here, laddy."

He swept clear a section of workbench with his forearm. Then, with a care bordering on reverence, he arranged the entire set with the grips touching the wall and the heels of the clubheads set precisely on line.

"I canna believe this," he said.

"Can't believe what?"

But Andy wasn't listening. He pulled down a thick leather bound volume from a rafter. The binding was broken, the pages loose, and most of the gold lettering on the cover had worn away. But I could see that the title was *Golf Arcana* by H.T. Hillthwaite. Andy carefully opened the pages to the proper spot and stepped back like a painter surveying a canvas.

"Yes," he finally decided. "Where the hell did you get these?"

"Never mind where I got them. What are they?"

"For the golf collector, they are Moby Dick, the Holy Grail, and El Dorado rolled into one. You know nothing about *Blitzklubs?*"

"Never heard of them before yesterday."

"You'll be needing a short history lesson, then," said Andy. "During World War Two, a high-ranking SS officer lost a golf match to a subordinate. Since he couldna believe his lack of talent was the reason, he decided his clubs were to blame and hit upon a plan to develop the perfect set of golf clubs. He knew nothing about clubmaking, so in typical Nazi fashion he confiscated a forge in a small Bavarian village and ordered a clubmaker to design a set of irons worthy of the master race. These are the result."

"Sounds like a fairy tale," I said.

"That's what most people say. The clubmaker manufactured only twelve sets, each with slight variations, before the war ended. No one on this side of the Atlantic has ever seen one. My father once had a customer who claimed to own a set, but those clubs turned out to be forgeries."

"How do you know these aren't?"

Andy handed me the book. There were no photographs, just carefully drawn artist's conceptions. They were Miles' clubs, all right. They had the same heel-toe balance, the same dull metal finish, the same gooseneck in the hosel, the same decorative swastikas and Maltese crosses, and the same lightning bolt underscoring Blitzklub.

The text confirmed everything Andy had told me, and added that all twelve sets disappeared when a platoon of Allied soldiers raided the forge shortly after Germany's surrender. The drawings were exact reproductions of the clubmaker's designs found buried in the forge sometime later.

"See these shafts?" said Andy.

"Graphite?"

"Aye," he said, suddenly unable to contain his excitement. "Fancy that, Kieran laddy. Graphite shafts in 1945. These things were the V-2s of the golf world."

He grabbed a camera from the drawer of a paint-splattered desk and snapped several photos of the clubs from different angles.

"They belonged to Sylvester Miles."

Andy kept snapping.

"Did you hear me?"

"That I did," said Andy. "He left them to you in his will, now did he?"

"Not exactly. He directed his executor to engage my services for expert advice in selling the clubs at auction for the highest possible price."

"Did it ever occur to Miles you know nothing about rare golf clubs?"

"That's why I'm here. What can a set like this command at auction?"

"Let me explain how clubs are appraised. These are in near mint condition, but that's less important than you might expect. The critical factor is rareness. Now we know only twelve Blitzklub sets exist. That's rare for clubs not owned by somebody famous, like Young Tom Morris' brassie or Bobby Jones' Calamity Jane putter. The main drawback is the missing pitching wedge. But even allowing for that, I'd say the mid-five figure range is reasonable. In the right market."

"For a set of golf clubs?"

"For mythology," said Andy.

"That's crazy."

"Aye, but consider this. A few months ago, an anonymous owner offered a rake iron at auction. The club isna legal now, but was very popular at the turn of the century when you wer'na restricted to four-teen clubs and designers invented all manner for nasty situation shots. The rake iron was built for hitting out of wet lies. Six vertical grooves in the clubface allowed the club to pass easily through the mud or water. Hence the name. Five Japanese collectors locked horns over that one club."

"They're into that, too?"

"Why not? What Japan lacks in an ancient golf heritage it's mak-ing up for in collectibles. The bidding lasted for hours. None of the five wanted to be the first to blink. Finally, a man named Hayagawa won out. His bid was ninety thousand."

"Ninety thousand dollars for one club!"

"That was the bid." Andy frowned. "Unfortunately, no one's veri-fied if the sale ever was consummated. Hayagawa isna the type to pay top dollar for something if it can be had any other way. If you know what I mean."

"We'll bar him from the auction."

"Might be pretty sticky. He keeps his ear well to the ground. I'd wager he already knows about these."

"Forget him for now. Where do we sell them?"

"Most of these auctions are held in connection with major golf tournaments," said Andy. "The biggest American auction was at the Memorial in May. The next big one will be at the World Series at Fire-

stone in late August. But the biggest of all will be at the British Open in
two weeks time."

"Is any one auction better than another?"

"They're all of a piece," said Andy. "The British one might yield
more because speculators flock there."

Two weeks, I mused. Judge Inglisi's lecture from the previous night
wound back into my consciousness. Coordinating a trip to the British
Open with competing in the Classic was crazy, if not damn near impossible.

"And what would the set be worth if the missing wedge turned
up?"

"Low six figures, unless the market suddenly is glutted with *Blitzklubs*. Which reminds me of one other factor. Say Sylvester Miles
owned all twelve sets. You could inflate the auction price of any one set
because you could guarantee the potential buyer the other sets wouldn't
pop up at another auction."

"Inflate the price how much?"

Andy stroked his chin. "A quarter million."

Golf is big business, and any big business spawns economic phenomena
that defy all logic. But the idea of intrinsically worthless objects com-
manding such value struck me as obscene. Why should a length of pipe
connecting a leather or rubber sleeve with a trapezoidal hunk of steel
cost as much as a house or attending med school? In my world, the *Blitzklubs* would better serve mankind as stakes for tomato plants.

But few people shared my world view, and Andy Anderson wasn't
one of them. I had arrived at his shop with the *Blitzklubs* strewn across
the back seat like a set of second-hand MacGregors. He refused to let
me leave without sheathing the clubheads in bubble plastic, wrapping
the grips in packing paper, and swaddling them all in a towel. The back
seat wasn't a fitting throne, and the trunk was out of the question. Andy

stood them upright on the passenger seat, lashed securely with the seat belt. "Drive carefully," he admonished, as if they were a Ming vase balanced on a dozen Faberge eggs.

I stashed the clubs behind the door of the cubby hole I called my office, then proceeded to sit on the info the rest of the day. Whatever my philosophical stance on the *Blitzklubs*, I was still dealing with estate property and was duty bound to report Andy's appraisal either to the executor or to the attorney. In this instance, however, a more intriguing alternative existed.

Adrienne Miles answered the door wearing a white body stocking and powder blue leg warmers, with a matching sweatshirt knotted loosely around her shoulders. Exertion flushed her cheeks, and two damp strands of blonde hair curlicued past her ears. Aerobics music thrummed in the background.

"May I come in? It's about the golf clubs."

Adrienne bit her lip, then snapped off a neat about-face. We went into a room completely devoid of furniture except for a hard rubber exercise mat, a boom box stereo, and a torchiere lamp. Adrienne shut off the stereo and settled onto the floor, tucking her legs beneath her. I crouched a discreet distance away, as if lining up a putt. The evening sun glared off the shiny surface of the mat.

"What do you know about the clubs?" I said.

"Very little," she said. "Golf doesn't interest me, so I never paid any attention. Syl kept them in his den and used them when he practiced in the evenings. I just assumed they were his practice clubs."

"He never mentioned them to you?"

"No, we—. No, he didn't."

I started to explain the mythology of the twelve *Blitzklub* sets. Bouncing off the eardrums of a nongolfer, it must have sounded hokey as hell. Adrienne spared me the embarrassment by cutting directly to the point.

"How valuable are they?"

"As is, with the missing pitching wedge, the set is worth approximately forty to fifty thousand dollars. With the wedge, the set is worth one hundred thousand, minimum."

Adrienne's eyes focused on infinity for a brief moment. Otherwise, she didn't react. No surprise, no disappointment. Nothing. She untucked her legs and rolled into a split. She may have been on the shady side of forty, but she was as lithe as an Olympic gymnast.

"Did Syl own any of the other eleven sets?" I said.

Adrienne shook her head as if the words jarred her out of deep thought.

"Sorry. I didn't catch that."

I repeated the question.

"I haven't seen any other ones, but I suppose I could rummage around. Why do you ask?"

"No special reason," I said.

The doorbell rang. Adrienne lifted out of her split and loosened the kinks with a heel-toe strut that looked very interesting from floor level. A wall blocked my view of the front door, but Adrienne said, "Hi, Bill," in a voice loud enough for my benefit. They spoke inaudibly for a time. I stood up, half with the idea of moving within earshot. Then Adrienne raised her voice again.

"Someone's here to see us, Billy."

They strolled into the room, St. Clare with his pudgy arm entwined around hers and Adrienne dragging her toes with each step like a blushing schoolgirl infatuated with the nerdy class president. The sight rankled me, though I wasn't quite sure why.

"Evening, Kieran," St. Clare said in a poor stab at bonhomie. He might as well have just told me to scram.

"Mr. Lenahan just stopped by for a moment," said Adrienne. "He has good news about those clubs."

"Oh really?" said St. Clare. "As executor, you should report your findings to me."

Adrienne squeezed his cheeks. "You're such a fogey, Billy. Does it really matter who finds out first?"

St. Clare reddened. He hated being called a fogey more than he hated being ignored as executor.

"I suppose not," he grumbled.

"Well," chirped Adrienne. "The clubs are worth about ten thousand dollars. Double that if the missing club turns up."

I didn't know Adrienne's game, but she had played her hand and I decided to pass.

"Ten thousand, huh?"

"Isn't that wonderful?" said Adrienne.

"Yes," said St. Clare, though he obviously didn't share her enthusiasm. Neither did I, for that matter. I bid them both a good evening and headed for home.

My digs were a two-bedroom garage apartment owned by a young Italian couple with a growing brood. An outdoor stairway shored by unpainted two-by-fours climbed the side of the garage. I snagged a six-pack from the refrigerator and sat on the steps to watch the sky turn dark. I kept replaying Adrienne's cheerful lie to St. Clare. Not that I gave a damn about St. Clare's sensibilities. The man was daft. He had served two undistinguished terms as mayor over thirty years ago, and still swaggered up Merchant Street like an incumbent. He even barked orders at the police during times of public emergency, which in Milton amounted to the occasional power blackout after a thunderstorm. I didn't know if he'd been shadowing DiRienzo's murder investigation. But he sure seemed to take a personal interest in the widow.

The lie was something else. If someone planned to use me, I wanted to know why.

Three beers past nightfall, headlights bored into the driveway and splashed against the garage doors. The light faded. A car engine kicked down, then shut off. Adrienne Miles gradually materialized in the dimness. Vaguely, I wasn't surprised. She fit herself onto a step below me, spine against the shingles and feet pressing a two-by-four. Jeans and a blouse had replaced the body suit, but the effect was the same. I handed her a beer. She popped the top and took a long, healthy draught.

"I owe you an explanation," she said.

"Damn right you do."

"You think I'm terrible for lying to St. Clare."

"What you tell St. Clare is your own damn business. You involve me and it's mine."

"Why didn't you tell him?"

"The clubs are worth whatever they're worth, not whatever you tell St. Clare. He'll learn the truth eventually."

"But you told me their value," she said. "You didn't have to. I know that much about the way an estate works."

"How did you know I hadn't already told St. Clare or Twomby?"

"I knew. You caught me completely off guard. I didn't think you would be so quick with a response about the clubs. And when he showed up I didn't know what to do."

"You didn't miss a beat," I said. "A minute ago you said you owed me an explanation. I'm still waiting."

Adrienne pressed the beer can lightly against her temple.

"I don't want St. Clare to know the real value of those clubs," she said. "Just for a little while."

"Why?"

"I have my reasons."

"Not good enough. The will charged me with a duty, and I take my duties very seriously. Like it or not, you need my help in whatever scheme you have planned."

"It's not a scheme!"

I couldn't see her face very well in the half-light, but her voice sounded genuinely desperate.

"Damn," she said. "When I heard you were named in the will, I thought finally here is someone I can talk to. And when you showed up tonight I thought you really were someone I could trust. But you're just like everyone else in this goddam town."

"Am I supposed to feel flattered or ashamed?"

"Go to hell." She clomped down the stairs and tossed the beer can onto the grass.

I didn't move. The same vague feeling that accompanied her arrival now told me she wouldn't leave. A moment later she was back at the foot of the stairs.

We went into my apartment. She wedged herself in a corner of the sofa, legs crossed and arms folded. A defensive posture, a student of body language might say. Beneath three hundred watts of ceiling spotlights, her skin looked less like butterscotch than too much time in a tanning salon. But she still cut a damn nice, if tightly wound, figure.

I'd cross-examined my share of witnesses. Sometimes it was as tough as cranking a frozen engine. Other times it was as easy as puncturing a tire and listening to the air rush out. I didn't expect Adrienne would be very talkative, so I gave her the old jump-start.

"I know something about Syl and his wills because my old law partner drew up the first dozen or so. You get the money from the *Blitzklubs*, right?"

Adrienne barely reacted at all, which I came to conclude was her way. She just smiled indulgently and trilled a tiny laugh in her throat.

"St. Clare is completely nuts," she said.

"I know all about the Mayor."

"It's far worse than you can imagine. St Clare's relationship with my husband went far beyond friendship. He revered Syl. Maybe it was the war hero thing. Or Syl's self-made business success. Or me. Maybe it was all these things. But with Syl gone, St. Clare's changed. I think a psychologist would call it a personality transference. He's starting to confuse himself with Syl. I wouldn't care so much, but with Syl dead St. Clare's become my husband in his own mind.

"The only thing I know about the will is that I'm entitled to half of what those clubs sell for. The secrecy is St. Clare's way of lording it over me, and that freak Twomby is just as happy not telling me anything. He's heard only Syl's side of the story for years and thinks the worst of me.

"All I want is to get out of this town. I hate it, I always have. Everyone probably thinks I killed Syl for the money just like they think I married him for the money. At least I've managed to convince the police I'm innocent. Detective DiRienzo believes me."

She smiled sweetly to invite my vote of confidence. I didn't oblige.

"Why don't you leave Milton?" I said.

Adrienne rubbed her fingers together in the universal sign for money.

"I don't have any. I don't even know if I have a roof over my head or if Syl left the house to charity, too."

"You can fight the will. There are laws."

"I know all about them. But it would be a fight. Just like a divorce would have been a fight. I don't have any fight left."

"What do you gain by keeping the truth from St. Clare?"

"The element of surprise," she said. "St. Clare has designs on me. He knows I can't afford to leave because I have nowhere to go. The only family I have won't take me in. My only cash is a piddling bank account I'd run through in a month. He actually believes I'll break down and marry him. But he also realizes I'd fly if I could afford it. As long as he thinks the clubs are worth ten or twenty thousand dollars, he won't worry. Half of that won't get me very far, so he'll let the clubs go to auction. But if he knows they're worth fifty to a hundred thousand, he'll hold up the sale forever."

"Of course, all of fifty or a hundred thousand will take you even farther."

"I have no desire to swindle money out of my husband's estate. I want only what is mine, not a penny more or less. When I leave this town, I leave no favors behind."

"Why the hell didn't St. Clare jump for joy when you told him ten grand?"

"He must have been nervous because you were there. After you left, he tried pumping me for what we talked about. I told him nothing. Then he focused on the figures, and I could feel him relax."

I didn't know how to take her. Good liars laced their stories with a ring of truth. Bad ones overcompensated with details. Adrienne had spoken from the heart, or what I fathomed to be her heart.

Don't get involved, the Judge had counseled. I already was involved, and with each passing minute that involvement deepened. I could help Adrienne without compromising my ethics. The auction would take weeks to arrange. By then the Classic would be over, and St. Clare's unrequited ardor may have cooled. Meanwhile, I could say nothing to anyone.

I escorted Adrienne to her car. I didn't tell her my intentions; she didn't ask. But before she pulled away, she lowered her window.

"Syl always thought highly of you. I can understand why."

CHAPTER
4

The next morning the cops beat me to the club. Three squad cars and an unmarked Plymouth drew a rough semicircle around the pro shop patio. Their doors were open and their gumballs flashed. Static crackled over the radios. The smell of burnt rubber hung in the air. Skid marks trailed back from the rear wheels of the Plymouth.

Two of the early morning regulars stood at the pro shop door and peeked at the festivities inside.

"We found it," one triumphantly told me. "We called the police."

I shouldered past. One cop pressed his nose against the sill of the shop's single small window. A second spread fingerprint dust on the glass top of the cash register counter. A third stood guard at the entrance to the bag room. Beyond him, harsh voices burped like machine gun fire.

"Where's DiRienzo?" I said.

The cop stepped aside to show DiRienzo pinning Pete against the workbench.

"Did you lock up last night?" DiRienzo shouted at Pete.

"I don't have to answer none of your dumb questions."

"I take you down to headquarters, we'll see how tough you are."

"Wow, like I never been there before."

"Hey!" I said.

DiRienzo straightened up. Pete rolled away and rubbed where the edge of the workbench cut into his spine.

"Finally, Lenahan," said DiRienzo. "You work banker's hours?"

"What the hell happened now?"

"That's what I'm trying to find out."

"Someone broke in last night," said Pete. "Sherlock thinks I know something about it."

"I asked routine questions. He gave me a bunch of crap."

"You wouldn't know crap if it dropped on your head."

"Cram it, Pete," I said. "You got work to do, do it."

Pete sneered at DiRienzo and swaggered back into the bag room.

"That kid's trouble," said DiRienzo.

"Used to be. Now he's a damn good worker when he isn't being harassed."

"Who's harassing? I asked him routine questions." He tapped the edge of his notebook against the heel of his hand. "Show you what happened."

We went back into the shop. The perpetrator or perpetrators, DiRienzo told me, entered through the window after forcing the crescent lock. The window was set high over the cash register. It would have taken two perps—or one very athletic one—to hitch up the outside wall and squirt through an opening barely eighteen inches square. At the moment, DiRienzo bet on the former, though he could change his mind.

"Pete has a key," I said, cutting through the veiled accusation. "Why would he climb in through a window?"

"Hey, I didn't say the kid did it. But when he comes at me with that attitude, I get suspicious." DiRienzo spread his paws. "This is how we found the place. Wasn't ransacked at all, but the cash register was open."

"I leave it that way every night," I said. "I'd rather have someone take the petty cash than break open the register with a hammer."

"What happens with the day's take?"

"I deposit it every night. Or Pete does."

DiRienzo smirked. "It gets to the bank?"

"Every damn night."

I took a rough inventory. Not a penny short in the petty cash. Every stick of merchandise sat on the shelves. Nothing moved a millimeter out of place. Then I looked into my office. The single piece of bubble plastic at the bottom of an otherwise empty trash can hit me like a body slam. I flung back the door. The *Blitzklubs* were gone.

"What?" said DiRienzo. Even he could read the expression on my face.

I told him.

"Those are the clubs Sylvester Miles left behind?"

I nodded.

"Very interesting," he said as he opened his notebook.

It was all so perfect, I thought as I drove across the golf course. She knew the true value of the clubs, drew me into her lie to William St. Clare, and scoped out my apartment. The only other possible hiding places were the pro shop or the trunk of my car, and she had guessed right. I could see her slinking her tight athletic body through the window, cartwheeling across the countertop, and landing on the floor in a perfect dismount. And I had been a complete fool, swallowing her tale of woe.

I was mad enough to barge into her house and toss the place. But an extra spin around the perimeter of the linksland allowed my better judgment to take over. A frontal attack wouldn't work, and she was too smart to hide the clubs anywhere obvious. My best bet was to tease information out of her by playing dumb.

Adrienne answered the door in sprightly fashion. Her bathrobe and wet hair reminded me of the early hour.

"I have some bad news," I said. "Someone broke into my pro shop last night and stole the *Blitzklubs*."

Adrienne took a step backwards. One hand groped for a small hallway desk. The other clutched at the collar of her bathrobe as if I'd swept in on a cold wind. She found the desk and lowered herself onto its chair, staring at infinity all the way. If she wasn't truly stunned, she was a damn good actress.

After a long moment, she raised her head and fixed her eyes on mine.

"You think I did it."

So much for teasing out info. "It crossed my mind."

"Oh boy," she said. "This isn't good. This is not good."

I told her all the particulars, scrutinizing her face for any hint of recognition, admission, or guilt. I saw nothing but eyes staring into the distance and a twitch in her dimples that might have been a prelude to a sob.

"Jack," she said softly.

"Who's Jack?"

Adrienne didn't answer. She pounded the desk and bit her lips together. "Goddam him."

"Who's Jack?"

"Syl's younger brother," she said. "He's a college professor. The obnoxious know-it-all type. He and Syl didn't get along very well. They saw each other only about once a year. Jack would show up at the door, usually at night and never with an invitation. They would talk in Syl's den. Actually, they would argue. And from what I could hear through the door, the arguments always were about money. Jack needed it for something. He kept saying he'd held up his end of the bargain and now Syl was reneging.

"I never heard what Syl said in return. He would put on this sweet, mellow voice like he was talking to a child. The same voice he used with me. I had the impression he wasn't completely refusing Jack the money. He was just delaying it.

"I don't know what Syl left him in the will, but it couldn't have been very much. If he still needed that money, he could assume those clubs are the only source of quick cash."

"How would Jack know anything about the *Blitzklubs?*"

"You told me the clubs were from Germany after the war, right? Jack fancies himself a World War Two expert. He also fancies himself a writer, but I never knew of anything he ever finished let alone published. We didn't get on so tremendously, either. When we first met, he promised to tell me the real story behind Syl's war exploits. I think he wanted me to know my husband had two very heavy feet of clay. He never delivered on the promise."

"But how would Jack know I had the *Blitzklubs?*"

"He saw you, didn't he?"

The face of the knock-kneed man took shape in my mind's eye. The resemblance to Syl suddenly came clear, like a silhouette drawing that changes shape when you switch your focus from black to white.

"The man who left here in a huff?" I said.

"That's Jack Miles."

———

I didn't necessarily believe Adrienne didn't steal the clubs, but I decided to back off. Even if she stole them, I doubted she could sell them without causing a stir. Besides, DiRienzo was on the trail, a thought I found strangely comforting.

According to Adrienne, Jack Miles taught at the State University at Purchase. He lived in a small rental apartment in university housing and owned a cottage on a lake in Putnam County. The cottage was supposedly his writing retreat. But he had been renovating it for as long as Adrienne knew him. She doubted he ever would finish it to his liking.

I found Jack Miles in his office in a stiflingly hot Humanities Building. The door was ajar. The single chair facing the front of his desk was unoccupied. He didn't seem busy, unless you consider daydreaming to be serious business. My plan was simple. If his animosity toward Adrienne equalled Adrienne's for him, all I needed was to start him talking. I rapped on the doorjamb, and he returned to earth.

He definitely recognized me, but neither of us let on. We dusted off the preliminaries. I was the golf pro at his brother's country club—technically Syl's employee. I needed his help with a problem.

"How can I help a golf pro?" he said.

"The problem involves World War Two. I understand you are an expert."

"Who told you that?"

"Adrienne."

"I see." Jack Miles steepled his hands in front of his face and let out a long breath. Seated behind the desk, he didn't appear to be as tall as I remembered. His spine bowed and his torso sank into itself. Now that I knew he was Syl's brother, I could discern the same hawkish bone structure beneath the tousled hair.

"And Syl," I added. "He mentioned you on several occasions."

"I have a fair amount of expertise on the subject," he said.

"If this is an inconvenient time . . ." I started to rise.

"It's just as good as any, Mr. Lenahan. Please, what is your problem?"

"Your brother named me in his will," I said. "I have no idea why, but he asked that I organize the auction of a set of golf clubs. They are of German origin, and I believe your brother picked them up in Germany after the war."

I recounted the *Blitzklub* mythology as told in the Hillthwaite book. Jack Miles scowled.

"Looting was quite common after the war," he said. "The Third Reich looted Eastern Europe of countless works of art, and all kinds of tangible goods. After the war, the allies looted it right back. Some were freelancers, like the G.I. who walked off with the Quedlinburg treasure under his raincoat. Some were organized on a national scale, like the old master drawings originally owned by a financier named Koenigs and stolen from a Saxon castle by the Russians.

"The golf club story sounds like a group of soldiers scrounging for souvenirs. I could imagine Syl taking part in that type of excursion. He never was oriented toward the finer arts. Anyway, I doubt these golf clubs would be worth very much. They may be interesting to some people, but not to most."

"I'm glad you think so," I said, "because someone stole them from my shop last night."

"That's unfortunate," said Jack Miles. "I hope you aren't held financially responsible."

"I honestly haven't thought that through," I said. "But that brings me to my next question. What do you know about Adrienne?"

"In what way?" he said cautiously.

"I have the impression she wasn't left too much in the will."

"And you think she stole these clubs in order to make up for what m' other failed to leave her?" There was the slightest hint of delight in voice. He drifted into thoughtful silence for a moment. Then his face hardened. "I don't know what she may have received, and frankly I don't care. Whatever it may be, it is too much."

That severed the bile duct. He pushed back from his desk and rearranged a pile of books already neatly stacked on the window ventilator.

"My brother and I drifted apart after he returned from the war," he said. "It went back to his first marriage. He married a woman from a wealthy Southern family and didn't have the decency to bring her home to Brooklyn to meet our folks. He simply stamped out the past in search of his next Platonic conception of himself, as F. Scott Fitzgerald might say. I resented him for it. We didn't speak for many years, but were just starting to patch up our own relationship when Adrienne came along.

"I had this project on the drawing board for some time. It was a post-modern novel set in the aftermath of World War Two. I approached Syl, and he expressed an interest in helping me. He wasn't to write any of it, of course. Writing is my forte. But his war experience was to be the core of the book.

"Syl wasn't the war hero everyone thought. I attended his memorial service and found it rather silly. My brother didn't capture a German mortar nest single-handedly, though he did participate in a similar mission. Syl acted along with a captain and a sergeant, both of whom were killed within a week. And those soldiers in the mortar nest were Polish. The Axis forces were in retreat and ethnic Germans rarely fought rearguard actions. But Syl perpetuated this legend about himself, and the gullibility of the post-war public is what interests me. I don't think Syl realized how deep my tongue would be in my cheek with my fictional treatment of his war record.

"We talked about his bankrolling the project. I estimated three years of solid writing, but only was entitled to one year of sabbatical leave. I don't live extravagantly, but I needed a hundred grand to see me through. I wasn't asking for charity. I fully intended to give Syl a lien on the royalties. He was a businessman about it. He wanted to see an outline. I spent a year putting one together. By the time I was finished, Syl wasn't interested. He was married to her."

"What did Syl leave you?" I said.

"What does that matter?"

"You seemed angry when you left his house after the will reading."

"You saw me?" Jack Miles narrowed his eyes. "I guess you would have. I was upset. Wouldn't you be?"

"Depends on why I was upset."

"My brother just died," he said as matter-of-factly as if discussing the weather.

"So it wasn't because of your legacy?"

"Not at all," he said. "Syl left me more than he ever dreamed he did."

And I left Jack Miles' office knowing my list of burglary suspects had doubled.

CHAPTER
5

I returned well past noon to an ominously quiet caddie yard. A lone caddie snoozed on a bench. A "be back in ten minutes" sign hung in the window of the caddymaster's shack. An old-timer impatiently tapped a spiked foot on the pro shop patio.

"About time somebody showed up," he said.

The pro shop door was locked. I quickly mated the old-timer with his clubs and searched for some clue why Pete deserted his assigned post. All I found were phone messages that trailed off in mid-morning and smudges of fingerprint dust on every surface.

The telephone answered the question. Well, sort of.

"He wants you here right away," said Judge Inglisi's law clerk.

"Can't he talk over the phone?"

"He's on the bench."

"I have a pro shop to run."

"Do you want my blood on your hands?"

Judge Inglisi presided in a courtroom on the top floor of the Westchester County Court Building, a twenty-story tower standing where glitzy '80s architecture met vacant '90s building pits. I slipped into the last row of the gallery while an attorney cross-examined a nervous young man about the particulars of an automobile accident. The Judge shot me a glance but betrayed no hint of recognition.

This was the first time I saw Big Jim in judicial action. I had expected something comic, a Humpty Dumpty in black robes scowling at inept attorneys and leering at pretty jurors. Instead, I found a man who was alert, decorous, witty, and—dare I say it—regal. He sat with his elbows on the bench and his head swiveling like an owl's between raised shoulders. His wispy white hair shined like neon in the glow of his desk lamp. Every nerve in his body tuned into the minutest detail in the courtroom. If the jury's attention wavered, he reined them in with a sly comment. If the cross-examining attorney asked an improper question and opposing counsel failed to object, he protected the witness from humiliation. He was completely in his element; I was impressed.

At precisely four o'clock, he declared a short recess in a voice that suggested adherence to ritual. A minute later, a court officer summoned me to chambers. Judge Inglisi wore a robe custom-tailored for optimum sleekness. He loosened his collar, and when he opened his mouth he was Big Jim.

"Where the hell have you been?"

"Chasing Sylvester Miles' golf clubs. Someone stole them from the pro shop last night."

"That's sweet. While you were gone, the police arrested Pete O'Meara for murdering Miles."

I sank into the nearest chair.

"Deirdre called to tell me," he said. "Actually she called to ask my advice on hiring a lawyer."

"What happened?"

"Deirdre didn't have many details. She was at the kid's house when he called from the Milton P.D. According to her, the mother went hysterical and the father came out of his daffy world long enough to ask what the hell the fuss was about. Deirdre rushed over to the station, but Pete already was on his way here for the arraignment."

"Who did you tell her to hire?"

"No one specific. I told her how to go about finding a good criminal lawyer and gave her a few names to steer clear of. Purely off the record, of course."

"When's the arraignment?"

"Whenever the ducks get lined up, you know that." The Judge zipped the front of his robe up to his jowls and prepared to be regal. "Fat lot of good this pep talk is doing. I know what you're thinking. We all stuck our necks out for this kid, and we shouldn't abandon him now. But neither of us is a criminal lawyer anymore. I'm going back on the bench. You should take the elevator down to your car, drive away very fast, and practice for the Classic. You might hate yourself now, but you'll thank me in the morning."

I rode the elevator only as far as the arraignment courtroom. Due to the notoriety of the crime, several dozen people milled in the corridor. Reporters in search of stories mingled with retirees in search of drama more interesting than the daily soaps. I shouldered through the crowd in search of the O'Mearas. Finding none of them, I slipped around a corner to a different corridor. Gina O'Meara sat forlornly on a wooden bench. Her jet black hair fanned out on her bony shoulders.

"Judge Inglisi told me about Pete," I said.

She muttered something in Spanish and nodded toward the opposite wall where Deirdre spoke into a pay phone. I hadn't seen Deirdre in close to a year. Her hair, pinned up for hospital work, shaded toward the browner side of red. A few extra pounds lurked beneath her nursing whites, but she still was lean and leggy by any standard. She signaled with a finger that she'd be a minute, then slowly pushed a tiny black notebook into her shoulder bag. The minute ended, and she joined us.

I repeated the exact words I had spoken to Gina, the idea being that Judge Inglisi's name legitimized anything. Deirdre squeaked her sneaker on the terrazzo floor.

"I'll get Tom," she finally said and headed off around a corner. She seemed to skate rather than walk, a trait I found endearing even at the height of our many battles. Gina immediately withdrew into something sounding like prayer. I wandered toward a window with the idea of staring at a sliver of the sky, but ended up within earshot of Deirdre's sharp tongue.

". . . because he's your son, that's why," she said and grabbed the arm of Tom O'Meara, who sat on the floor.

"Give me a second willya, goddammit." He waved a wooden cane. "My leg."

"Your leg isn't half as bad as you make it out to be."

I rejoined Gina. Tom hobbled toward us, prodded by Deirdre walking behind. Tight jeans showed exactly how the accident had rearranged the bones and muscles of his bum leg. His whole body was crooked as a hunchback's. He lowered himself onto a section of the bench Gina hastily cleared for him. He had deep-set eyes and Deirdre's angular face, though with far less flesh to soften the bones. Longish red hair laced with springy whites swirled to conceal the onset of pattern baldness. A two-day growth bristled along his jawline.

For the third time I stated the reason for my presence.

"Judge Inglisi?" said Tom. "What's he got to do with this?"

"Nothing, Tom," said Deirdre. "I called him."

"Whydja call him? Can he spring Pete?"

"I called Judge Inglisi because he's my friend." She looked at me. "Oh, don't pay him any attention. He's in a foul mood."

"Like I don't got a right to be. My leg, my job, now my kid gets arrested for murder. No, I don't got no right to be in a foul mood."

"My baby a murderer!" wailed Gina.

"Shaddup," said Tom, and pounded his cane on the floor. Gina shut up. Tom focused on Deirdre. "Is this the lawyer you hired?"

"No."

"Then what the hell's he doin' here?"

"He's here because he cares about Pete," said Deirdre.

"He's here because he wants to see us in our misery."

"Tom, that's not fair," said Deirdre.

"Whydja want me to talk to him?"

"This is Kieran Lenahan. You remember him, right? He's a lawyer, remember? He can—"

"I know who he is," said Tom. "You don't have to talk to me like I'm a kid. I'm just saying I don't know why it is I gotta talk to him."

Deirdre started to respond, but I waved her off.

"I'm here for two reasons," I said. "Deirdre's right. I do care about Pete. I also know how confusing and terrifying the system can be."

"Do I look scared?" Tom arched his back and pounded the top of his cane on his chest, challenging me to disagree.

"No, you look angry," I allowed diplomatically. But with his wild eyes and trembling mouth he looked terrified.

My explanation of an arraignment wasn't very complicated, but people in their straits didn't have clear heads, so I chopped it into small pieces and played it out slowly. I didn't get very far before Tom lurched to his feet.

"What the hell planet are you talking about?" he said. "We're poor and a rich man is dead. That's the only thing that matters."

"Tom—" said Deirdre, but he was already limping down the hall-way.

"Sorry," she said.

"Forget it," I said. "By the way, who did you hire?"

"Someone named Cooper. Arthur is his first name, I think."

"Arturo Cooper? Can't be."

"I know who I hired, Kieran," she snapped.

"Can't be. Arturo Cooper is a corporate lawyer. I dealt with him when Texaco bought that land from the Spencer twins a few years back. He doesn't do criminal defense work."

"I'll show you. His card's somewhere." She fumbled through her notebook. "First thing I did I called Big Jim. He told me to get my ass to the courthouse because good criminal lawyers are never in their of-fices."

"You met Arturo Cooper hanging around the courthouse?" Now I was convinced there were two Arturo Coopers in town. My Arturo Cooper cultivated an image of British gentility. He dressed only in grey or black and spoke with his lower lip thrust forward to lend an upper class limpness to his speech. He rarely saw the inside of any courtroom, much less one used for arraignments.

"Not exactly hanging around. I stood outside a courtroom and checked out the lawyers Big Jim mentioned. They looked like sleaze-balls. The kind of men who wear chalk stripe suits and have about four strands of hair they comb all over their heads."

"Appearances are important," I said.

Deirdre ignored me. "Cooper didn't look like a sleazeball. I ex-plained the problem, and he agreed to take the case for five hundred dollars. He said he'd put in an appearance ticket, or something like that."

"A notice of appearance," I said. "It means the court will call him when the arraignment is ready to begin. He charged you only five hundred dollars?"

"That's all the cash I had. I offered to write him a check for more, but he said we'd discuss fees after the arraignment."

I still doubted we were talking about the same guy, but then Deirdre found the card. It belonged to my Arturo Cooper because it bore the name of the fancy law firm in which he ran a fast track to partner. Someone had marked out the direct dial phone number and written in one with a different exchange, but I didn't think much of it. Instead, I wondered what blinding light of social consciousness had driven the effete Cooper to represent "a client with a face." The words belonged to him.

I scouted out the courtroom. The reporters ignored me, probably because my golf attire didn't identify me as anyone important. The officer on duty inside the courtroom recollected me slightly from my practice days. I told him I was with the O'Meara family and asked if he would please call us out of hiding when the arraignment was about to begin.

Gina had wandered away in search of Tom, leaving Deirdre alone on the bench. She sat pigeon-toed, elbows on knees, hands propping her chin. I settled beside her, and she slid ever so slightly away. An underbite gave a bratty tilt to her mouth. Her eyes beamed a bright turquoise other women needed contact lenses to match.

Deirdre and I came from similar working-class Limerick backgrounds. We had both "risen above" them in ways society applauds. I had become a lawyer, then a golf pro; she was a skilled cardiac intensive care nurse and lived in a condo with the insipid name of Waterledge at Milton. We understood each other on a primal, nonverbal level. Though we hadn't been lovers in several years, we constantly smoldered in each other's presence and occasionally erupted with emotions we couldn't control. But today we tried to hold things together, bound by the threat to our last common interest.

"You know, Kieran, there was something you said a long time ago when you left for Florida. You said you were tired of being a lawyer because all you did was clean up other people's shit for them." Deirdre unfolded herself, stretching her long legs and staring at her feet. "I was so mad at you that I didn't focus on what you said. But when Mom got sick, and I had to cancel my plans because the O'Meara men aren't worth a damn in an emergency, I understood. Here I am cleaning up the shit again.

"I thought Pete was straightening out. I really thought so. He seemed less mixed up. No more trouble at school. It seemed like he found himself. That job means something to him. He loves golf. He never loved anything before. Anything he tried to do with Tom, Tom belittled him. Fishing, basketball, baseball. Tom always did a number on his head. Big man, my big brother. But golf is something Tom doesn't understand."

There's a lot Tom doesn't understand, I said to myself.

Deirdre ran her hand over her hair. She had long slender fingers with chopped nails, an occupational hazard. She forced her mouth into a smile, but her eyes didn't cooperate.

"Do you think he killed Miles?"

"Gut reaction, no," I said.

"But?" she added.

"Pete's a funny kid. You think you know him, then he'll react in a situation and leaves you scratching your head. And he has that temper."

"A gift from his father." Deirdre gripped her elbows and shuddered as if a chill passed through her body. "Tom's right in a way. Who the hell are we compared to someone like Sylvester Miles? Now that Pete's been arrested, who's going to believe he didn't do it?"

I had several answers, but none worth mentioning. Deirdre was miserable about Pete, and so was I. We said nothing for several minutes.

"My father, old full o' shit Corny, used to brag that he and Miles were army buddies," she finally said. "I never paid much attention. He talked mainly to Tom about that sort of stuff. And after Tom got tired of listening, he talked to Pete. One day, after I learned what was really going on between him and my mother, I heard him telling that story again. I couldn't take it. I just snapped back, 'If you and Miles were so tight, why is he rich and you're working on the railroad?' He never mentioned Miles or the war in front of me again."

An hour passed. Gina returned and said Tom had gone for cigarettes. Deirdre made some phone calls to the hospital. Most carried the crisp tones of business, but during one she leaned against the wall with the receiver cradled against her chin and slowly ran her hand along the cord. Adrenalin welled in my chest. Old habits die hard.

My court officer friend stuck his head around the corner. The arraignment was about to begin.

I hustled Gina and Deirdre into the first row of the gallery. Several reporters, instantly recognizing people fitting the general description of "suspect's family," swooped in for comments. Deirdre told them to get lost. No one on this earth can make Deirdre talk against her will. The reporters slinked away.

Meanwhile, I assessed the scene. The Legal Aid catcher reclined in the jury box and spoke easily to a reporter. His job was to "catch," or represent, any defendant appearing for arraignment without private counsel. Since Deirdre already had hired Cooper, the catcher would watch. The assistant D.A. assigned to the case sat at a counsel's table and serenely shuffled papers. His name was Fowler, and he had a cherub's face. But appearances were deceiving, and in this regard the practice of law paralleled golf: you couldn't predict the toughness of your opponent by the shape of his face.

The defense counsel's table was empty, as was the bench. Nothing strange there. The defense lawyer usually was the last to learn the exact time of an arraignment, and judges rarely took the bench without all players present. No sense asking my friendly court officer who would be presiding. Judges handled after-hours arraignments on an emergency basis, so anyone who happened to be in the building was fair game.

A steel door opened in the wall. Pete, flanked by two burly guards, shuffled toward the defense table. Chains running from handcuffs to ankle irons rattled with every shuffling step. He flicked a glance in our direction, but his eyes stared right through us.

Gina swooned. Deirdre righted her and leaned toward my ear.

"Where's our lawyer?" she said.

I turned toward the courtroom entrance. People shouldered their way down the aisle, but Arturo Cooper wasn't among them. A guard shoved Pete into a chair.

"Where's the damn lawyer?" said Deirdre.

"If he put in a notice of appearance, they should have called him."

A bouffant-haired woman ascended to the bench. The court clerk, banging his hand on the wood rail and demanding order, identified her as Judge Betty Hartnett. She must have been newly elected because I'd never heard of her and because she was eager enough to be in the building at this late hour. The veterans usually split before five.

"Where is defense counsel?" Her voice bounced around the large courtroom. She leveled her gaze at the catcher, who scrambled out of the jury box as if poked by a cattle prod.

"Kieran, what's happening?" whispered Deirdre.

"Are the People ready?" said Judge Hartnett.

"Ready, Your Honor."

"Counsel, do you wish to confer with your client?"

"Yes, Your Honor," said the catcher.

"Do it. Three minutes."

"Kieran, what's going on? Where's Cooper?"

The doors parted again, but the man who entered wasn't Cooper.

"You paid him cash?" I said.

"Five hundred dollars."

"Give me his business card."

I ran out to the corridor pay phones and hastily punched in the number. An obnoxious electronically synthesized voice informed me the number had been disconnected.

I pounded down the courtroom aisle and kicked open the gate in the rail. I don't know why the officers didn't tackle me. Maybe it was my honest face. Maybe the sight of a man wearing golf clothes didn't strike terror into anyone's heart. Whatever the reason, I captured Judge Hartnett's full attention before anyone reached me.

"What the . . . Who the . . ." she sputtered.

"Kieran Lenahan, Your Honor. I'm here on behalf of Mr. O'Meara."

"That's nice," she said sarcastically as two sets of hands clamped onto my arms and two elbows dug into my spine. "Are you an attorney?"

"Yes. I know I don't look like one. But I definitely am and . . . Your Honor, may I approach?"

She leaned back in her chair and stared at me with narrowed eyes as if calculating what I might have up my sleeve. Finally, she nodded her head. The two officers bent my arms behind my back and pushed me toward the bench. Fowler joined us there, a well-practiced wince of exasperation spreading his cheeks.

"What is the meaning of this circus act?" Judge Hartnett said through her teeth.

"The woman in the first row is Mr. O'Meara's aunt. She paid an attorney five hundred dollars to handle this arraignment, and he hasn't shown up. I wanted to bring this to the court's attention before you ordered Legal Aid to stand in."

"Who is this other attorney?"

"Arturo Cooper."

She pursed her lips as if the name meant something, then rolled her chair to the far side of the bench. A court clerk spoke into her ear. When he finished, the judge shook her head in obvious disapproval and rolled back.

"My clerk informs me that no one by that name has entered a notice of appearance for this case," she said. "Whatever arrangement the defendant's family made with a member of the bar is not the business of this court."

"Okay, I'm representing him."

"This is highly irregular."

"Is it highly regular that a member of the bar bilks an unsuspecting woman out of five hundred dollars?"

Judge Hartnett stared daggers. "How do I know you are a lawyer?"

My wallet contained all manner of identification, but nothing to prove membership in the bar. Then I realized that the officer bracing my right arm was my old buddy.

"Ask him," I said.

The officer vouched for me, and Judge Hartnett granted my request.

"Can I have ten minutes with my client?" I said, smoothing the finger marks out of my shirt sleeves.

"Three."

"How about five?"

"Don't push me, Counselor."

Pete and I huddled at the defense table. An alligator patch hung by a single thread from a golf shirt spattered with bleach stains.

"Kieran, what are you doing here?" His voice quaked.

"Never mind. It's a long story. How are they treating you?"

"It was okay in Milton. But they got some big guys here. They made kissing noises at me." He lowered his head and raised his hands, but the chain tightened before they met. "Kieran, I'm scared."

"I know. We don't have much time. This is called an arraignment. It's where the D.A. tells you what you're charged with and the judge asks how you plead. Of course, you're going to say not guilty."

"That guy, the D.A., he came to Milton and asked me questions." Pete swallowed hard. "He really thinks I did it."

"It's his job to think you did it. Did you tell him anything?"

"Nope. I know all about that. Things you say incriminate you."

"Right. Remember I'm on your side, and whoever we ultimately hire to represent you will be on your side, too. No one else. Got it?"

He nodded. "Who are all those people out there?"

"Reporters, nosey people. Your Mom and Aunt Dee, too. Listen, we have only another minute. You let me do the talking. The judge will ask you one question, and when I nudge you, say 'not guilty.' And say it loud like you mean it. Then I'm going to try to get you released on bail. I don't see how the judge can deny that."

The glint of hope in Pete's eyes was so bright it scared me.

"Are we *finally* ready to proceed?" said Judge Hartnett.

Fowler and I both answered yes. Technically, Pete could request a formal reading of the charges against him. But I waived the formal reading to save Pete a lengthy scene. The charges ran from murder in the second degree to the milder forms of manslaughter. Fowler made his brief statement in a snippy, arrogant manner, as if anyone he charged with a crime was automatically guilty and the legal process was a game dreamed up by the Founding Fathers.

"How do you plead?" said Judge Hartnett.

I kicked Pete's foot.

"Not guilty," he said in two different octaves.

I made my pitch for his release on bail. He was a young boy, I said, a student with roots in his community, a part-time job, a family obviously concerned about his welfare. Fowler disputed everything, even the job.

"He works for me," I said, laying the sarcasm on thick.

Laughter coursed through the courtroom. Judge Hartnett donned a pair of half-glasses to read a sheet of paper handed up by the court clerk.

"This bail evaluation comports with the defense argument," she said. "However, now that I see the defendant has a prior criminal record, I am inclined to agree with the People. This crime was particularly heinous. The victim was a man of some stature in his community. Accordingly, I am ordering a remand."

"Your Honor—"

"The defense may renew its bail application at a later date."

"But—"

"Mr. Lenahan, I have indulged you enough for one day. Another word out of you and I will hold you in contempt."

"Kieran, what's this mean?" said Pete. His shaking hands rattled the chains.

Words of apology, explanation, hollow encouragement froze in my throat as the two guards hauled him away. His screams echoed in the tunnel to the holding pens.

"I thought I was going home! Kieran, you promised! You promised!"

CHAPTER
6

As the courtroom emptied, I asked the court clerk what he had told Judge Hartnett about Arturo Cooper. I couldn't believe my ears.

Cooper's law firm sprouted branches in several major cities. The White Plains office had been a backwater operation until major corporate clients fled New York City for the northern suburbs. Now it hummed round the clock, grinding out whole forests of paper in the name of the great god Litigation.

I banged into an antiseptic reception area. Having sprinted four blocks from the courthouse, my neck sizzled in the refrigerated air. A receptionist wearing gobs of blue eye shadow stopped buffing her nails long enough to answer my question.

"Never heard of him," she said and snapped her gum.

I lifted a plastic clipboard from the desk and flipped through the firm directory until I spotted an extension for someone named Cooper.

"Whaddaya know. Learn something new everyday," she said,

though her tone of voice lacked any sense of discovery. She punched up
the number. "Someone here to see you. No, I didn't get it." She covered
the receiver. "What's your name?"

I told her and she told him.

"He never heard of you."

"Mention the Texaco-Spencer deal. About seven years ago."

"He says something about a Texaco deal. I don't know. Look, he
wanted to talk to Alex Cooper. I'm supposed to know you're busy?"

"Arturo Cooper."

"Wait," she said. "It's Arturo Cooper he wants. Do you know his
extension? Really? Should I tell him? No? What if he wants to know?
Okay." She slammed down the phone. "Jerk. Not you, I mean him. Arturo Cooper left the firm last year. He has an office at One William
Street."

"What shouldn't you tell me?"

She cupped her hand next to her mouth. "He was fired," she whispered.

One William Street was a mid-rise office building with Art Deco flourishes. A potted corn plant hovered near death in the lobby, and the
elevator buttons refused to light up. I tracked signs along a labyrinthine
corridor to a door with "Law Offices" unevenly lettered in gold decals.
Behind it, a typewriter pattered.

I rapped politely. The typing eased off to a trickle, then gushed
again. I pounded hard enough to rattle the hinges. The typing stopped.
A blonde sourpuss wearing a lavender jogging outfit opened the door as
far as a security chain allowed. Over her shoulder I saw a receptionist's
desk, a typing bay, a semblance of a law library, and two doors leading
from the common area to private offices. One door was ajar, the other
closed. The name plate on the latter read: "Arturo Cooper, Esq."

"I want to see Mr. Cooper."

"The office is closed. Are you a client?"

"The office is not closed because I see lights. And, no, I'm not a client."

"Mr. Cooper will be in at nine tomorrow."

If she had been any taller or I had been any shorter, I wouldn't have seen Cooper's door quickly open and shut.

"Would you step back, please?" I said, wedging my foot inside the doorjamb.

"I told you, Mr. Cooper isn't here."

I repeated my request. When she realized I wouldn't budge, she stepped back. One shoulder butt snapped the security chain.

"You can't do this. I'm calling the police." She lifted a phone from a nearby desk.

"Be my guest," I said. "Save me the trouble."

She chased after me, yapping at my heels like a bad-tempered poodle.

I banged open Cooper's door. He knelt on the floor with his face buried in the cottage cheese thighs of a woman stretched obliquely on a leather chesterfield. The woman instantly covered herself with a file folder. Cooper wobbled to his feet. His pants puddled around his ankles.

"What is this?" he said, flailing for his suspenders.

"You know what the hell it is. You took, strike that, counselor, you *stole* five hundred dollars from a desperate lady." I grabbed a wad of tee-shirt and flung Cooper against the desk. The edge caught him squarely in the stomach, and he melted to the floor. The woman whimpered. I threw a red skirt the size of a handkerchief at her.

Cooper rocked on his side and tried to catch his breath. The woman squirmed into her skirt. That's when I saw Deirdre's five hundred dollars. It wasn't in the form of currency because Cooper had converted it into tangible goods: a tiny pyramid of cocaine nicely arranged on a slab of glass. I grabbed a decorative gavel and smashed it all into a useless pile. Then I shoved Cooper's face into the remains.

"You pull that shit again," I said, "and I'll come back for whatever's left of your license."

I beached Cooper on his desk and shouldered past sourpuss, who stood frozen in the doorway.

"Who the hell are you?" she said.

"Bar disciplinary committee."

The Milton Police Department shared a massive stone building with the town court in Station Square. The desk sergeant, a Limerick neighbor, allowed me past without too much hassle. DiRienzo's office was anally neat. Perfect X's crossed off the days on a hunting calendar. A phalanx of needle-sharp pencils stood at the ready on a fresh green blotter. Criminal law texts lined a pressboard bookcase. Colored thumbtacks speared announcements, notices, and wanted posters to a bulletin board. I was about to crack DiRienzo's secret color code when a toilet flushed and a door opened. DiRienzo emerged tucking in his shirttails.

"Figured I'd see you sooner or later," he said. "I heard what you did in court. You some kind of grandstander?"

"I did what was necessary. And now that it's done, I'm here to talk about Pete."

"What about him?" DiRienzo lowered himself into his chair and straightened his tie. A tight collar kept the blood close to his head.

"What do you have on him?"

"Is that a specific question? If it is, I already made a statement to the press. Read about it in tomorrow's paper."

"I'm not here as a nosey citizen. Right now I'm Pete's attorney of record."

"Talk to your client."

"He's damn near incoherent," I said.

"Too bad. You need to know something, you contact the D.A.'s office like the criminal procedure law says." He folded his arms and grinned smugly, though he did glance quickly at the bookcase for support.

"You know, Lenahan, I'm not the one to say I told you so. But two years ago I wanted that kid to do time. Even if it was only six months at a youth farm, he might have learned something instead of you taking him in and teaching him golf. Everyone called me a fascist for doing the things I did as Youth Officer. That's because this town doesn't want to face the fact it has some bad kids behind its neat shutters. Well, now one of the town's leading citizens is dead. But I'm not going to say I told you so.

"You start nosing around trying to spring this kid, you'll be up against it. Just remember that. I closed this case fast because I know this town better than anyone."

For all his puffing, DiRienzo didn't own the monopoly on inside dope. His main competition came from Gloria Zanazzi. Gloria had been the Inglisi & Lenahan receptionist until the firm folded. She now logged traffic tickets in the Milton Town Court, a job well-suited to her avocation as town gossip. Unfortunately, my call raised only her answering machine. I hung up without leaving a message and buzzed up county to Judge Inglisi's house.

Big Jim's den featured a massive air conditioner pumping thousands of British Thermal Units past fluorescent green streamers tied to the grill. The Judge himself took up most of a leather couch. A wet towel curled around the back of his neck. The remains of a six-pack littered the floor around his slippers. On a giant TV screen, two Amazons in g-strings bashed each other in the middle of a wrestling ring.

"What the hell are you watching?" I said. I hadn't been there two minutes, and I was already irritated by his attitude. I also was freezing my ass.

The Judge arced a peanut from thumb to mouth, then dabbed at his forehead with the towel.

"Are you criticizing my choice of entertainment?"

"It's fake as hell."

"Let me tell you something about television sports," said the Judge. "Every damn one of them is fake. Football, baseball, basketball, women's wrestling. They're all the same. I'm not disputing that professional athletes play hard and bring pride to their performances. But that doesn't mean shit to the people on our side of the TV screen. We're not playing the games. Our job is to stay amused enough to sit through the commercials."

"Who sponsors this?"

"A company selling pick-up trucks with balloon tires. I might buy me one." The Judge yanked the towel from his neck and threw it into a corner. "Now what's the problem?"

I told him first about Cooper, a safe topic that would lay a foundation for the real purpose of my visit. The Judge didn't take his eyes from the television screen. The only hint that he even listened was a barely audible titter when I described the scene in Cooper's office.

"Cooper left his firm about two years ago," he said when I finished. "No one is officially fired from a firm like that one. You 'associate' with someone else or 'announce the opening' of your own office. Cooper did the latter. That is, he rented space with a few solo practitioners who work hand to mouth at One William Street. There've been rumors about him neglecting court appearances and screwing around with clients' escrow money. He's stayed one step ahead of the disciplinary committee. Guess he still is a pretty good lawyer when he wants to be. He's saved his own ass longer than it deserves."

"Takes balls to walk out of his own arraignment and scam money from Deirdre," I said.

"Sit where I sit long enough and you realize that people are amazingly creative in how they can fuck over one another."

I told him about Pete's arraignment. This time he didn't watch the television. His eyes bored into me with a stare that could turn a brain pan as hot as a griddle.

"I see this afternoon's conversation made some impact," he said.

"I didn't intend to represent Pete. But now that I'm involved I need to know what's going on."

The Judge dragged a fresh towel across the back of his neck. "Are we getting anywhere near a point?"

I explained DiRienzo's refusal to tell me what evidence the police had on Pete.

"What about Gloria?" said the Judge.

"I can't find her. And I don't want the extraneous gossip if I can avoid it."

The Judge groped through the empties around his feet until he found a fresh beer. Froth gushed onto the carpet. He didn't bat an eye.

"I was wrong," he said. "This isn't Florida all over again. You think you can put things back together with Deirdre by helping Pete. If that's it, you're making a big mistake for all three of you."

On the screen, the two Amazons screamed at each other over the cringing shoulders of a male announcer.

"I like these ladies," said the Judge. "They're honest."

I extracted another Judge Inglisi promise to help, all with the usual trouble, and drove back to Limerick. Light from my landlords' kitchen window cast a fuzzy glow on the small plot of grass between the house and the garage. In an upstairs bedroom, their newest baby wailed.

I draped an old carpet over the clothesline and gathered half a dozen golf balls scattered around the grass. My mind worked best while I swung a golf club. As I pumped shot after shot into the carpet, I thought about how inextricably bound my life was with the O'Mearas.

One night, shortly after joining Big Jim's law firm, I walked into one of Milton's upscale bars and walked out with my life turned on its ear. Limerick wasn't large enough a neighborhood to permit total strangers among its residents. I knew Deirdre as Tom O'Meara's younger sister, a lanky redhead who finally grew into her legs. We talked and drank and flirted and went out on a date that lasted an entire weekend. When it ended, I had fallen unabashedly in love with her luxuriant red hair, lean legs, and *carpe diem* attitude; she with my sanity, stability, and charm.

We spent the next five years chasing that one weekend.

We weren't together more than a few months before people pegged us for marriage. Now in Limerick, marriage talk didn't surface like a normal topic of conversation. You felt a sense of bated expectation in the neighborhood, from the significant silences of the biddies camped on their porches, to the raunchy laughter of the regulars at Toner's Pub, to the teasing voices of my landlords' gremlins.

I guess we withstood the pressure because the only people who mattered exerted none. Corny O'Meara never sat me down and grilled me about my intentions toward his daughter; Dolores treated me like a son. And in an odd way, the family's relaxed attitude contributed to my own misgivings about marrying Deirdre. I didn't understand the full impact of my doubts until much later.

My memories of the O'Meara family were holiday snapshots: Corny at the head of the dinner table, owl eyes behind thick glasses, dabbing his chin after every mouthful; Dolores at the opposite end, brown hair pulled tightly back from a broad forehead, nipping at a plastic tumbler awash with whiskey; hyperactive Pete beside Corny, prodding his grandfather to tell stories about the war; Tom, ramrod straight before his accident, cautioning Pete that Grandpa's stories were just that—stories like Mother Goose would tell; Gina, skittish as always, sensing a face-off between husband and father-in-law, hurrying into the kitchen for more bread or butter or gravy; and Deirdre beside me, her leg thrown over mine beneath the lace tablecloth, whispering devilish promises in my ear.

Later, after exchanging gifts, we sat in the living room and watched flames engulf tattered wrapping paper.

"He has a girlfriend," said Deirdre.

"Who does?"

"My father, the host of this great feast. And yes, my mother knows. And no, she won't do a thing about it except say the rosary. Not me. You ever put me in that position, Kieran Lenahan, and I swear to God I'll kill you."

Corny never saw another Christmas. He died from an aneurysm the following autumn just before he was about to retire from the railroad. Tom, laid up in the hospital after his accident, attended neither wake nor funeral. Corny's girlfriend jumped on his casket at the cemetery. Dolores said the rosary.

Deirdre and I tripped along, leading lives circumscribed by our respective jobs. Big Jim promoted me to partner. Deirdre rose to head nurse of the cardiac intensive care unit at the County Medical Center. My hours were long. Hers were unpredictable. It took a year to figure out she'd been cheating on me.

We broke up, though Deirdre continued to barge into my apartment at any and all hours, usually in the aftermath of a date gone sour. I tossed her out the first half dozen times, but eventually we talked. She admitted that discovering her father's affair had been the most devastating event of her life. She was sixteen at the time, and had stumbled across the love letters and photographs while cleaning out an old desk in the basement. She collapsed on the floor and cried until her brother found her. Tom was skeptical. He idolized his father, hung on his every word no matter how exaggerated or preposterous. They staked out the girlfriend's apartment in an Irish section of the Bronx; saw Corny go in and not come out. Tom grasped for innocent motives. "He's never been too swift," Deirdre told me back then. "Never could stare at garbage like I can."

Tom eventually accepted the evidence and turned an icy shoulder to his father. Deirdre, in deference to her mother's wish for harmony, maintained a pleasant exterior. But deep in her heart she vowed that no man would ever treat her so shabbily. In psycho-babble, her cheating on me was a subconscious attempt to sabotage our relationship before I did the same to her.

We decided to live together. The novelty injected a temporary zest into our relationship, but soon we descended into suspicion. The relationship was dead; neither of us wanted to hammer the last nail into the coffin. Then Big Jim won his election. With nothing to keep me moored to Milton, I packed up for Florida.

My professional apprenticeship had been a snap, and after earning my PGA card I concentrated on winning a spot on the PGA Tour. Each year the Tour held a tournament known as the Qualifying School, in which hundreds of hopefuls slogged through eight rounds over a course designed by the Marquis de Sade. At stake were a handful of Tour exemptions—the unrestricted right to play on the Tour for an entire year. The exact number available for any Qualifying School class depended on how many touring pros lost their exemptions for not winning enough prize money the previous year.

Most apprentices prepared for the Qualifying School by competing on mini-tours, weekly tournaments held during the winter months. Prize money was minimal, but competition was keen. Success on the minis closely correlated with winning a Tour exemption.

I won three mini-tour events and placed second in two others. I had no doubt that I would play well enough in the Qualifying School to achieve my dream of becoming a touring pro. The Florida State Attorney's Office had other ideas.

In a vacationland that offered wagering on jai alai, thoroughbreds, trotters, greyhounds, and alligators, someone had devised a method of betting on golfers. While I pocketed prize money that barely covered expenses, several of my fellow pros supplemented their incomes by co-operating in an illegal gambling scheme. The details were fuzzy—and ultimately nothing was proven—but the State Attorney launched an investigation that attracted the intense interest of the Tour brass.

I wasn't a target, but several of my friends were. The investigators' tactics were unfair and intimidating. I advised my friends on how best to gum up the investigation. The Tour brass, upset with my storefront legal activities, rejected my entry application for the Qualifying School. In other words, I was a troublemaker. With no other options, I returned to Limerick. Milton Country Club had lost its long-time pro, and I submitted my resume.

The board handed me the job. My landlords re-let my old apartment to me. Suddenly, I was back in my hometown, newly incarnated, my previous life a dream. Dolores O'Meara suffered a stroke, and Deirdre cancelled plans to move to Texas in order to stay and care for her. Somehow, I knew neither of us would ever leave Milton.

Judge Inglisi was right: if I had kept to myself in Florida I would have been on the Tour, away from Pete, Deirdre, the whole lot of them. From a slightly different perspective: if Corny O'Meara had been a decent family man, I would have married Deirdre on the first pass and never become a golf pro.

CHAPTER
7

I found part of the answer the next morning in, of all places, the local newspaper. Randall Fisk's column oozed down the entire length of page one of the sports section under the headline "Third Reich Claims Another Victim."

The column juxtaposed an idyllic description of Milton Country Club's linksland with the lurid details of Sylvester Miles' murder. It then leaped back to a short history of the *Blitzklubs*, skillfully paraphrasing H.L. Hillthwaite's text, and concluded with the presumption that Miles was among the G.I.s who raided the forge of the Bavarian metalsmith in 1945.

Then came the innuendoes:

The story grows curiouser. Miles' last will directed newly crowned Met champ Kieran Lenahan to sell the *Blitzklubs* at auction with the proceeds going to unspecified heirs. The kicker is the *Blitzklubs* disappeared from Lenahan's MCC pro shop the other night in what police describe as a "suspicious burglary." Aren't all burglaries suspicious? A police spokesman had this to say: "We found a window forced open, but we aren't convinced it was the means of entry." Question, then: Are the *Blitzklubs* and the murder connected? The same spokesman replied: "It is one of our working hypotheses."

DiRienzo undoubtedly was the police spokesman, and the implication of his working hypotheses disturbed me. Most people who aren't very smart tend to underestimate the intellectual abilities of others. DiRienzo had the opposite tendency. Once he fixated on a suspect, he ascribed all sorts of diabolical schemes to the suspect's mind. A week ago, he wouldn't have known a *Blitzklub* from a nightclub. Now these German artifacts were the linchpin of his murder investigation.

I turned things over in my mind. Fisk's column hinted that the police believed Miles was killed because of the *Blitzklubs*. Did the missing wedge disappear from the murder scene? Did the murderer track down the rest of the set later? Pete must have seen the strange set of clubs. He went into my office dozens of times each day. Did he know they belonged to Miles? Did he know how valuable they were? Did he, as the column also hinted, screw around with the window to make the burglary look like an outside job?

I probably could have solved the entire mystery if the telephone hadn't sent my train of thought careening off a cliff. Deirdre's Irish was up higher than a kite.

"They showed up at the house eight o'clock this morning to look for a set of golf clubs. Tom didn't stop them."

Bingo, Randall Fisk. "Did they have a warrant?"

"I guess so."

"If they did, there was nothing Tom could do."

Deirdre's breath hissed. She wanted to be mad at Tom, someone, anyone. Next stop, Arturo Cooper. Did I ever contact him?

"We met in his office," I said.

"Did he explain why he never showed up?"

"He didn't have a valid excuse."

"What about my money?"

I opened a cigar box stuffed with accounts receivable. If I collected half I could cover her $500 without dipping into my Met winnings.

"He didn't protest when I took it," I said.

"Must have been some conversation."

"We reached an agreement."

"So now what? Pete's still in jail."

"Let me work on it for awhile."

"Kieran, you have other things—"

"I know. Other things can wait. I've already started—"

She hung up, miffed at the implication she had done a poor job. That was Deirdre. She had a few chinks in an otherwise thick hide.

The Judge blew in at lunchtime.

"I didn't find out much, but what I found isn't good." He squeezed into my office and propped himself on a stool. "They have a witness who can place Pete at the scene, which isn't necessarily the golf course. The police don't think he was killed near the pond. I don't know where they think it happened, but it wasn't there. Miles was dragged because the tops of his shoes were turned back and there was dirt in the toes. But whether it was thirty yards or three hundred yards, I don't know. They have physical evidence linking Pete to the scene. Don't ask me what because I didn't find that out either."

"Do they know when Miles was killed?"

"A dawn to dusk range is as fine as it'll get. I talked to the Medical Examiner's office myself. Something about water affecting the blood pooling and coagulation. I don't understand that scientific talk. But they know what killed him. A blunt instrument blow to the shoulder broke his collarbone and severed an artery. A second blow to the occipital lobe of the skull was window dressing."

"Could the murder weapon have been a golf club?"

"Is a golf club a blunt instrument?" said the Judge. "Maybe the way I swing one."

I tossed the sports section to the Judge. He tossed it right back.

"I already read that column," he said. "Fisk isn't too far off the mark. The police diver didn't find any club belonging to Miles in the pond."

"Which could mean Miles wasn't killed while he was practicing," I said.

"Or it could mean the kid, or the killer, took the club off Miles. Then he found out how valuable they were and burgled your shop for the rest."

"So at some time we don't know, Pete killed Miles someplace not on the golf course, dragged his body to the pond, sunk it with stones, and made off with the *Blitzklub* pitching wedge."

I paused so the absurdity of the scenario could dawn on the Judge. He only shrugged.

"Then he saw the rest of the set in the shop and faked a burglary. Did he sell the clubs before his arrest, or are they hidden somewhere?" I didn't wait for the Judge to answer. "Sorry, I don't buy any of this. I don't think Pete is capable."

"Are you finished?" said the Judge. "Because there is one more tidbit you might consider before you nominate Pete for canonization. Drug tests found traces of cocaine in his system. Enough so that he would have been flying high the night of the murder."

The Westchester County Jail is a low-slung concrete building located beside the County Medical Center in the town of Valhalla. A home of the gods it isn't. The jail houses inmates doing time for misdemeanors as well as felony suspects bound over for trials in White Plains. Pete O'Meara fell into the latter category.

A corrections officer asked me questions at the entrance. One metal detector and two sets of steel doors later, I stood at the glass-enclosed control room known as the Bubble. The officer inside asked me for identification. I slipped my wallet through a slot.

"Lenahan, huh? You the fella called before. Who you here to see again?"

I filled out a form and received a card with Pete's name lettered in red grease pencil. The officer pressed a button, and a door opened with a metallic rumble.

The visitors' room felt like the bottom of a mine shaft. The sky had been blue and the sunlight brilliant, but here only bleak gray light filtered through the tiny barred windows twenty feet above the floor. Obscenities peppered the dull green surface of a small metal table. Hand prints dappled the cinderblock walls. Rancid body odor lingered in the air. I shivered involuntarily. I never understood why deterrence didn't work for everyone as well as it did for me.

A guard produced Pete, removed his handcuffs, and locked us inside. Pete rubbed his wrists before taking a seat across the table. He wore white chinos and a denim shirt. Tension straightened his serpentine posture.

"Are you still my lawyer?" he said.

"Until I find someone we can trust to do a better job."

"When will that be?"

"That isn't important right now," I said. "What happened yesterday after I left the shop?"

"DiRienzo left when you did," said Pete. "He came back an hour later with a couple of cops and said he had a warrant for my arrest. I thought he was kidding. But then he smacked this piece of paper across my face, and the two cops grabbed my arms. DiRienzo slapped the cuffs on me and told me all that stuff about how I didn't have to answer any questions and I could call a lawyer. Then they took me down to the station."

"Did they question you?"

"Nope. They fingerprinted me and booked me, and then they waited around for that fat-assed D.A. to show up."

"They didn't ask you any questions?"

"The D.A. did. He told me all that stuff about not having to answer and said I could call a lawyer. I was hoping you'd show up looking for me, but then I figured I'd better call home instead. The D.A. asked me stuff like what did I do the night of the murder. A witness said I did it, what did I think of that."

"Did you say anything?"

"Hey, Kieran, I know something about all this legal shit." Pete tried to act hard, but he shuddered and became a kid again.

I puzzled over the arrest. DiRienzo had a warrant and a witness to back it up. He probably sought the warrant after investigating the burglary, which meant he'd been focusing on Pete for awhile. Strange he didn't question Pete. But maybe he wanted to be extra careful with the biggest case of his life. No need to risk coercing a confession some liberal judge might quash.

We turned back to the night of the murder. Pete covered the same ground as he had with me and DiRienzo the afternoon the body turned up. It had been a misty evening with no golfers on the course. Just before Pete locked up the shop, Dr. Frank Gabriel asked to borrow a cart to inspect sprinkler heads on the back nine. He kept Pete waiting approximately half an hour, and tipped him two dollars for his trouble. Pete tried hitching a ride home on the Post Road rather than walking the most direct route, which was across the course and past the Miles house.

"What time did you get home?" I said.

"Quarter to eight, maybe."

"Anyone home when you got there?"

"Nope. Dad was out fishing. He's been doing a lot of that lately, taking the boat out in the late afternoon and not coming home till dark. All he brings home are friggin' bergalls. Real proud, you know, like they're tuna or swordfish or something. Mom was out shopping, but she always leaves my dinner wrapped in aluminum foil on the stove. I brought it upstairs to eat while I got ready."

"For what?"

"Just stuff. I heard Dad come in while I was upstairs. It must have been eight-thirty or so. He put on the TV. I could hear 'Victory at Sea' playing on the porch. I didn't want him to see me leave because he was pissed at me for all the time I spend at the golf course. So when I finished getting ready, I went real quiet down the stairs and ducked past the porch. I slipped on some wet stuff dripping on the hallway floor. I don't know if he heard me because I ran like hell."

"Where were you going?"

"To meet a kid named Todd Verno. We hung out a lot in eighth and ninth grade. I'm not supposed to hang out with him now. I mean, if Aunt Dee found out, she'd be mad. But Dad doesn't pay attention, and Mom doesn't know what the hell is going on. And I really don't hang around with Todd much anyway. He knows these two girls from Port Chester. They were supposed to meet us at our spot. Have a few beers. You know, that kind of stuff."

"Where is the spot?"

"The linksland," he said. "If you drag the bench off the tenth tee into the Marshlands, there's this spot you can see New York City and the bridges."

"Great," I said without enthusiasm. "What time were you there?"

"After nine. The girls were supposed to meet us at nine-thirty. We went a little early, like to set stuff up. Drag the bench off the tee. You know, make sure the beer was cold."

"Who are the girls?"

"I don't know. They're Todd's friends. They never showed, anyway. Probably because of the weather. So we drank the beer. Almost a whole case between us. We got pretty ripped."

"What happened to the beer cans?"

"I threw them all into the trash basket on the tee. I won't litter the golf course, you know that."

"Then what?"

"We left."

"You walked down Harbor Terrace Drive right past Miles' house."

"That's the quickest way home."

"And what time did you get home?"

"Midnight. Maybe a little later."

"And that was it."

"Yep."

I leaned across the table. "Who the hell do you think you're trying to fool?"

"Kieran, I—"

I slammed my fist so hard the table bounced off the cement floor. Pete's skin blanched. The corners of his mouth turned down.

"You and Todd didn't just chug a case of beer. You guys blew some coke. You think those tests you took after your arrest were a joke? You think the D.A. doesn't know this?"

Pete didn't once meet my eye. He whimpered and sniffled and dragged both sleeves across his nose. And then he talked.

"Okay, Todd had some coke. I don't do it much. Really, I don't. It makes me feel all jazzed up, even the next day. But these chicks didn't show up, so I did some. We finished all Todd had. Must have been half a gram. Todd knew someone who could sell us more, but we didn't have enough money. So we had an idea we'd try and get some."

"You broke into Sylvester Miles' house."

"No way, man. I mean, my memory's a little fuzzy with all that beer and shit. And I guess we looked at the house because it's the closest to the golf course. But we didn't break in."

"You just said your memory is fuzzy."

"Hey, I don't need a good memory to know I stayed away from those Harbor Terrace houses. They all got burglar alarms or watch-dogs."

"What do you remember?"

"Runnin' like hell. We heard something, I think. But I can't re-member what. I got home about midnight. Dad was sleeping on the porch in front of the TV, as usual. I don't think he heard me."

The doorlock slid back with a clank.

"Someone else here to see the kid," a guard said and stepped aside.

Brendan Collins swept in with a nylon raincoat billowing from his shoulders. His face was freshly tanned, and his bleached hair was wind-blown as if he'd driven up from Milton in a convertible.

"What the hell's going on here, Brendan?" I said.

"I've been retained to handle this case. I'm here to interview my client." He slid an alligator skin briefcase on the table and obviously enjoyed the loud pops of its brass latches. "I understand you handled the arraignment when Pete's first lawyer didn't appear. Very plucky of you. I appreciate it."

"Who retained you?"

"The family."

"They didn't say anything to me."

"We spoke only an hour ago. I can show you the retainer if you like."

Collins grew up in Limerick and had succeeded beyond everyone's dreams except his own. I always envied his style. Not his house or his car or his boat or his clothes, but his relaxed demeanor. No matter how much shit fell around his ears, he always remembered it was the client's shit. He was just doing his job. If I had cultivated the same attitude, I might have enjoyed the practice of law. Instead, I took the shit home and wrestled with it every night.

Collins didn't need to handle a notorious criminal case just to keep his name in the headlines. His interest had to be money, and plenty of it. I doubted Tom O'Meara could afford him.

"Kieran, what's going on?" said Pete. Fear and confusion swirled in his wide eyes.

Collins handed me the retainer agreement. I skipped over the boilerplate babble and concentrated on the numbers filling the blanks and the name gracing the signature line. I immediately understood how the O'Meara clan swung Collins. The fee was surprisingly small, even by my old standards. The signature explained the rest.

"I'm your lawyer now, son," said Collins.

"I'm not your son," snapped Pete.

Collins nodded amiably, as if prepared to hear much worse from his new client. He pushed the briefcase across the table and nudged me from my seat. I took my time standing.

Pete grabbed my arm. "Kieran!"

"He's right, Pete. Your Aunt Dee hired him. But don't worry, I'll be around."

"What's that supposed to mean?" said Collins, taking the chair and arranging his tape recorder and legal pad on the table.

"Exactly what it sounds like."

"No one looks over my shoulder."

I leaned close to his ear.

"Then don't make any mistakes," I whispered.

I skidded into the O'Meara's driveway behind a powder blue hatchback with a County Medical Center parking sticker in its rear window. A poorly laid flagstone path curved across a bare dirt yard. I cupped my hand against the screen door. A long hallway cluttered with fishing tackle and broken lawn furniture receded to a brightly lit kitchen where a blue flame licked a large pot on a stove. Deirdre's voice, distinct but unintelligible, rose above the maritime strains of "Victory at Sea." I rapped on the door.

Gina O'Meara shuffled cautiously down the hallway, squinting in confusion until she finally recognized me. I followed her, pausing only to peek in at Tom, who lay asleep on a recliner while the Battle of Midway roared on the TV.

Deirdre sat at the kitchen table with a bowl of freshly peeled potatoes near her elbow. She immediately leaped to the offensive.

"You want to know why?" she said. "I did what's best for Pete. That's why."

"You could have told me."

"I didn't know until this afternoon that I'd even be able to hire another lawyer. I called the pro shop to tell you, but you were already gone."

"Why Collins?"

"He called and asked if he could help."

"He called you?"

"That's what I said. He knew all about Arturo Cooper and the arraignment. He said there were lots of sleazeballs out there ready to pounce on people in trouble like us. Then he offered to defend Pete, if we hadn't already hired someone to replace Cooper."

I scowled. When I was in practice I always waited for prospective clients to call me. No ambulance chasing, no dropping business cards at funerals. Certainly no calls to families of murder suspects.

"He charged you only half the normal rate."

"I know," said Deirdre. "He charged what we . . . what I . . . could afford."

"That isn't the Brendan Collins I know."

"Who is the Brendan Collins you know? You're not the only knight in shining armor on this planet."

"No one ever accused Collins of chivalry."

"That's your opinion. Collins said he wanted to defend Pete because he was once a Limerick boy, too."

"What a joke!"

"And I suppose you're the only one who knows what he's doing. That's why Pete's out on bail."

"Bail for Pete wasn't possible, not with his record and that judge. My mistake was promising something I couldn't deliver."

"That's what I mean. The old Kieran wouldn't have made a false promise. Let's face it. You chucked your law career to play games. Fine, that was your decision."

"Now you know that's too simple."

"Is it?"

"You remember those days."

"Oh, so I'm the reason you quit."

"Quitting the practice of law doesn't mean I've stopped being a lawyer."

"So you can flip from one role to the other as you see fit? You're not going to dabble with my nephew."

"I'm trying to help him."

"So am I."

"By selling him to Brendan Collins?"

The pot on the stove boiled over with a piercing hiss. Midway's background score suddenly went silent.

"*Jesu Christi*," said Gina, nervously smoothing her faded shift over her bony hips.

"—the hell's goin' on here?" Tom limped stiffly down the hallway. His shoulder dislodged a pair of hip boots hanging from the wall. They tumbled slowly, and he whacked them with his cane before they hit the floor. He looked crossly at each of us before lowering himself onto a chair Gina hastily pushed behind him.

"What's all this shouting about Brendan Collins?"

"I hired him to represent Pete."

"Who's gonna pay for the likes of Brendan Collins?" said Tom.

"He offered to defend Pete. Don't worry about the fee."

"I'm not accepting charity. The man must be paid."

"He will be, Tom. Don't you worry. Remember, this is Pete we're talking about."

"The money has to come from somewhere, sister dear. Someone has to think realistically."

"You're a fine one to talk about reality."

"Shut your trap," snarled Tom, his fingers twitching on his cane.

Deirdre slid her hand toward a paring knife. They glared hard at each other. I tensed my muscles, ready to jump between them.

"I'm paying for it, okay, Tom," said Deirdre. "I had money put away for his college. I gave that to Collins. Are you happy now?"

"College, huh? You got a lot of big ideas about my kid without including me."

"As if you're interested. College isn't such a big idea. It's just bigger than any ideas he hears in this house." Deirdre's face reddened. Her lips stretched thin and white across her teeth as she fought to control a sudden surge of anger. "Damn you!" she said. She scattered the potatoes across the table and ran out the back door.

"I suppose you'll say I taught him to murder," Tom yelled after her. He turned to me. "None of this woulda happened if you didn't give him that job. He shoulda gone to that youth farm instead of thinking life is a game."

He limped down the hallway. With one deft movement of his cane, he swept the hip boots back onto their hook. Seconds later, Midway resumed. Gina wrung her hands. The pot boiled over again.

I went after Deirdre. The back gate hung open. Beyond a lopsided garage, a tin can rattled as she stomped down the alleys and footpaths that coursed through Limerick like a maze. I knew what she struggled against; I had struggled against it myself. The Limerick mentality. We were a neighborhood of begrudgers. Another's success highlighted our own failures; another's goals reminded us of our own faded ambitions. The legacy passed down the generations. Don't ask for too much; be grateful for your lot; life may not improve, but it can worsen. I could forgive the ignorance or the stupidity that gave rise to this mentality. But a thick streak of bitterness ran through Tom's particular strain. That I couldn't forgive, and neither could Deirdre.

Across the backyard, an old flagstick leaned out of a cup cut into the crabgrass. Golf balls surrounded it like the stars of an unknown constellation. I picked one up. It was dirty, scuffed from countless collisions with rocks, fenceposts, aluminum siding. The name of a Tour heavyweight was lettered in red marking pen. I picked up another; saw another name. A laugh rumbled in my throat, almost on its own. I once told Pete about this game I devised as a boy. My own private Tour, with golf balls instead of players vying for mythical championships on golf courses sketched over neighborhood landmarks. I sorted through the rest of the balls, discovering the names Pete idolized.

The last one was mine.

To hell with Tom, to hell with Deirdre. To hell with the whole crazy family right back to you, Corny. I'd save Pete despite all of you.

CHAPTER
8

Lucky for me Jack Miles was an easy tail. I caught him coming out of campus, weaved behind him through the westbound rush on the expressway, then let out some slack on the long sweeping curves of the Taconic Parkway. By the time we hit Putnam County, the sun dipped below the hills, and we were the only two cars in sight.

Miles turned onto a dirt road descending sharply through a thick stand of pines. I stashed my car fifty yards farther on. Enough light still filtered through the green canopy for me to see the glimmer of water far below.

I picked my way down through the brush, conscious of how easily sound traveled in the perfect quiet of evening. The cottage was mostly clapboard, with tarpaper taking over where Jack Miles had run out of energy or patience or money. The front porch sagged between two stone pilings. A screen door, unhinged, leaned against a post.

I ducked around the Volvo, which was parked on a battered patch of weeds beside the cottage. Around back a window glowed like an aquarium.

Jack Miles hunched over a word processor, his head angled toward a stack of papers lit by the beam of a high intensity lamp. Line after line of wispy white text ascended the blue monitor screen as his hands played over the keyboard. He typed at a furious pace for several minutes, then leaned toward the screen like a nearsighted giraffe. He shook his head. A quick swipe of his hand sent several loose pages fluttering to the floor.

Miles swiveled his chair around as if suddenly aware of me. I pulled back from the window. When I peeked in again, the screen was dark, and Miles stared at the ceiling with that same daydreaming expression I'd seen the day before in his office. He slowly returned from his trance, cocking his head as if puzzled by the mess on the floor. He gathered the papers into a neat pile, switched off the lamp, and melted into the shadows.

The front door slammed. Leaves swished and twigs cracked in the direction of the lake. I moved from tree to tree until I sighted him. He paced along the lake bank, sucking a cigarette and loosening stones from the mud with his toe. He lit a second cigarette, immediately stubbed it out, and walked quickly to his car. The engine turned over with a wheeze, then tires crunched up the road. I waited until his taillights completely disappeared before making my move.

The front door opened easily with a credit card. A plywood floor, dotted with odd pieces of carpet remnants, creaked beneath my feet. Acoustical tiles made up part of the ceiling, bare rafters the rest. A dirty sheet screened off the toilet and wash basin. None of the closets had doors.

I quickly searched anyplace large enough to hide a set of golf clubs. I even hiked myself onto the ceiling rafters and shined a flashlight conveniently left standing on a file cabinet. No *Blitzklubs* anywhere.

Jack Miles' writing corner had an air of studied professorial disorder—piles of maps, back issues of *Stars & Stripes*, photocopies of several Bill Mauldin cartoons thumbtacked to a bulletin board. Beside the word processor were two manuscript boxes with labels designating them as draft five and draft six of *The Death of the Future*. Draft six was empty. Draft five contained about thirty typewritten pages heavily edited in pencil and three different colored pens. In the opening paragraph, a French army doctor told a G.I. named Sam Mills that his leg would have to be amputated. I replaced the cover on the box. Jack Miles' narrative hook hadn't hooked me. At least not under the circumstances.

A large blackboard stood against the wall with a flow chart resembling an Einsteinian formula scrawled across it. Initials, dates, and abbreviations. Boxes, triangles, and circles. All connected by arrows and arcs, lines and loops.

I turned to leave when something caught my eye: a brown paper bag wedged in a half-open drawer. The bag was filled with old letters banded together in four separate stacks. I spread the letters on the desk. All were written to Sylvester Miles in the early years after the war. One stack was from M. Velge in Brussels, Belgium; another from Hank Press in East Orange, New Jersey; the third from Eddie "Z" in Pittsburgh; and the last from Corny O'Meara in Milton. I felt my eyes bug out. Then I remembered Deirdre mentioning her father had known Sylvester Miles in the army. Beneath the paper bag lay three letters written by Sylvester to Jack and mailed from Nuremburg, Germany.

I had no idea how long Jack would be gone. Reading every letter would take hours. So I chose the ones written by Syl and skimmed as quickly as I knew how.

The ink had faded on the onionskin paper, and Sylvester Miles hadn't honed his penmanship in Catholic grammar school. But the letters were readable enough. He wrote of joining a transportation company stationed at the railyards in Nuremburg after the war ended. The company coordinated all supply shipments into Nuremburg for distribution to outlying areas. He described the house of a former SS officer the men had commandeered for lodging ("not exactly the Ritz for the master race"); he mentioned the war trials ("boring, even the defendants are asleep"); he occasionally waxed philosophical ("the infantry discourages getting close to your buddies, but here you can develop close friendships"); and he commented on the economics of the day ("cigarettes are better than cash").

I found no specific reference to the *Blitzklubs*. But in the last paragraph of the final letter, Syl vaguely wrote of finding souvenirs he could develop into valuable artifacts someday "if I get all the right breaks."

I remembered Jack Miles' snooty remark about his brother. Syl might scrounge for souvenirs, but he never was oriented toward the finer arts.

Maybe Syl had linked both.

I lay the letters back in the drawer and replaced the paper bag precisely as I found it.

I tried raising Pete on the jailhouse phone several times the next day. He finally called me in the early afternoon.

"He thinks I did it. Everyone thinks I did it. Kieran, I didn't do it."

"Slow down," I said. "What happened?"

"Collins talked to me for about two hours. He asked me all kinds of questions. What I did that night. What did I remember? Who saw me? How good a friend is Todd Verno? I told him everything. Told him the truth. And at the end, all he said was whether I did it or not doesn't matter right now. I'm in big trouble, and I'll do jail time. But he'll get me the best deal he can get."

"He used the word 'deal'?"

"Yep. I asked what that meant. Like did it mean I'd get off without going to jail. Maybe a youth farm or something. He said he and the

D.A. could work something out and tell the judge how much jail time I should get. The judge didn't have to go by that, but he said they usually did."

"Did you agree to anything?"

"No."

"Did you? Be very sure."

"No. Nothing."

"Good. You don't agree to anything without talking to me first."

I asked about the *Blitzklubs*, as I had intended when Collins interrupted us yesterday.

"What the hell are they?" said Pete.

"The clubs that were in my office, all wrapped in bubble plastic and paper. The stolen ones."

"Those clubs? What about them?"

"DiRienzo thinks they are the reason you killed Miles."

"I didn't kill him."

"Allegedly killed him. He thinks so enough he searched your house yesterday."

"He did?"

"Aunt Dee told me. Your father and mother let him. They had to, he had a warrant."

"Did he find them?"

"Would he?"

"DiRienzo does things like that," said Pete. "He's planted drugs on a few kids in town. Stuff no one hears about."

No one heard about that stuff because that stuff didn't happen. Not in the Milton I knew. But even if DiRienzo's tactics weren't a figment of Pete's hyperbolic imagination, he couldn't pull the same crap here. Drugs were fungible; the *Blitzklubs* weren't.

"What do you know about those clubs?" I said.

"I don't know dick about them. Are they worth lots of money?"

"Yeah, but I'm not sure if DiRienzo knows how much. He thinks you took one of the clubs from Miles' house, then stole the rest from the shop and faked the burglary."

"Hey, man, that's crazy."

"It isn't the first time DiRienzo's added two plus two and come up with five. But this is what you're up against."

Brendan Collins hung his ornate shingle on a crooked pedestrian lane off Merchant Street. He rarely opened the office because he billed most of his hours from his house on Poningo Point. The Point, as proper Miltonians called it, was a pricey spit of land separating Milton Harbor from Long Island Sound. The homes were larger, the lawns wider, and the pocketbooks deeper than anywhere in Milton.

Mrs. Mulranny, the housekeeper, answered the door. She lived not far from me in Limerick.

"Well, I knew you'd be turnin' up here sooner or later," she said, waving a feather duster under my chin. She wore a black and white uniform and, in deference to her bunions, pink powderpuff slippers.

I waited in a sunroom the size of my entire apartment while she shuffled off to ask if himself would see me. Beyond the seamless glass wall, a lawn as lush as a fairway sloped down to a cove where Collins' sloop bobbed in the gentle swells raised by a passing yacht.

Mrs. Mulranny announced that her master could spare me five minutes of his busy schedule, her tone suggesting she had argued the point with him. She led me to Collins' office, where he stood behind a large oak desk littered with papers and stared at me like I was a bill collector.

"You're not on this case twenty-four hours, and you already have Pete pleading out."

"Now wait a second, Kieran."

"Pete's a scared, confused kid. You're supposed to be his friend.

And if you're not his friend, at least his ally. He just called me. He doesn't understand what the hell's going on. He told you a story. He said he's innocent. And all he gets in return is a promise you'll cut him a deal."

"I thought I told you not to look over my shoulder."

"Forget it, Brendan. You have to live with me on this one."

Collins could be smooth as silk, but press him, and he frayed at the edges. Right now, his cheek twitched.

"All I did was lower the kid's expectations," he said, one lawyer to another. "My job isn't to prove who committed the murder."

"And it isn't to bite the first time Fowler makes plea bargain sounds. Or to make them yourself."

Collins waved a hand. "The family understands the trouble he's in. The father does, anyway. He's a testy sort. Very suspicious of the legal process. You know the type."

"I thought Deirdre hired you."

"She did, but I can't very well represent Pete and snub his father for the simple reason that he doesn't have the money to pay my fee."

"What about your fee? Did you suddenly develop a sense of charity?"

"I grew up in Limerick, too. Just like you. And just like Pete O'Meara."

"And the only time you see the old neighborhood now is barreling through on your way to Merchant Street."

"My idea of remembering the past doesn't include living there." Collins must have felt he cut pretty deep because he settled into his chair and took a long breath.

"You know my clearest memory of Sylvester Miles?" he said. "I worked my way through college, just as you did. You remember how we found summer jobs in those days. We would come home for spring break and beat a path up and down Merchant Street, buttonholing shopkeepers for work. Miles talked to me for an hour. Oh yes, he was very impressed with me. The grand opening of his new store was set for the first of June that year, and he needed an assistant manager for the summer. I was his man, he told me in those exact words. I went back to school with that secure feeling of a preordained summer. Money for tuition and enough left over to spend on myself.

"I showed up at the store June one and found out Miles didn't need an assistant manager. He walked me out onto the street, as if he thought I would create a scene and frighten his customers away. 'Sorry, son,' he told me, 'there just isn't any room on the payroll.' I was livid. The bastard betrayed me. All I could say was, 'I'm not your son,' just as Pete said to me yesterday.

"You know, I never found a job that summer. It took me eight years to pay off the loan I needed to cover that lost tuition money. Only fifty dollars a month, a trifle as it turned out. But I always remembered it as Sylvester Miles' loan." Collins blinked himself out of the memory. "Of course, my personal animosity doesn't justify a man's murder. But you can understand why I want to make certain the boy gets a fair shake. On the other hand, I must be honest with the family. I don't want anyone expecting miracles, especially since it looks like reasonable doubt may be a horse race."

"You've already come to that conclusion?"

"Kieran, there's a big problem. I talked to DiRienzo. He was a bit more forthcoming than with you. The police found Pete's footprints inside Miles' house."

I felt like I'd been sucker punched.

"Pete told me he never went inside."

"He told me the same thing," said Collins. "I believed him. I still want to believe him. But the evidence says otherwise."

"Did you speak to the Verno kid?"

"Not yet."

"Why didn't the police arrest him?"

Collins leaped out of his chair. Now that I moved the conversation back to case particulars, his old Limerick boy shell molted away like the exoskeleton of a locust.

"How the hell do I know?" he said. "I don't know their strategy. Right now I'm concerned about my own client rather than a possible co-defendant."

I wasn't so sure that was true, but we defined concern differently.

"What about Frank Gabriel?" I said.

"Pete told me he was on the golf course around seven that evening and might have seen something." Collins sighed. "But the police believe Miles was killed at least three hours later."

"I heard they don't have a fixed time."

"Not to the minute. But ten or ten-thirty is consistent with the other evidence, and with Pete's own story. I'll talk to Dr. Gabriel soon. Maybe he'll know something everyone else has missed."

Not before I do, I thought.

"Hey, Kieran," Collins called after me. "Bottom line is this is still a business."

That was the difference between us.

CHAPTER
9

Dr. Frank Gabriel was a Milton institution. His dental office occupied a three-room suite above the old Woolworth's on Merchant Street. The Woolworth Company had quit Milton due to decreasing sales and increasing rents. A sign in the soaped-over display window promised a mini-mall of boutiques coming soon. Gabriel hadn't abandoned his hometown so cavalierly. Though he performed complicated oral surgery in a professional building he owned in White Plains, he devoted two weekday afternoons to the teeth and gums of the good people of Milton.

The waiting room smelled of mouthwash sprayed from an atomizer. Static crackled in the Muzak. Gabriel's longtime receptionist wrestled with a bad temper as she spoke over the telephone.

"Dr. Gabriel does not want to commence legal proceedings. . . . Your rent is already one month overdue . . . I realize you lost your job. . . . Of course I told Dr. Gabriel. But you must understand his situation."

The door to the inner office opened, and out stepped a young girl clinging to her mother's arm. Gabriel followed closely behind, wiping his hands on a towel. The girl's eyes were red.

"She's a very brave girl," said Gabriel. He patted her hair, and she buried her face in her mother's skirt.

"Thank you for seeing us," said the mother.

"I'm glad I did. Another week and I mightn't have saved that tooth." Gabriel spied me. "Ah, Kieran Lenahan, fresh from victory. Don't tell me you have a toothache."

"No, but I would like a few minutes of your time."

"You may have an hour." He cocked an ear to the receptionist's conversation, frowned momentarily, then ushered me into his office.

The room was sparsely furnished: a desk, three chairs, a cabinet, a light box for viewing x-rays, and plaques citing Gabriel as Lions Club Man of the Year and commending him for service as a Milton Town Councilman.

I'd known Frank Gabriel for a good number of years and always suspected his public persona to be a carefully planned facade. His manners bordered on the saccharin, his friendliness could be a damn pain in the ass, and his placid disposition rivaled the linksland in its monotony. Judge Inglisi claimed once to have baited Gabriel into shouting an authentic "Goddammit" instead of his prissy "God blessed." Then again, the Judge could reduce a saint to tears of frustration.

But everyone erected facades, and if Gabriel's included false kindness to little girls scared stiff of dentists, it suited me fine. Besides, the good doctor supported my pro shop in yeoman fashion. He launched each of my first two seasons by purchasing elaborate equipment packages priced well into four figures. This past April, he stood pat. "Hard times?" I'd kidded him. He hadn't laughed.

Gabriel settled onto a chair and loosened the buttons of his smock. For a man in his late sixties, he was the picture of heartiness with youthfully square shoulders and dark hair curling thickly on well-muscled arms. A gold watch and gold bracelet circled wrists that could launch a golf ball a country mile. His only concession to age was a perfectly bald dome, which gleamed in the sunlight streaming through the venetian blinds.

"Well, if it isn't a tooth, I hope you're looking for an apartment. I could use a solvent tenant for a change."

"I want to talk to you about Sylvester Miles."

"Poor Syl." Gabriel removed his wire-rimmed glasses and buffed them with a corner of his smock. His eyes, large and brown behind the lenses, shrank to colorless slits. "I must say, the police were God blessed fast in arresting someone. In this day and age, unfortunately, that is the finest way of paying tribute to a murder victim. We are all going to miss him. Now, how may I help you?"

"You were on the golf course the evening of the murder. Did you see Syl?"

Gabriel's features stiffened. He worked the glasses onto his nose. "What possible reason could you have for asking me this?"

I told him about standing up for Pete at the arraignment.

"But you aren't representing him now."

"I didn't say that, but you are right."

Gabriel narrowed his eyes. Then a light seemed to go on in his head, and most of his smile returned.

"I see. You're taking an unofficial interest in the case. I've always commended your efforts on behalf of that boy, always commended them."

He wasn't lying. When I decided to hire Pete as a condition of his probation, I needed to justify my reasons at a board meeting. All three board members knew about Pete's troubles, so I wasn't exactly dropping bombs. Gabriel spoke in favor of giving the boy a chance, and the board unanimously agreed.

I explained that Pete had told DiRienzo about the evening cart ride during the early stages of the investigation; he also had mentioned it to me the day after his arrest.

"The boy is entirely correct," said Gabriel, "and I volunteered that exact information to the police. I inspected some of the automatic sprinkler heads on the back nine as part of a report I'm preparing for the board. They haven't been operating properly, you know."

"Did you see Syl out on the course?"

"I didn't. As I said, I was on the back nine, and Syl usually practiced fairly close to his house."

"You didn't notice him from a distance, say, across the linksland from the seventeenth tee."

"I didn't see a soul. No golfers, no joggers, no dog walkers. In fact, I remember thinking it was the first time in my memory I was completely alone on the golf course. You know how it can be out there. You spot someone two hundred yards away, and you feel you're being crowded. Not that night. I felt perfectly alone. It must have been the weather. That damp mist went right to my bones. I regretted not wearing a windbreaker."

"Pete says you were out there half an hour or so."

"I wasn't checking my watch, but that sounds about right. I tried to hurry because the boy seemed annoyed when I asked to borrow the cart. I guess he wanted to go home. I felt badly for delaying him, so I tipped him for his trouble. He must have told you."

I assured Gabriel he had.

"God knows I want Syl's killer brought to justice," he said. "But if that boy is guilty, the tragedy is doubled."

Not a very heartening interview. An empty golf course between seven and seven-thirty barely narrowed the time of death and didn't place Sylvester Miles on the linksland. I thanked Gabriel for his time. One question remained. But it was slightly far afield and best asked from a distance.

I paused at the door.

"This is off the subject, Doc. Is there any truth to the rumor that Milton Country Club is up for sale?"

Gabriel's automatic grin lasted a split second, no more.

"This God blessed town never ceases to amaze me," he said. "Tragedy strikes and all sorts of extraneous rumors fly. Selling the club after all the sweat and effort Syl put into its creation? I'd just as likely spit on his grave as vote for a sale."

"I heard this before the murder," I lied. "It was all over Wykagyl during the Met. Something about a Japanese group looking to buy a local club. I even heard one rumor that Miko Onizaka would be club pro."

"It's an absolute falsehood."

I smiled my best relieved smile. "You understand why I'm concerned. Head professional jobs are scarce, and at my age I don't have the patience to be anyone's assistant."

"I'm surprised, Kieran. Someone like you always could return to the practice of law."

"I have even less patience for that."

"Let me put your fears to rest. As long as I own my share of the club, you can stay on as pro. You are doing a fine job. Not every club has the distinction of employing the Met champ."

"Thanks for the vote of confidence, Doc."

Gabriel walked me to the front door, no doubt to stay under the guns for any more parting shots. As we passed through the waiting room, the receptionist launched into another fruitless plea for rent money.

———————

The Milton phone book listed only one Verno family, living in a mixed-use area cut off from the rest of Milton by the same industrial park where Andy Anderson kept his shop. The lone dead end street seemed forgotten by village services. Telephone poles skewed over rutted macadam sidewalks. Last year's leaves choked the storm drains like dry brown mush. The house itself sat above a slab of bedrock scarred from blasting. A corrugated metal swimming pool slouched in the yard, filter tubes leading to nowhere. A little girl romped on a mound of dirt where weeds had gained a foothold. At the curb, a teenaged boy with a baseball cap turned backward waxed a newly painted clunker. The car had no license plates, and its front wheels were up on blocks.

"Todd Verno live here?" I said.

"Who wants to know?" He didn't look up. Grease streaked his angular cheeks like the lampblack used by wide receivers.

"I need to talk to him about Pete O'Meara."

"You a cop or something?"

"More like the something."

"I ain't talking to nobody." He slapped a wad of rubbing compound onto the hood and went at it with a soggy cheesecloth.

The little girl tumbled off the mound and started to cry.

"Shut up, Joannie," yelled Todd.

I could see the girl was hurt. Blood dappled the front of her dirty green playsuit. I lifted her up and dabbed at her cut lip with a handkerchief.

"Is your mother home?"

She nodded, blubbering.

"Go inside and ask her to run cold water on your lip."

She wobbled off toward the front steps. I grabbed a handful of rotten leaves from the curbside and dumped it onto Todd's cheesecloth.

"Hey, what the fuck you doin'?"

I spun Todd around, flicked the cap off his head, and bent him backwards over the hood.

"You can bully your little sister, but you're not going to bully me. We are talking about Pete O'Meara. Now."

Todd gagged. I eased off enough to let some air into his lungs.

"Not sayin' nothin'."

I pounded the hood next to his ear hard enough to ring his eardrum.

"Hey, man, you nuts or somethin'?"

"DiRienzo squeezed you, right? He hauled you in and made you talk, and you said you were with Pete that night. Now what else did you tell him?"

"Nothin'."

I creased the car's hood with one punch.

"You want anything left of this shitcan, you don't insult my intelligence. Dig?"

"Yeah, yeah. Okay, man. Just don't fuck with the car anymore."

I let him up. He began wiping at the mess, but I stopped him.

"First we talk. What did DiRienzo pull with you?"

"He came by the next morning when I was still asleep." Todd tapped the toe of one black boot against the cinderblock wedged under the wheel. "I didn't know nothin' about no murder yet, and he just asked me a bunch of questions, like what I did that night. I told him I was with Pete. That was it. Nothin' about what we did. Then he said he wanted to look in my car because it wasn't registered and I couldn't keep it on a public street. Like the public comes down this shittin' street, right? Then he said if he looked he might find something he didn't want to find. So I better tell him what Pete and I did."

Todd's story pretty much jibed with Pete's: the beers on the linksland, the Port Chester chicks who never showed, the coke, the idea to hit a house to buy more.

"We tried the first house we came to on Harbor Terrace Drive. I didn't know who the hell lived there, but Pete said he did. Guy who owned the golf course, he told me.

"There were a few lights on inside, but Pete said he could tell no one was home. We went around back and found a door that wasn't locked. Pete went into the kitchen. I only went as far as the door because this whole thing was nuts, and I wasn't so sure nobody was home. Pete like tiptoed around. He looked through a bunch of stuff on the counters, like jars where people would leave cash. Then all of a sudden he stopped like he heard something. I thought I heard something too, like floorboards squeaking upstairs. I waved for him to come on, but he kept looking around, only faster now. Then he stopped again. Shit, I decided I was dashing. No way I was gonna get caught in a Harbor Terrace house. I'd really get my ass fried. So I ran."

"Pete followed?" I said.

"The last thing I saw, there were some golf clubs leaning against the wall beside the refrigerator. Pete grabbed one."

CHAPTER
10

I finally hooked up with Adrienne late the next morning. She didn't
have any explanation for where she'd been during the several runs I
took past her house since my talk with Todd Verno. After an embarrassed, almost guilty silence that reminded me of too many one-sided
arguments with Deirdre, she peppered me with questions about the
Blitzklubs and Jack Miles. I didn't know what pissed me off more, her
self-interest or her desire to change the subject.

"I talked to Jack Miles. I searched his cottage. I don't have the
Blitzklubs. End of story."

I pushed past her down the hallway before she could invite me
anywhere particular. The kitchen belonged on the cover of a home
decorating magazine. Lots of butcherblock cabinets and a white tile
floor perfect for footprints. Bright orange tape bounded a six foot square
just inside the door to the patio.

"Why didn't you tell me about this?" I said, crouching just outside the tape.

"I didn't know you are a cop, too." If she'd been a cat, her back would have arched to the ceiling.

I studied the floor. Vague footprints pointed in every direction as if describing frantic dance steps. Distinctive sneaker treads, but no other detail. I played with the door. The piston pulled it shut too fast, and the latch didn't line up with the striker. Without a guiding hand, the door slammed hard and flapped on its hinges. A thin film of fingerprint dust covered the doorknob.

Adrienne started to speak, but I shot her a glance, and whatever she meant to say bubbled to a stop in her throat.

I sized up the kitchen as Pete might have sized it up that night. Tried to see what he saw and hear what he heard. Tried to imagine the golf clubs Todd Verno mentioned. None were here now.

"Did Syl keep clubs in the kitchen?"

"He kept clubs all over the house. Sometimes I felt it was an obstacle course."

"The kitchen," I said.

Adrienne pointed to a narrow section of wall beside the refrigerator. "He wanted them handy in case a sudden urge overtook him."

"Were any there the night of the murder?"

"I suppose so. I don't remember."

"Didn't the police ask you?"

"Yes. And I gave them the same answer."

"Any possibility the missing *Blitzklub* was there that night?"

"I already told you, I can't tell one club from another."

"But you told the police it could have been."

She didn't answer. I stepped over the taped area and onto the patio. A wide lawn rolled to a rocky cliff overlooking the public marina. Brambles and hedges covered the stone wall running between the

Miles' property and the golf course. The wall had no gate, just a two-foot gap in the foliage and a stile cut into the stone. If the murder had occurred here, why haul the body over the wall and drag it three hundred yards to the pond? Why not just roll it off the cliff?

Adrienne hovered at my shoulder.

"I don't want to fight you," she said. "I understand how you feel. You're close to him, the boy they arrested."

"I've been to bat for him before."

"You think he's innocent."

"I don't think he did what the police say he did."

"They must have good reason to think he killed Syl."

"The police have lots of good reasons for what they do. Finding the truth isn't always one of them."

"I told them what I knew. I told them what I didn't know. I can't help the conclusions they draw."

"Try me."

Adrienne sighed as if preparing to tell the same story for the hundredth time. She leaned against the patio rail and gripped her elbows.

"I was upstairs getting dressed around five o'clock. I heard the door slam shut. You can see it needs to be fixed, and Syl never bothered to call a carpenter. About half an hour later, just as I was about to leave, I heard the door slam again and someone puttering around in the kitchen. I remember thinking Syl probably didn't stay on the golf course too long because of the weather."

"You didn't see him actually go onto the golf course," I said.

"No, but he usually did around that time."

"Did you see him in the kitchen?"

"No," she said. "But it had to be him."

"You left while he was still in the house."

Adrienne nodded. "That was around six. I came home after midnight. Since Syl and I slept in different rooms, I didn't immediately notice him missing. The next morning I saw the back door was open and the footprints on the floor. I looked for Syl, but he wasn't home, and his bed hadn't been slept in. I called the police. When I saw the commotion at the pond later that day, I knew they found Syl."

"Was there any sign that Syl returned to the golf course that evening?"

"None that he did, and none that he didn't."

"His clothes?"

"They found him in the same ones he wore the last time I saw him, which was before five."

"Where did you go that night?"

"Out."

"Where?"

"Dinner."

"Alone?"

"No."

"With who?"

Adrienne crossed the patio and set up defenses along another part of the rail.

"I don't want to argue with you."

"You already said that."

"I've been over everything with Detective DiRienzo. He's satisfied. Can't you just believe I was out somewhere?"

"I can't."

She sighed deeply, and turned away.

"You're not going to explain yourself," I said.

She shook her head. "You don't understand what's happening. It's too complicated. Too . . . You wouldn't understand."

"I guess I wouldn't."

She stayed on the patio while I took one more look around the kitchen. Out of the corner of my eye, I could see her pacing. At one point, she kicked the rail.

"You'll let me know if those clubs turn up," she called in.

"Oh sure, I'll jump right on the horn," I said, and escorted myself to the front door. I had the definite feeling we had declared war. I just didn't know how to fight it.

I found Gloria Zanazzi in a diner near the Milton Town Court. She sat alone in the last booth with her back to the door and her nose buried in a menu I bet she knew by heart. Lunch hour always had been Gloria's sacred time, something she declared on numerous occasions during her tenure as the Inglisi & Lenahan receptionist. I tapped her shoulder and learned nothing had changed. She sprang up like an angry frog.

"Dammit, Kieran, don't scare me like that." A film of sweat plastered ringlets of black hair to her forehead.

"Sorry, Gloria, I need a favor." I slid into the booth.

"You're lucky I don't brain you." Gloria fanned herself with a menu. Her lipstick didn't quite coincide with her lips. "All right, what is it? This oughtta be good."

"I need to know about the Miles murder investigation."

"Jesus, you too now? The Judge wanted to know yesterday. Am I on the payroll again?"

"You're still the best source around."

"I don't know about this one. The lid's on pretty tight. That big lunkhead DiRienzo wants it that way. He must think Miles was CIA or something."

"I want to know what the police did about the widow."

"Adrienne? They had her down for questioning a few times."

"What did they ask her?"

"Do you think I walk around the building with a stethoscope in my ears?"

I didn't think exactly that. But when people use the old expression "the walls have ears," they mean Gloria's.

"She's the widow. She should be a prime suspect. But they dropped her too fast."

"That's because a better suspect came along," said Gloria. "Look, I know you tried helping that boy. It makes sense you'll help him now. But this is a tough one."

"I'll make it easier for you. Adrienne Miles had an alibi. She won't tell me what it is. That's all I want to know."

Gloria threw a glance over each shoulder and leaned low across the table. "Are you onto something?"

"Find that out and we'll both know."

A bank of mini-blinds shaded Randall Fisk's glass cubicle from the rest of the newsroom. Fisk himself sat chest high at a word processor keyboard. He didn't look up until I shut the cubicle door.

"I'm not saying a word about that column," he said. "If you have a complaint, speak to the newspaper's counsel. She cleared every word."

"I don't give a damn about what you already wrote. I have information for you."

"You what?" For a second, I saw a spark of interest in Fisk's eyes. Then he knit his brow. "Don't bother me. I'm working."

I yanked the word processor's plug from the wall. "Now you're not."

"Hey, asshole, that was tomorrow's column." Fisk fell to his knees and pounded the plug into the socket.

"The world will survive."

"If I don't meet my deadline, I won't." He booted up the machine.

"I know who stole Sylvester Miles' *Blitzklubs*," I said.

"Big deal. So do the cops."

"The cops are wrong."

"Not according to my source."

"DiRienzo, right? Did he show them to you? I didn't think so. He doesn't have them."

"The O'Meara kid hid them someplace. It's only a question of time."

I shook my head smugly. Acting smug toward someone like Fisk ranked among life's rarest pleasures.

"All right. Who do you say stole the clubs?"

"Not so fast, Randy. I want something from you first."

"Like what?"

"Everything you know about the sale of Milton Country Club."

"Forget it. Trading information with you isn't a fair deal." He started typing. I moved off his shoulder. Either his diction was atrocious or something more momentous than the use of power carts on the Senior Tour weighed on his mind. After several turgid sentences, he pushed away from the keyboard.

"Goddammit, Lenahan, let's get this over with. Who stole the damn clubs?"

"Uh-uh. First you tell me about the sale. Then I give you the name."

"Go to hell."

"Fine." I opened the door.

"All right, all right," he said. "We'll do it your way. But I'll warn you up front, I don't know that much."

Fisk's only other chair was one of those Scandinavian contraptions that looked like a futuristic *prie dieu*. I folded myself into it.

"I hear about country clubs going up for sale all the time," he said. "Some of the rumors are just rumors. Other ones are true. I'd say the Milton deal—if there is a deal—is more of the former than the latter."

"Frank Gabriel flatly denied the club is up for sale," I said.

"You asked him, huh? When?"

"Yesterday."

"Hmmm." Fisk raised a hand to his mouth and worked his teeth across his fingernails like corn on the cob. "As I said, this deal strikes me as a rumor except for one detail that sticks in my craw."

He switched hands. After several moments of vicious chomping, I wondered if he needed to draw blood before relating this one detail. Finally, he came up for air.

"Frank Gabriel has been in financial trouble for over a year," he said. "A few years ago, he was worth millions. He had twenty or twenty-five houses in Milton, two office buildings in White Plains, ten or so empty lots primed for development. Then the real estate market tanked and brought him down with it. Dwindling rent income, no buyers, and a huge monthly nut. He's been playing a shell game with the banks for months. They're fed up. He's desperate to avoid foreclosure because he sees it as the ultimate humiliation. From what I hear, he's come this close to filing for bankruptcy several times."

He pressed his thumb and forefinger together.

"But he has one salable asset that can put him more than flush. His one-third share in Milton Country Club. So around the end of last year, he started making discreet inquiries with several Japanese corporations to see if there were any interested buyers. He had a specific type in mind. A corporation with a large local office that could afford a golf course as a company playground.

"Gabriel came up with a buyer, and for the life of me I couldn't find out who. Apparently, he negotiated the whole deal without Miles' or St. Clare's knowledge, then presented it at a board meeting in April as a *fait accompli*. My sources have been radio silent ever since. No one knows whether it's been voted up or down or even voted on at all."

"What was the offering price?"

"Seventy million."

I mulled that for a minute. One-third of seventy million could make most people flush. It also could make one willing to kill an old friend.

"Where did you learn that Miko Onizaka would be the club pro?"

Fisk grinned tightly and lifted a hand for another go at his fingernails. I grabbed his wrist.

"Tell me, Randall."

"All right, all right," he said, trying to shake free. "I made that up. Not completely. I did hear something about that in April, too. Then I heard it wasn't true. Then I heard nothing more either way. I only said it the other day to get a rise out of you."

I let go of his wrist. My fingermarks blazed red on his pale skin.

"Now who has those German clubs?" he said.

"Sylvester Miles had a brother named Jack," I said. "He's a history professor at SUNY Purchase and an expert on World War Two."

I explained the contentious relationship between the brothers, and how Jack obviously saw me in possession of the *Blitzklubs*. I described my fruitless search of the cottage and quoted the salient part of Syl's post-war letter to Jack. I didn't mention Jack probably lacked the physical ability to enter my shop through the single tiny window. Fisk could draw his own conclusion after he chased down Jack.

"Who else knows this?" said Fisk.

"No one. Just us."

Fisk smiled wryly. "Why don't you tell the police?"

"The time isn't right just yet," I said. "And quite honestly, until the clubs turn up, I don't have proof."

Fisk tapped a pencil on his computer console.

"This is on the level, right?" he said. "You aren't kidding, are you?"

I shook my head and grinned my best lawyer's grin. The kind you couldn't pin down to a direct answer.

———————

The board of directors conducted business on the second floor of MCC's neo-gothic clubhouse. The building had been the Tilford family seat, and the room the board chose for its sanctum once served as a chapel. I had seen the boardroom on only two previous occasions, once for my own interview and again to make my pitch for hiring Pete O'Meara. I remembered a cathedral ceiling, ornate wood moldings, a circular window of stained glass, and most importantly, a row of neatly shelved binders holding the minutes of the meetings.

A permanently locked door at the base of the clubhouse flag tower barred access to the second floor. Luckily, a passkey kept in the club administration office worked. I slipped through the tower door and took the spiral stairway three steps at a time.

A full moon painted stained glass colors on the conference table. I waited for my eyes to adjust, then used a penlight to find my way to the back of the room. Thirty looseleaf binders, one for each year of the club's existence, lined the shelves.

I opened this year's and hastily flipped the pages to the April minutes. At the beginning of the meeting, Frank Gabriel introduced Tomiro Hayagawa. Otherwise, the meeting went just as Fisk described. Frank Gabriel revealed his secret negotiations with Tomiro Enterprises, Ltd., and asked for a vote on the sale. Miles and St. Clare protested a fellow board member offering the club for sale without prior consultation. Even the antiseptic language of the recording secretary couldn't mask the truth: they were damn angry. St. Clare railed for twenty-two minutes (9:03 to 9:25 pm, by the secretary's watch) over Gabriel's "unmitigated gall". The board then tabled the subject for further discussion.

I flipped ahead to May. This time, only the board members attended. More discussion ensued, highlighted by another St. Clare filibuster. Miles, however, seemed to change his tack. He wanted to "study the matter."

Ahead to June. Tomiro Enterprises, Ltd., apparently had issued an ultimatum. If the board failed to approve the sale by the regularly scheduled July meeting, the corporation would rescind its offer. Gabriel pressed for an immediate vote. St. Clare violently opposed it, but Miles sided with Gabriel. He must have seen himself as a peacemaker because the vote came down one yea, one nay, and an abstention by Miles. The issue again was tabled for . . .

I checked my watch. The July board meeting was due to begin in two minutes. I shoved the binder onto the shelf and hurried to the door. Footsteps plunked on the stairs, voices echoed in the corridor. Shit, no place to run. Then I remembered: two thin closets with louvered doors stood on either side of the bookshelves. I closed myself into one just as the ceiling lights blazed.

Frank Gabriel took a seat at the head of the conference table. His office receptionist pulled the current year's binder from the shelf and settled to his right. Gabriel smoked a cigarette in long pulls. The receptionist paged through the minutes of the previous meeting. Neither said a word until St. Clare arrived.

"We shouldn't be holding this meeting," said the ex-Mayor.

"Why not?" said Gabriel. "We're alive and we make up a quorum."

"It doesn't seem right," said St. Clare. But he sat down, and the meeting began. Gabriel announced, for the record, that he was assuming Sylvester Miles' seat as chairman based on the order of succession set out in the by-laws. St. Clare grumbled. A handful of resolutions, mostly approving routine maintenance expenditures, passed unanimously. St. Clare grew increasingly sullen as the inevitable approached.

"We now turn to old business," Gabriel dictated to his receptionist. "The proposed sale of Milton Country Club to Tomiro Enterprises, Ltd., for a total price of seventy million dollars."

The vote, predictably, was a deadlock. If Gabriel reacted at all, I didn't see it. He noted the result, adjourned the meeting, and asked his receptionist to leave the room.

"I can't indulge you anymore," he said when she was gone. "The Japanese need our answer tomorrow."

"We're deadlocked," said St. Clare. "Just like when Syl was around. That means the answer is no."

"That isn't a good answer, Billy. In fact, it's a dangerous answer."

"What is that supposed to mean?"

"Exactly as it sounds. Let's just say there are forces demanding the club be sold."

"Syl was killed because of the club sale?"

Gabriel lit a cigarette and blew a long draught of smoke toward the ceiling.

"If you know something, Frank, tell me. That boy killed Syl just like the cops say, right?"

"That boy no more killed Syl than you or I."

"Jesus Christ," said St. Clare. "Frank, I know you have your troubles. We all do. But Syl—"

"This goes beyond any of our problems. We own something someone else wants. It's as simple as that."

"But murdering Syl? What did he do?"

"I'll tell you what Syl's problem was," said Gabriel. "He had no follow through. Just like his golf swing. He always thought he could bend people to his will. People would make demands on him. He would brush them aside with false promises, then hope they would go away or magically accede to his wishes. Maybe that approach worked in the clothing industry. It didn't work here. He wrecked his life by marrying Adrienne, and played catch-up ever since. He thought he could fix her by not voting for the sale. He thought he could abstain, and the Japanese would retreat. He was wrong."

"But I can't sell," said St. Clare.

"Your reason is no better than Syl's. In fact, it's worse."

"But what we did could come out."

"So what? We committed no crime. It was thirty years ago."

"But it could ruin me."

"You and your reputation. Your four years as the Honorable William St. Clare, Lord Mayor of Milton. Nobody gives a damn, Billy. And if they did, the best way to preserve your reputation would be to sell. Pawn off the problem on the Japanese. They're clever enough to solve it."

St. Clare puffed furiously on the cigar, pulled it from his mouth, and stuck it back in. Smoke curled in slender arabesques in front of his pudgy features.

"We built this place," said Gabriel. "The three of us took the big gamble when everyone was ready to laugh us out of town. And we won. This is the payoff."

"There's more to a payoff than just money."

"Don't romance me, Billy. You've been involved since day one, like it or not. What's done is done. Syl's gone and there's no bringing him back. There are just the two of us, and we have to see this through."

"The Japs won't buy now. They're very sensitive to public opinion. They would look like scavengers if this deal went through after a murder."

"That's no problem, Billy. They have assured me they will close the deal as long as the criminal case ends quickly and the negative publicity blows over."

St. Clare pulled himself upright and paced behind Gabriel. Each pass came so close to the closet door I needed to hold my breath.

"What about Kieran Lenahan?" he said. "Syl's estate hired him to arrange the auction of a set of golf clubs Syl left behind. He's been asking uncomfortable questions."

"I've already talked to him. He's just worried about his job."

"No, he's trying to save that kid. He's been hounding Adrienne about the murder. I don't like the idea he has an excuse to poke around in our business. He might find something."

"Relax, Billy. Brendan Collins is handling the criminal end of this. Lenahan will poke around for awhile, then get tired when he doesn't find anything. It's hidden in plain sight for years, and no one's noticed."

"No one had a reason."

"No one has a reason now, either. And if Lenahan persists, we will deal with him."

"But—"

"Goddammit, Billy, don't you understand? If you don't vote to sell, you won't be around to enjoy your reputation, good or bad."

St. Clare collapsed into a chair. He pounded his heart and coughed up cigar smoke while Gabriel stared at him with utter revulsion. And right then I realized that if St. Clare went into cardiac arrest, Gabriel would have let him die.

St. Clare's breathing slowly evened out, though the red didn't drain from his face. Gabriel called his receptionist in from the corridor. The meeting reconvened, and the last two living owners of Milton Country Club approved the sale to Tomiro Enterprises, Ltd.

CHAPTER
11

I didn't sleep well. Two hours in the closet left me with a sore back and stiff joints. Sporadic dreams returned me to the linksland of Milton Country Club. Only it wasn't any linksland I'd ever seen. A pale sun rode low in a gray sky. Ocean-sized swells fueled by a gale swamped the marina. Reeds and cattails grew shoulder high in the fairways, and so thick the wind barely swayed them. I chopped through with a club fashioned from a knobby tree branch, fighting my way toward the green. But with each labored step, the red flag receded deeper into the cold wind.

First thing at the shop the next morning, I punched up Demo Mike's work number. Demo, whose real name was Demosthenes Michaelides, was a Limerick boy whose mechanical aptitude had earned him the genius reputation often hung on intelligent kids in blue-collar neighborhoods. But a stroke at the age of seventeen left him with a limp and an arm too weak to handle tools. He took a job as a computer input clerk in the Surrogates Court, worked his way through college, and avoided the Limerick curse of becoming a regular at the neighborhood pub. In September, he was to begin night classes at Pace University Law School.

"Do you have time for outside research?" I said.

"About seven hours a day."

"I won't tell the taxpayers if you don't. How expert are you with land records?"

"They aren't my bailiwick, but I can find my way around."

"Good. Get yourself a pencil."

I spoke slowly so Demo couldn't mistake what I needed. I heard nothing from the other end but the scratching of lead on paper. That's what I liked about Demo: the craziest request didn't faze him.

"May take some time," he said when I finished. "Records this old are on microfiche. I'll need to put in a requisition, and the microfiche guys don't move very fast."

"Snap them up the best you can."

"Righto, Kieran," he said and rang off, leaving me to wonder how cheery I'd be in his straits.

The white sky cast no discernible shadows, but sunbathers lay like a glistening carpet beneath the Art Deco towers of Milton Beach. I found Tony La Salle exactly where I expected—camped outside his board-walk clam bar with a cigarette dangling from his mouth. The normal mollusk-eating crowd wasn't bellied up to his counter.

"Business worse than sucks." Tony skimmed a handful of ice chips from a tray and scattered them on the boardwalk. They quickly melted on the hot wood. "A few cases of food poisoning at some ritzy seafood joint up in Connecticut and some dildo of a health inspector traced it to clams taken from polluted waters. I ain't sold a clam since."

He rapped his knuckles against a sign pleading: "My clams are from Maryland."

"Dumb bastards don't believe me." Tony winged the sign across the boardwalk. "They think I get my clams from the Sound. Me? I ain't sold a Sound clam in ten years, twenty maybe. Dumb bastards."

He stomped into the bar and opened a can of beer.

"You want me to do what?"

"Light salvage work," I said.

"Don't tell me in the same pond I found the dead guy."

"Close."

"What am I looking for?" he said.

"A golf club."

"Any club?"

I described the missing *Blitzklub* pitching wedge.

"Shit, a pond that size'd take days."

"You cleaned out the golf balls in less than a day."

"You'da known if I forgot any? Finding something special is different."

"I don't think it's in the pond, anyway. I want you to search the inlet."

"You're crazy," said Tony.

I named a figure that made me a lot less crazy. Tony spit his cigarette onto the boardwalk. A couple wheeling a baby carriage stopped in front of the clam bar and studied the menu. The woman whispered something to the man, and they moved on.

Tony snorted. "When do I start?"

My undeclared war with Adrienne Miles left me with very few avenues to her late husband's intentions. Both Frank Gabriel and William St. Clare posed their own set of roadblocks. Judge Inglisi's trail went cold fifteen years ago, and Jack Miles' forked into a forest of lies and revisionist history. The only remaining route, and a narrow footpath at that, ran through Roger Twomby, Esq.

A midday commuter train dumped me at Grand Central Terminal. I escalated into the Pan Am Building, then elevated to Twomby's office. Twomby obviously ordered the receptionist to keep me at bay, so I paged through the legal profession rags scattered on a coffee table. One lead article, written with Fiskian verve, focused on a sudden drop in profits experienced by several large New York City firms. Twomby's firm headed the list.

Time dragged. I ran out of reading matter. Several times the receptionist glanced my way and whispered into her intercom. Finally, Twomby relented. The receptionist directed me to an office with a sterling view of Park Avenue receding into midsummer smog. Twomby sat in the jaws of a huge leather swivel chair. His handshake felt even deader than at Miles' house.

"If you came here to report to me about the *Blitzklubs*, you have wasted your time," he said. "The executor already informed me they were stolen by the boy charged with murdering Sylvester Miles. The police are confident they will soon be recovered. In any event, they represent only a minimal estate asset."

"The ex-Mayor misinformed you on every count."

"Indeed!" said Twomby, though his face registered no emotion. "I assume you know who stole those clubs."

"I have ideas, and they are damn closer to the truth than the Milton police department's. And I also know those *Blitzklubs* are more than a minimal estate asset. Unless the estate can sneer at a quarter of a million dollars."

"You reported ten to twenty thousand."

"William St. Clare reported ten to twenty thousand," I said. "The actual figures were lost in translation."

A single furrow appeared in Twomby's brow.

"Then I have no choice but to file a civil suit against you for conversion of estate property," he said.

I paced slowly in front of his desk, running my fingers on the gold inlay, then idly admiring a ceramic figurine of an English judge.

"I read an interesting article while you kept me waiting," I said. "This firm is in a slump."

"I cannot deny we experienced a subpar fiscal year," said Twomby. A second furrow rippled across his brow.

"I find it extremely interesting that a wealthy man with a history of jumping from law firm to law firm happened to die—excuse me—happened to be murdered at the precise time a firm in dire financial straits was certain to inherit his probate work."

"Are you implying we had Sylvester Miles killed in order to administer his estate? That is beyond preposterous. It is libellous."

"You'll sue me for that, too, right? Just what a foundering firm needs, bad publicity."

Twomby suddenly began shuffling papers.

"What is the purpose behind this invasion of my time, Mr. Lenahan?"

"I thought you'd never ask." I stopped pacing and leaned across the desk. "I want to know whatever you know about Sylvester Miles' intentions."

"What kind of intentions? What he intended to eat for supper the night he died?"

"His donative intent. Isn't that what you will-drafting jocks call it?"

"I cannot reveal a client's intentions," he said.

"Don't throw attorney-client privilege at me, pal. The will named me as an agent of the executor. You can discuss any aspect of Sylvester Miles' intent without violating one of your ethical principles."

Twomby swiveled back and forth in his chair. First one furrow in his brow disappeared, then the other. I guess he couldn't think and register emotion at the same time.

"All right," he said, stopping the chair by grasping the desk with both claw-like hands. "Miles left one-half the value of the *Blitzklubs* outright to his wife. He left his brother a set of old letters, with the precatory statement that he use them as source material for his great American novel. Miles considered his brother a worthless dreamer. I'd rather not say what he thought of his wife."

"I can imagine," I said.

"The residuary estate is to be administered by me, as trustee, for five years," continued Twomby. "At the end of the trust term, all assets are to be liquidated to establish the Sylvester Miles Foundation. The foundation is to provide grants to college golfers who meet certain criteria.

"I advised Sylvester that this will might not withstand probate. His brother probably could not successfully contest his pitiful legacy, but Adrienne certainly could tie up the trust in litigation for several years. He disagreed. He truly believed she would be satisfied with her legacy and not endanger the trust. I told him he was taking a huge risk. I advised him, as his probate counsel, to leave Adrienne a proper marital share. Obviously, he refused.

"In April, he asked me to draft a codicil leaving his one-third share in Milton Country Club to the town of Milton. He believed this particular legacy would be less of a target than a full-blown trust in the event Adrienne sued. I drafted the codicil and scheduled several appointments for Sylvester to execute it. He repeatedly begged off. He told me he definitely intended to sign the codicil but simply was too busy.

"Finally, he admitted he had discovered something that, in his words, 'needed to be checked' before he could sign. I offered to aid in any sort of investigation he wanted, but he insisted he act alone. The situation was potentially embarrassing on a personal level, he told me.

"He called me the day before he died and said he was ready to sign the codicil. Could I bring it to him? I jumped on the next train to Milton, but when I reached his house he was gone. Adrienne said he suddenly was called out of town. She couldn't say where or why or for how long. I left the codicil with instructions that Sylvester should sign it before a notary." Twomby opened a file folder and slid a sheet of parchment paper across his desk. "You can see the codicil is not executed."

I skimmed the legalese.

"Did Adrienne know what Sylvester was about to sign?"

"I certainly did not tell her," Twomby said indignantly. "The codicil was in a sealed envelope. My verbal instructions on execution could have applied to anything."

"When did you receive the codicil back?"

"The day of the will reading. It was in the top drawer of the desk in Sylvester's den."

"The envelope was open?"

"Yes, of course it was open," said Twomby. "Obviously, he had read it."

"Obviously." I slid the codicil back across the desk and thanked Twomby for his time. His voice stopped me at the door.

"I meant what I said about a civil suit," he said.

"And I meant what I said about bad publicity," I replied.

My conversation with Roger Twomby posed more questions than it answered, I realized as the commuter train banged toward Milton. First off, neither of us could prove Sylvester Miles ever saw the codicil when he returned from his sudden trip out of town. Adrienne was no dummy. A lawyer leaving a sealed document for her husband with instructions to sign it in the presence of a notary would have set off a cacophony of bells, whistles, and sirens. Adrienne could have steamed open the envelope, read the codicil, and decided to lose it somewhere in the house.

After the murder, she could have ripped open the envelope and placed it in Syl's desk. Anyone would then conclude Syl had refused to sign.

But what if Adrienne dutifully delivered the codicil to her husband? Did Syl's refusal to execute mean he had reached a conclusion on the MCC sale? Obviously, he couldn't vote to sell MCC to Tomiro Enterprises and leave his share in the country club to the town of Milton. Or was it related to his potentially embarrassing problem? Or were they one and the same?

No matter how long I wrestled with the questions, the bottom line still seemed to be the club sale. Spending three months on the fence made Miles the most likely target for persuasion. Frank Gabriel certainly needed the money. But William St. Clare opposed the sale for reasons I did not understand. Yet I couldn't see St. Clare as a murderer. Someone who capitulated so easily at the board meeting would not kill to prevent the sale. Even factoring in his misguided ardor for Adrienne made no sense. Killing his "rival" under the cover of the club sale controversy ascribed too much guile to the ex-Mayor.

We own something someone else wants, Gabriel had told St. Clare. Both the we and the something were obvious. The someone else—Tomiro Enterprises, Ltd.,—was a complete blank. I probably needed the resources of the Justice Department and the FBI to prove a Japanese corporation directed the murder of Sylvester Miles to insure the sale of Milton Country Club. But one advantage to knowing nothing about a subject was that any meager information was an improvement. So I jumped off the train at Milton Station and called Randall Fisk from a pay phone.

"Did you ever hear of Tomiro Hayagawa or Tomiro Enterprises?" I said.

"Yeah," he said cautiously.

"Know anything about them?"

"Why do you care?"

"They are Milton Country Club's buyers."

Fisk clucked like he had a chicken bone caught in his throat. "Hold on," he said.

His phone crashed to the floor. In the background, file cabinets rumbled and papers rustled. Fisk cursed and cursed, then crowed with satisfaction as he found whatever he was looking for.

"Knew I had a file someplace," he said, back on the line. "Forget about Tomiro Enterprises. Tommy Hayagawa is your man. Let's see, he's about sixty. No, fifty-eight to be exact. If I had to describe him in one sentence, I'd say he's a *yakuza* leader who went legit."

"What's a *yakuza*?"

"Japanese term for an organized crime group," said Fisk. "Okay, here's what I'm looking for. I have clippings from all kinds of business magazines, but my notes digest them better.

"Hayagawa started as a leader of a *yakuza* in Osaka. They specialized in back-alley activities. You know, gambling, prostitution, drugs. He had a reputation for being fast with a gun and even faster with nunchucks. Those are two sticks connected by a chain or string. In the right hands, they feel like a whole windmill of blackjacks.

"But violent as Tommy could be, he had a wily streak. He always believed the ultimate goal of any successful *yakuza* should be legitimate businesses and accommodation with the authorities. That's a direct quote, though he probably didn't talk like that in his back-alley days.

"He directed the transition in the late seventies through a stock manipulation scheme involving a corporation called Osaka Dynamics. The government tried to prosecute him and his cohorts for fraud, but several witnesses met accidental deaths and the case folded. The Hayagawa-*kai*, that was the name of his *yakuza*, came away with untold capital. It invested in real estate, rode that crest for awhile, then diversified into a variety of industries like seafood processing, resort management, and golf course development. Now he's trying to expand beyond the Pacific rim.

"I don't know anything about Tomiro Enterprises. Actually, this is the first I've heard of it. I imagine it's some form of holding company to oversee his affairs."

"How do you know so much about Hayagawa?" I said. "International crime isn't your beat."

"Hayagawa is a passionate golfer. He's assembled a collection of rare golf memorabilia that would knock your eyes out. Claims some of the pieces cost him six figures. And he supports young Japanese golf pros trying to make it in Europe and the U.S."

"Could he be Miko Onizaka's sponsor?"

"You want what I think or what I know for a fact?" said Fisk. "What I think is that Miko is exactly the type of pro Hayagawa would sponsor. He's a good golfer, and carries just a hint of the ruffian onto the golf course. But I don't know anything for a fact. Hayagawa is very discreet about who he helps."

My conversation with Andy Anderson wound back in my mind.

"Didn't Hayagawa outbid four other collectors for a rake iron recently?"

"Oh that," said Fisk. I could sense him smiling over the phone. "The bidding lasted an entire day. Very intense. But the auction was conducted over the phone, so no one knew who they were bidding against. Gradually, the others realized Hayagawa was involved. One by one they dropped out."

"He's that bad?" I said.

"He can be as charming as any CEO. He's on the thin side, rangy for a Jap. Not the type you would expect to rise very high in a *yakuza*. But he still has a lot of the street in him. His face is seamed. Some of the lines are wrinkles, but most, when you look closely, are scars.

"I met him once while researching a feature I planned to write about him. As we shook hands, he said, 'I hope you tell the truth.' Only it wasn't a hope. It was a command. And he squeezed my hand just a little too tightly and for a shade too long. Just enough to let me know I was a mouse in a trap, and only he could let me go. I never wrote the feature."

I hung up and beelined down Merchant Street to the Milton Public Library. Fifteen minutes later, I was ensconced at a table in the reference room. Books and magazines rose around me like the parapets of a fortress. I waded through *Dun & Bradstreet* and *Standard & Poor's*. I rifled through slick business magazines and glossy trade manuals. Then I struck the motherlode: an article in a trashy magazine that feeds the egos of the corporate elite.

Tomiro Enterprises began in 1974 as a real estate investment company named T.H.Y., Ltd. During the early 1980s, it transformed itself into a holding company for all manner of industries: textiles, electronics, aviation, agricultural machinery, and investment banking. In 1985, it re-christened itself Tomiro Enterprises and entered the sports/vacation industry with the purchase of a Hawaiian resort complex. In 1989, it created a subsidiary named Ichi-Ni-San to market hi-tech golf equipment worldwide. According to the article, Hayagawa had turned over most of the operation of Tomiro Enterprises to his son. But he devoted ninety percent of his time to Ichi-Ni-San.

An unexpected thrill coursed through my body. Ichi-Ni-San Golf was Miko Onizaka's employer.

The Stamford Ichi-Ni-San Golf World Pro Shop stood in the shadows of the beehive office towers lining the Connecticut Turnpike. Warehouse or outlet would have been a more appropriate term, since the pro shop occupied a converted supermarket. The grand opening, I remembered, caused quite a stir among the club professionals in Westchester and Fairfield counties. These pros feared high volume marketing tactics would siphon off sales from their own shops. But the economic disaster never materialized. Ichi-Ni-San mainly sold its own line of equipment, and stocked only a smattering of clubs manufactured by American competitors. After a brief flurry of interest, American golfers avoided the Golf World in droves. The overwhelming majority of its patrons were the Japanese who lived and worked in the New York metropolitan area.

I stepped through the automatic doors and found myself quite literally in another world. The feeling transcended the obvious fact that everyone else in the store, customer and salesperson alike, was Japanese. I simply never had seen such a collection of golf equipment under one roof. Racks upon racks of golf clubs stretched as far as I could see. Shafts glistened and trademark blue grips shimmered in the fluorescent light. One sturdy rack displayed a bilingual sign boasting "2,000 drivers, and no two alike". Kangaroo golf bags dangled from the ceiling like squadrons of dirigibles. Short, sleek Japanese men in blue and gold golf attire patrolled the aisles and offered assistance to customers. This world was far different from the cluttered shop of Andy Anderson, but I wasn't sure it was progress.

I systematically searched each of the aisles. Not one of the blue and gold clad staff members was Onizaka. In the rear of the store, I found twelve lesson bays in operation. In each bay, a golfer smacked balls into a huge green net under the watchful eye of a professional. After each shot, pro and pupil huddled at a video screen and analyzed every aspect of the swing. Again, no Onizaka.

Beside the last bay, a man stood in an office doorway. One arm dangled at his side, smoke from a cigarette curling out from his cupped fingers. His blue and gold outfit sagged on his scrawny frame. Gray streaked his slick hair. Bags puffed under eyes that may have been watching me for a moment or an hour.

"May I help you?" he said. A metallic name plate pinned to his shirt read: H. Ishoki.

"Not especially," I said.

"You are looking for someone in particular?"

"I'm just looking around," I said. "Nice place. Twenty-first century golf."

He leaned back into the office and stubbed out the cigarette in an ashtray.

"I have given you two chances to speak the truth, and you have failed," he said. "I know who you are, and I know who you are looking for. He is gone. We preferred he not work here."

"You fired Onizaka?"

Ishoki nodded grimly.

"He lost many tournaments in terrible ways. But losing these tournaments was not his sin. His acts of frustration and anger after the Met tournament led to our decision."

"You fired him after the Met?" I said, remembering my conversation with Andy. "But I thought you pulled your backing before the Met."

"We paid Mr. Onizaka a salary, as we do all our staff pros. We encourage them to play in all local tournaments, and we applaud their successes when they win. But we do not provide formal financial backing as a sponsor would."

"But Miko had a sponsor, right?"

"Mr. Hayagawa himself took an interest in Mr. Onizaka's career," said Ishoki. "Mr. Hayagawa thought very highly of him. In my opinion, I believe Miko reminded him of his younger self. But they fell out many months ago. Mr. Hayagawa is very sensitive about the reputation of his companies in America. He knows that many Americans resent Japanese activities here, and demands that all of us act with politeness and discretion. Mr. Onizaka acted in a headstrong manner. He drank too often at the wrong time. Mr. Hayagawa suggested I fire him. But I said Mr. Onizaka is a good pro. He brings much business here. Mr.

Hayagawa relented. But I could not ignore what happened after the Met tournament."

"Where can I find Miko?" I said.

Ishoki slipped behind his desk and wrote out an address.

"I would move very quickly," he said. "Mr. Onizaka's work visa automatically expired when we fired him. It was our duty to notify the Immigration Service."

Miko Onizaka's address brought me to the penthouse level of a posh waterfront condo. I knew what staff pros earned, and even the upper end of the scale couldn't pay for a spread like this. Neither, apparently, could a sponsorless pro named Miko. A heavy-duty padlock, courtesy of the City Marshall, barred entry. The eviction notice plastered across the door was three weeks stale.

I called Andy from the lobby phone. Naturally, he wanted to talk about the missing *Blitzklubs*, but I kept the conversation on Miko.

"He picked up his clubs two days ago," said Andy. "Only paid half the charge."

I wished him luck on collecting the balance.

Stuck in traffic on the turnpike, I reconstructed the Met. Like all of our local tournaments, the Met format consisted of fifty-four holes of stroke play. The entire field of 120 golfers played thirty-six holes on the first day. The 60 golfers with the lowest scores qualified for the final round.

I had completed my thirty-sixth hole in a misty dusk. My two-round total of 141 tied me for second place, six shots behind Onizaka. Dozens of pros, caddies, and spectators milled around the scorer's tent as the tournament committee determined the cut and assigned starting times for the following day. Miko would lose his lead, and ultimately the tournament, in the final round. But at that moment, his 135 stood out like a beacon among the other scores. If Miko had been part of that crowd, I would have seen him.

I pulled into Wykagyl at sundown. The caddymaster's shack was closed, the benches empty. I walked around the clubhouse terrace and descended a shrub-lined path to the eighteenth green. Far out in the fairway, the last foursome of the day meandered through the shadows toward home. Even at this distance, I knew neither of the caddies was Hawkeye.

I circled the clubhouse and found a young caddie perched on a fencepost at the edge of the parking lot.

"Do you know Hawkeye?" I said.

"Doesn't everybody?" he said.

"Any idea where I can find him?"

The caddie rolled his eyes and, with a jerk of his thumb, directed me toward an old Mustang parked beneath a maple at the far end of the lot.

I heard the music at fifty yards but didn't spot Hawkeye until I pressed against the passenger side window. He lolled boozily under the steering wheel. The Grateful Dead pounded through stereo speakers, and marijuana smoke curled thickly in the orange light of dusk.

I thumped on the window. Hawkeye rolled his head toward me. The twin scars trailing back from the corner of each eye blazed fiery red. He pulled himself upright and slapped at the window crank. The window opened a crack, and the acrid smoke wafted past my nose.

"Hey, Kier'n Len'han, man. You wanna hit?" A joint the size of a carrot floated in front of his face.

"No hit. Talk." I always spoke pidgin to the impaired.

"Talk. Sure, man. C'mon in."

"No. Out here."

Hawkeye shrugged. He was too high not to be compliant. I hoped he wasn't too high to remember the Met. He carefully extinguished the joint against the side of a beer can. Then he wrestled with the door handle and staggered out of the car.

"Talk." He squinted against the last rays of the sun slicing through the maple leaves. "Good thing you caught me early. What's up?"

"You remember the Met," I said.

Hawkeye winced. "Sure as hell do. You played outta your ass. Made up six shots the last round, three in the last three holes. My man didn't know what hit him."

"Your man is who I want to talk about."

"Flatted me," said Hawkeye, which meant Onizaka had paid him the bare minimum caddie fee for three rounds. Hawkeye couldn't figure out how to frown, so he giggled.

"What happened after the first two rounds?" I said.

"Like what?"

"Like where was Onizaka when the committee made the cut and fixed the final pairings?"

Hawkeye stroked the stubble on his chin. "Shit, let's see. We finished real early. And On'zaka, he knew he had a big lead, and it wouldn't fade because the bad weather was settin' in. He hung out for awhile and talked to some of the sportswriters. Sorta surprised me because he gave me lots of credit for his rounds. Then this Japanese guy came up to him. An older guy. Tall and thin, with lots of scars on his face. Onizaka told me to leave them. It was like he was nervous about the guy.

"I watched them from across the tent. They talked for awhile. Actually, the other guy talked and On'zaka listened. He had his head bent like he was getting yelled at, only not so loud. Then they bowed to each other, and the old guy left.

"After that, On'zaka seemed like he had something on his mind. Like maybe this guy told him something he didn't want to hear. Then all of a sudden he told me he had to split and make sure I was here early tomorrow. I told him all the groups weren't even in yet. The committee still had to cut the pairings. He said forget it, he'd be here early enough. Then he was gone like a bat outta hell."

CHAPTER
12

Demo Mike intercepted me as I pulled into my driveway.

"I stuck it in your door," he said, straddling the balloon-tire bike he rode around Limerick to strengthen his weak leg. He was a beanpole of a kid with bright eyes set off by dark curly hair and olive skin.

I loosened a twenty from my money clip.

"What's this?"

"Payment for services rendered."

"It only took me ten minutes after I got the microfiche."

"You want to be a lawyer, you should learn how to charge for your time."

The deed was much thicker than I expected, and when I spread it on the coffee table I could see why: the metes and bounds description of the boundaries read like a pirate's treasure map, making reference to stakes and rocks, roads and high-water marks. The deed conveyed property from the Estate of Josiah Park to the Town of Milton for use as a nature conservancy. The signatory was I.W. Frippy, Esq., Executor and Trustee of the Park Land Trust. The purchase price was the ubiquitous legal ambiguity, "TEN DOLLARS and other good and valuable consideration." Incorporated in the deed was a resolution of the Town Council establishing "the Marshlands as a nature conservancy for the benefit of the public forever."

I quickly sketched an outline of the property and compared it with my memory of the golf course. Something was very wrong.

I drove to the club extra early the next morning. MCC's clubhouse and the Park mansion stood on opposite ends of the same knoll. Between them ran a stone fence constructed by Caleb Park in 1899, the height of the Park-Tilford feud. Many of the stones had tumbled one way or another, but a hedgerow planted for good measure by Caleb's son Josiah grew thick enough to shield one building from the other.

With the deed and hastily sketched map tucked under my arm, I parted the hedges and hopped down onto the Park Estate. The Park mansion was as American as the clubhouse was British. Constructed of brick and decorated in the Federal Style of the late 18th century, it was a landmark registered with the National Historical Society. Across a back lawn the size of a postage stamp, a bronze plaque marked the entrance to the Marshlands Nature Conservancy. The plaque recited Josiah Park's love of nature and commitment to the preservation of wildlife and wetlands. Beneath the year of dedication were the names of the politicians instrumental in bestowing the Marshlands Conservancy upon the people of Milton. The mayor was William St. Clare. One of the town councilmen was Dr. Francis Gabriel.

Through all my years in Milton, I'd never once set foot in the Conservancy except to search for golf balls badly hooked off the eighteenth tee. A narrow woodchip path wound through the same ancient forest of oak and ash that had given way to the original twelve holes of MCC. Rustic signs described the species of flora and fauna visible to the patient eye. Thick underbrush blotted any hint of the groomed fairways barely fifty yards away.

As the path descended, the oak and ash gave way to scrub pine. A brook gushed beneath a footbridge, the water swirling toward the tidal stream that skirted the eighteenth tee then meandered through mud-flats and bulrushes to the harbor.

I skipped across tiny pools to an islet of mud, grass, and crushed stone. The tide was in; brackish water eddied thick as gravy. Standing at the tidal stream cast the golf course in a new perspective. The trees, so massive when blocking your line of flight, resembled cotton puffs on match sticks. The sixteenth and eighteenth fairways, pouring down off a ridge, seemed more the product of a garish paint brush than nature. Three hundred yards in the opposite direction, the water of the harbor sparkled silver and blue. In the foreground, the dun-colored fairways of the linksland marched deep into the Conservancy, the red flags on the greens licking in the breeze like the standard of an invading army.

I sighted a boundary stake and oriented the map. Unless I was blind, Dr. Frank Gabriel and the Hon. William St. Clare had much to hide.

Shortly after passing the bar exam, I treated myself to a month-long vacation backpacking in the West of Ireland. Being an American of Irish descent, I felt duty bound to seek out the branch of the family still rooted to the Old Sod. I knew precious little about my ancestry—just the name of one grandfather and the approximate date of his emigration from County Clare. But in so sparsely populated a region, I thought this information would suffice.

I tacked from village to village, talking to priests and leafing through ancient baptismal records but finding no trace of the Peter

Lenahan who sold his stony farm for a pittance on the eve of the Easter
Rising. Disgruntled and thirsty, I stopped into a country pub at the fall
of the day. After my second pint of stout, I told the barman my tale of
woe. If you want to find your roots, he told me, don't ask the priests.
Seek out the oldest man you can find.

The barman's own father was 96 years old and lived in a one-room
cottage with a tiny fireplace and an ancient radio. Despite the summer
weather, he wore a gray wool suit with waistcoat and tie. While pursuing his daily chores of sweeping out the fireplace and pouring milk for
his cats, he delivered a monologue about the days when a pint of porter
cost tuppence or thruppence. Finally, he closed his eyes and said, "Peter
Lenahan. Peter Lenahan. I knew a Peter Lenahan who left for America." And he named a tiny village across the border in County Galway.
I bid him farewell, certain that my search had reached a dead end.
Three days later, while passing through the town the old man had mentioned, I detoured to the church. Baptismal records confirmed the accuracy of his memory.

And because of him I now spent the last evening before the start of
the Classic with the Dutchman.

The Dutchman was an elderly tailor I once saved from a disastrous
investment in an import business. Now retired, he spent his time sew-
ing patches. No pattern was too complicated for his nimble fingers: corporate logos, family coats of arms, insignias from the most obscure
armies on earth. His mind was a little fuzzy at times. But plug into the
right channels, and he spoke with encyclopedic accuracy on the history
of Milton and its citizens.

The Dutchman answered the door wearing an oversized cardigan
sweater that hung from his shoulders like the mainsail of a schooner.
Professional football team logos covered every square inch.

"We'll have to talk around back. Miriam's rules." He patted his
sweater self-consciously. "I'm testing these."

Meeting the Dutchman around back proved difficult. The path was unlit and choked with wildly overgrown privet hedges. I hadn't tangled with such thick underbrush since dribbling a drive off the second tee at MCC.

"Don't you believe in gardeners?" I said as I picked thorns from my shirtsleeves.

"I do, Miriam doesn't. That's her idea of a burglar alarm. Last time I pruned she didn't sleep for a month."

He admitted me onto a tiny screened-in porch lit by a single ceiling bulb. Pencil sketches and snippets of colored thread littered a card table. Books on heraldry crammed a tiny cherry bookcase. When I first met the Dutchman, he lived alone and kept a well-furnished office in a second floor bedroom. Then his newly widowed sister moved in. Miriam forced him into the first floor den, and now threatened to sweep him into the backyard.

He unstacked a pair of plastic chairs. The porch opened onto a parlor, where cardboard placards propped on the sofa, coffee table, piano bench, and carpet prohibited sitting, smoking, piano playing, and the wearing of shoes.

"Something to drink?" said the Dutchman, kicking off his loafers. "I'm having apple juice."

I decided to join him lest the beer I preferred run afoul of one of Miriam's rules. He returned and we made ourselves as comfortable as possible. Between the two of us, the tiny porch had barely enough leg room.

"A special order," he said, thumbing the lapel of his sweater. "Is that why you're here?"

"I haven't said yet."

"Doesn't matter. Always good to see you. And before I forget, good luck in the Classic. If you win it, I'll design a special commemorative patch."

"I'd like that, Dutchman." I leaned in close enough to whisper. "The reason I'm here is I want to know how Milton Country Club was organized."

The Dutchman neither flinched nor asked why I was interested. Like most old men, no one paid him any heed except other old men. He had survived his friends. His life now consisted of creating his patches and keeping his sister out of an institution. I might as well have told him he'd won the state lottery.

"You're asking after Sylvester Miles, aren't you?" he said. "Never thought I'd see the day the police would fish a body out of a water hazard."

The Dutchman stroked his goatee, which was as smooth and as white as cornsilk.

"I remember when he first climbed down from the train at Milton Station. It was August, nineteen and forty-six. The eleventh or twelfth, I think, but don't hold me to it. One of those hot days when the dust hung heavy in the air. Lots of dust back then because some of the streets were dirt, especially near the railroad station.

"Anyway, I was driving a cab for old man Shea. Miles was in uniform, and what caught my eye were his patches. He was with his wife. She was a shy girl. Wore a bonnet and kept her head turned sidewise. When I picked up her bags—I was giving them a ride—all she said was, 'Much obliged.' Later, I found out she was sickly instead of shy, but I'm jumping ahead.

"I asked Miles where they wanted to go, and he said someplace where they could get a room for a few days. 'Passin' through?' I said. And he said no. He wanted to buy a house and start a new life. 'Why do you want to live in a one-horse town like Milton when you have New York City so close by?' I asked. He said he didn't like cities. Too easy to get lost in. He heard about Milton from some army buddies, and it sounded like a nice place to live. So he and his wife—Hannah, I just remembered her name—he and his wife just got married down in Florida and come up by train."

I didn't see how Sylvester Miles' arrival in Milton shortly after World War II connected with my suspicions. But I knew from my experience with the old man of Clare that I should keep my mouth shut.

" 'Well, if it's work you want, we got it,' I told him. But he insisted he wanted to know about houses first. 'Don't you have that backwards?' I said. And he said no and asked if there were any houses for sale. I told him about the Projects they just built over in the flats by Marie's Neck. Lots of nice new homes built for returning GIs. Small capes, no basements, sat on slabs. Nice by the standards of the day, but Miles just sneered and said he wanted a real house.

"I drove them around to all the fancy neighborhoods, like Poningo Point and Soundview and Harbor Terrace because I thought the size of the houses would knock his eyes out. But he just took it all in and occasionally whispered something to Hannah.

"I expected if Miles stayed in town I'd see a good bit of him. Boys were still coming home from the war, and the bars were full every night. Guys like Teddy Byrne, Phil Harrigan, Corny O'Meara, Mickey Aldrich. They'd walk in wearing their uniforms and arguing about which service was the toughest, and civilians like me would buy them drinks because we didn't care what they did in the war. Just going overseas made them heroes to us, and a round of drinks was small payment for their sacrifice. I thought I'd see Miles. But I never did except once, and then it wasn't in a bar but in McMillan's Pharmacy. I asked him how he was making out, and he said fine, except his wife was sick. Fact was, he was filling a prescription. They were living in the Projects, and he was working in a shop on Merchant Street. And I remember thinking he wasn't so brash as I thought. Here I knew he was a real war hero. I'd seen the Purple Heart and a Distinguished Service Cross pinned to his uniform that first day off the train. But he was quiet as a church mouse while blowhards like Corny O'Meara talked like they personally put a bullet in Hitler's brain. Isn't that always the way, though?

"Well, the next thing you know, Hannah dies. A few months after that, Miles buys the store he's working in and changes it into Miles Clothiers. Then he sells the house in the Projects and buys that damn monstrosity over in Harbor Terrace. People started wondering who he was because he kept such a low profile. But I just smiled because I knew him when he first set foot here, and it was good to see a good man become a success. Makes you think we did right by winning the war.

"I swear, for years I was the only person in town who knew Miles was a war hero, and that was only because I saw him in his uniform that day. In fact, it was Miles who gave me my start in heraldry by offering family coats of arms for blazers. He sold the blazers and hired me to sew the coats of arms. I wanted to sew him a Miles family coat of arms big enough to hang on a wall. But he wasn't interested. Funny thing was he never spoke about the past. It was like he was born the day he climbed down from the train at Milton Station. Never even talked about Hannah much, except he once hinted that she left him pretty well off. I took it to prove what everyone else in town thought, that she left him with family money.

"Miles hooked up with Gabriel and St. Clare when they all were members of the Lions Club. Gabriel had his dental practice over the old Woolworth's, but he always treated it like a sideline. He preferred wheeling and dealing in real estate, and dabbled some in town politics. Saint always was crazy as a loon. People call him Mayor nowadays because he used to be the mayor. But they were calling him Mayor way before he ever ran because he used to swagger up and down Merchant Street like he owned it. And he was such a terrible gossip, always thinking he knew exactly what everyone did and why they did it. I always said Saint is proof you don't need brains to make money. All you need is a good line of shit.

"Each of them was successful in his own way, which caused a lot of resentment among the old guard of the Lions Club. And that's what drove the Three Musketeers of Merchant Street together, this reaction to all those stuffed shirts.

"Their biggest coup was getting Saint elected. In those days, the Republican Party was a joke in Milton. Every election year it put up a slate of candidates, and they'd get murdered like a flock of sacrificial lambs. One year, the party leader thought it would be funny to run Saint for mayor. Like I said, people called him Mayor anyway. Maybe they'd get confused and vote for him. Saint accepted and Gabriel volunteered to be his campaign manager. One of them, it must have been Gabriel because he's always been pretty smart, came up with this brilliant idea. The traditional kickoff to the campaign was always the Republican Town Picnic on Labor Day. There'd be a parade down Merchant Street to Station Park, then a bunch of speeches no one listened to and lots of hamburgers and fried chicken everyone ate, regardless of political affiliation.

"Gabriel inveigled Miles to dress up in full uniform and ride in an open car with Saint and make a speech about the war. That was the first time people in town came to realize they had a real live war hero living in Milton. And it was early enough in the sixties that people still appreciated that stuff.

"Saint followed up that act by buying space in the *Milton Weekly Chronicle* to run stories about Miles' heroics. It created enough of a stir that Saint stole the election by riding on the coattails of a man with no political aspirations at all. Saint set up that display in Town Hall, and Syl was grand marshall of the Memorial Day Parade until the Vietnam War protests put a stop to that sort of truck.

"The whole thing about the country club started off kinda funny, though no one thought much of it at the time. From what I recall, Gabriel wanted to join a country club. Problem was that he had trouble finding a club to accept him. See, his real name is Gabrielli, and in those days there was still some resistance to Italians. Seems sorta funny now, especially the way Gabriel turned out owning those big professional buildings in White Plains, plus all those houses he rents out around Milton.

"So one day the Three Musketeers decided what the hell, if Frank can't join a club they'll start their own. Rich as Miles was, people still considered him an outsider. So he figured organizing a club would put him solid in the community. And Saint, well he had no mind of his own. He just went along with Gabriel and Miles. Mostly Miles. The two of them were real buddies after the election.

"They tried to interest the other Lions and the Jaycees, but no one wanted to buy shares in a pie-in-the-sky idea. The only club they could afford was the Tilford Estate, and that wasn't even a club. Just a rich family's playground and pretty run down at that because the last of the Tilfords lived in France most of the time and lost interest in maintaining the place. But they scraped enough money together for a down payment.

"No one else in town took the idea of a club very seriously, especially one with only twelve holes. Miles' Boondoggle, they called it, because Syl was the front man for the deal. Saint was the mayor, and Gabriel was a councilman by then, so they had to take a back seat for appearance sake.

"Anyway, what turned the club around was the Three Musketeers bringing in an architect from Scotland. He found a way to turn about forty acres of scrub into six holes, what you folks call the linksland part of your golf course. Then everybody jumped on the bandwagon."

"That was around the time the Park Estate became the Marshlands Conservancy?" I said.

"Afterwards, but not by much."

"Why hadn't the Tilfords used the same land when they built their golf course?"

"Didn't know what they were doing, that's what the Scotsman said. He could tell from the way the first twelve holes were laid out. Lots of waste. Besides, being a Scotsman, he had a natural affinity for links-land. Saw all the scrub in a different way than an American architect. Or so he said."

"The club didn't try to buy any land from the Parks?"

"Hell yeah, it did," said the Dutchman. "Miles himself tried to ne-gotiate a deal with Josie Park. Being a newcomer, he was innocent of what'd gone on all those years between the Parks and the Tilfords, whatever it was. No one in town seemed to remember how the feud got started, but like most feuds that wasn't the point. Miles visited old Josie and waved a bunch of money in his face for all the land from the man-sion clear down to the waterline. Old Josie answered by stringing chicken wire along the stone fence and smearing it with grease. He was in his seventies, then. All piss and vinegar. No wife, no kids, probably never had a girlfriend. Devoted his whole life to continuing his father's feud against the Tilfords, and like most followers, took it ten steps far-ther than the originators would have."

"So there was no easing of the feud after the Tilford family sold to Miles and the others?"

"Not a whit. Josie was fixated on the land. Jesus Christ Himself could have owned that Tilford property, and Josie still would have run that chicken wire and smeared it with grease. Hell, he left the land to the town for a nature conservancy. People think he did that because of some secret tax break he got. Uh-uh. As long as he had power over that land, from the grave or otherwise, there was no way his land ever would be joined with Tilford land. Actually, the conservancy idea probably was I.W. Frippy's. Josie didn't know a goose from a moose."

"Do you remember anything about Frippy?"

"Oh sure," said the Dutchman. "Clever bastard, but a real odd duck. The only person he ever lawyered for was Josie Park. Made a career out of him until old Josie died. A very prim and proper little man. Delicate, you might say. A bachelor who always kept to himself. Left town not long after Josie died. I heard he was the main beneficiary of Josie's will, except for the land. Josie was the last of them, you know."

"Frippy still alive?"

"Far as I know, which means I ain't seen his name in the obituaries."

CHAPTER
13

Dawn of the Classic, Day One, found me pacing the floor in a pre-tournament funk. A new golf bag, red and white and thick as a sequoia, leaned against the back of the sofa. My arsenal of replacement clubs stood at the ready along the living room wall. I had awakened with butterflies, but as the skies brightened the butterflies transformed into an army of angry bats. I rushed to the bathroom and stared at the open toilet while clawed wings raked the walls of my stomach. As I waited to retch, all the old questions percolated into my consciousness. Why am I torturing myself? Why did I choose this profession? Isn't there a less stressful way to satisfy the ego?

They were all the questions I'd ask myself on the eve of a trial.

Today was only a practice round, I told myself. No one can kill you for playing badly.

It suddenly occurred to me that my actions on behalf of Pete might be an elaborate psychological scheme to divert my attention from the reality of finally playing in a PGA Tour event. I still pondered this newest version of the old question when a familiar rumble shook the front windows. My stomach finally heaved, though with no real result, and I returned to the living room to find Judge Inglisi hefting my golf bag. He wore huge linen pants and a loud shirt depicting a jungle of flora.

"Some poor bastard of a caddie's heading for a hernia," he said.

"Mind telling me why you're here?"

"I arranged my vacation to coach you to your first Tour victory."

"You're wasting your time."

"This is no time for pessimism," he said. "Besides, you'll make a better impression if you arrive in my Ferrari instead of your bomb."

I tried to dissuade him. I would likely play thirty-six holes, then practice on the range until dark. Spectators weren't allowed golf carts, so he'd have to follow me on foot over terrain fit only for mountain goats. Naturally, he parried each of my arguments.

"You're using this old shillelagh?" he said, sliding my putter out of the bag.

"I preferred you not taking an interest in my golf career."

The Classic resembled any other golf tournament with a million dollar purse. Contestants dribbled in for Tuesday practice rounds. Local society figures donated exorbitant sums for the privilege of playing in Wednesday's Pro-Am. Then the tournament proper began—72 holes with the field cut in half for the weekend rounds.

We pulled into the contestants' parking lot. Judge Inglisi stayed in his car and barked orders to his law clerk over a cellular phone while I lugged my golf bag to the caddie yard. The clubhouse area buzzed with activity. PGA officials shouted over walkie-talkies, TV people snaked camera cables through the dewy grass, college kids manned refreshment stands, and sales reps erected display tents. In a strange way, the frenetic activity calmed me. Everyone seemed too busy to notice the travails of a local club professional.

I told my caddie to meet me on the practice range in ten minutes, then waded into the locker room. Valets circled like barracudas. For a twenty dollar tip, I received a locker, a footstool, and a surly *gratias* from a cutthroat in livery.

The Judge caught me at the practice range, a large, perfectly flat expanse of grass known as the Polo Field. Later in the week, when the tournament proper would begin and the crowds thicken, the Polo Field would become a parking lot and the players would practice on a cozier range beside the clubhouse. Right now several dozen pros already fanned out along the teeing area. Club shafts whipped in the early morning sunlight, and balls whistled toward distant mansions poking out of the treeline. My golf bag lay on the dewy grass beside a pile of pearly golf balls. My caddie switched a towel at invisible bugs.

I cold-topped my first three shots. The balls skittered through the grass, leaving ugly dash marks in the dew. I walked in a slow circle to collect myself. The Judge started to speak, but I shot him a glance that stifled any comment. The last thing I needed was his expertise.

I finally fashioned a decent swing. The ball flew skyward, bounced crisply, then spun to a stop. Years of muscle memory instantly returned. I methodically worked my way through the irons, admiring each shot to its finish before scooping another ball from the pile, settling into my address, and hitting again. The routine quickly bored the Judge, so I suggested he drop by the marshal's tent and set me up with a partner for a practice round. He muttered something discernibly sarcastic and billowed away.

I rounded off my warm-ups with a dozen whistling drives, then hunted up a telephone bank the local phone company furnished for the players. Last night's attempts to locate I. W. Frippy had reached nothing but dead ends. No listing appeared in any recent lawyers' directory;

calls to his old Milton residential number raised a Chinese restaurant. That left me one last avenue—the Office of Court Administration.

The state government created the OCA to oversee the workings of its sprawling court system. Like all good bureaucracies, the OCA quickly invented more duties for itself to execute. Soon, its tentacles wound not only around the court system but around every lawyer in the state. It demanded filings of retainer statements, trust accountings, and a steeply escalating biennial registration fee. More to the point, it tracked every member of the New York bar until the grave.

After being shunted through various extensions, I connected with a woman in charge of attorney addresses.

"Who are you looking for?"

"I.W. Frippy."

"Are you an attorney yourself?"

I told her my name. She must have verified it by computer because seconds later she shot back my social security number.

"Just a moment for your request."

I sighed, thinking that maybe, just maybe, OCA would prove its worth. I thought too soon.

"I can't release Mr. Frippy's address or telephone number."

"Why not?"

"He lists only his residence, and that information cannot be divulged over the telephone."

"This is an emergency."

"Sorry, that's the rule. And it protects you, too."

I didn't need protection; I needed his address.

"Make your request in writing to any OCA office," she told me, and hung up.

Demo Mike sounded overjoyed to hear from me. I told him to type a letter pronto and hand-deliver it to OCA's White Plains office.

"This will cost you thirty bucks for my time," he said.

"Don't be a wiseass."

At nine-thirty I stood on the first tee with a paunchy veteran who couldn't wait for his next birthday and the Senior Tour. The first hole is a long par three that would exact its share of bogeys in the tournament. I bored a five-iron into a gentle breeze. The ball flew dead straight between the two yawning bunkers guarding the green, but landed about thirty feet short of the flag.

"Passable," snorted the Judge, who harbored the delusion that he could shame me into winning a golf tournament as easily as he had challenged me to win verdicts.

The marshals hadn't erected the gallery ropes, so spectators strolled the fairways. The Judge padded behind me for the first two holes, both of which covered flat terrain. The third hole dipped into a valley, then rose sharply to the green. An easy par, but a difficult march if you carried three hundred pounds on bunioned feet. I wasn't surprised when the Judge disappeared after my tee shot.

I paused to savor my first official day on the PGA Tour. Non-golfers who know the game only through golf jokes or the sad tales of abandoned spouses never experience the feel of a golf course early on a summer morning. Lush fairways curve gently through cathedrals of trees. The aroma of freshly mown grass sweetens the air like incense. Sprinklers chuck softly, folding and unfolding gossamer wings as they turn slowly in the distance. Your cleats crunch the gravel of a cart path, then sink firmly into the turf. You thumb a scorecard out of the box. It is crisp, new, unsullied by any pencil mark.

The true devotee knows golf is more than a weekend diversion or a time-killer for Florida retirees. Golf reaffirms our belief in perfection—for a round, a hole, maybe just the wink of a single golf swing. We crave the melding of body, club, ball, turf, and sky. We yearn to be wrenched out of time, watching our shot trace and trace across the sky long after our ball comes to rest on the physical earth. Duffers play for love and pros play for money. But in those sudden moments of ghostly perfection, we all remember why we took up golf to begin with.

I didn't know what the Classic held for me. I could blow myself out of contention on the very first hole. I could fail to make the cut by a single stroke and spend the next year agonizing over every shot, a Tantalus in my personal Underworld. Or I could still be here on Sunday, scurrying among the thunderous hooves of the big boys, a mouse in a herd of buffalo. The scorecard, with its pencilled reality, would tell me soon enough.

The Judge returned midway through the front nine. He sported a marshal's cap and had commandeered an electric cart to ferry his bulk around the course. I expected the vet would complain about the distraction. Instead, he took an instant shine to the Judge, who can turn flattery into a fine art. They traded reminiscences about the vet's ancient duels with Palmer and Nicklaus, while I concentrated on tailoring strategies for each hole. The course played tough. The rough felt like three inches of steel, and the greens were mowed to glass. The pin placements for the tournament would be the trickiest the greenskeeper could conjure.

After the round, I wandered through the mobile village that followed the Tour like a circus caravan. One trailer housed an exercise room more elaborate than most health clubs. Another sparkled with all manner of shafts, clubheads, and grips for anyone who blamed their equipment for that dismal 75 in the final round. A third, jammed with computer terminals, offered legal advice, accounting services, and instantaneous nationwide banking. The only missing aspect of modern life was a trailer of certified mental health therapists.

I was back at the phone booth, dialing for Gloria Zanazzi at the Milton Town Court, when the Judge collared me.

"Get your ass to the first tee. I set you up for a round with a couple of guys." He named the current British Open champ and last year's second leading money winner on the Tour.

"How did you fix that?" I said.

"The power of persuasion. I told them I was your business manager."

"Can they wait?"

"You dumb bastard, this is the highest profile round you'll ever play. I can't ask golfers of this caliber to wait for you."

"Use your powers of persuasion. I'll be there as soon as I can."

The Judge shagged off in mid-expletive.

Gloria came on the line and whispered that she'd struck paydirt with the information. In the background, an angry male voice screamed about the inaccuracy of the police department's radar guns.

"You were right. DiRienzo eased off because Adrienne had an alibi. She went out to dinner with someone the night of the murder and didn't get home until late."

"Who did she have dinner with?"

The line went silent, but didn't disconnect. Something in the courtroom could have needed her attention. More likely she wanted to relish this last morsel of gossip before she forked it over.

"Who with?" I said when she returned.

"Jack Miles."

I hooked the receiver and shoved off into the crowd thronging the mobile village. Thoughts of Adrienne and Jack Miles swirled so thick they might have been visible, like the birds and stars circling the head of a cartoon hero knocked for a loop. I staggered to an empty first tee. Someone yelled my name. The Judge spun into focus, sitting in a cart parked alongside a concession stand.

"Get in here," he bellowed. "They teed off ten minutes ago."

"I'll join someone else," I said absently, so stunned I forgot who *they* were.

"The hell you will. I twisted enough arms for one day."

The British Open champ and last year's second leading money winner graciously welcomed me at the second tee. They each boomed a drive, and then stepped politely aside for my turn. Everything around me tilted askew. The tee sloped away from my feet. The fairway corkscrewed to the horizon. The gallery faces looked like images in a funhouse mirror.

I tried to focus on the ball. The club felt too short. The ground seemed too far away. Christ, I said to myself. Not this. Not now.

I swung the club mightily and struck the ball minimally. It looped over the gallery and buried itself in a thicket of brambles far to the right of the fairway. The British Open champ and the second leading money winner exhaled deep sighs of regret. My self-styled business manager looked mortified.

I dropped a new golf ball onto the turf and burned a four wood down 75 yards of fairway. For my next trick I planted the blade of my six-iron an inch behind the ball. Then I fluttered a wedge to the fringe of the green and rounded out the performance by three-putting. The gallery tittered; the Judge steamed.

I played best with a disengaged mind, and Gloria's news engaged me like the high gear of an Indy racer. I buried myself in a corner of the third tee to try to refocus while the others blasted drives. I know this game. Don't attack, I remembered. Play within limits. Concentrate.

My drive chugged like an airborne jalopy but covered 250 yards. For the second shot, I used an extra club and shortened my swing. Very conservative, but right now I didn't need heroics. I needed a long string of pars. The ball drifted lazily onto the right fringe of the green. I chipped back to eight feet, and sunk the putt. Not pretty, but a par.

I parred the next six holes in workmanlike fashion. No great birdie chances, but no severe trouble. The gallery paid me little mind because my playing partners traded birdies like baseball cards.

"At least you're not a total embarrassment," said the Judge as I walked off the ninth green.

Waiting to hit off the tenth tee, I spotted Miko Onizaka on the practice green. He rapped a long putt. The ball smoothly mounted a rise, curved down a twisty slope, and found the bottom of the target cup with a crisp click. Onizaka straightened up and stared across the green at an older Japanese man standing with two television people. The man, taller and rangier than most Japanese, wore smartly tailored golf clothes.

A second Onizaka putt dropped loudly into the cup. Again, he stared at the older Japanese as if begging to be noticed.

"You're wondering why your rival is here." Randall Fisk swung under the gallery rope and popped up beside me. Two marshals immediately rushed in, but he flashed a press pass as though it were a crucifix to ward off vampires.

"Mildly interested," I said, though I couldn't mask the edge in my voice.

"Simple," said Fisk. "Onizaka's an alternate because he placed second to you in the Met. The tournament committee is allowing him to practice in case you decide not to play."

"He's wasting his time."

"That's exactly what I told him."

A third ball plunked into the cup. Onizaka raised his fist as if he just won the Masters. The older Japanese laughed easily with the two TV people, either completely unaware or pointedly ignoring the putting display staged for his benefit.

"Who is that older fella?" I said.

"You mean you don't know?" said Fisk.

My question immediately answered itself. The TV people broke away, and the Japanese glanced briefly in our direction. His face, seamed like a pumpkin, could belong to only one man. He strode across the practice green and passed close to Onizaka without any hint of acknowledgement. Onizaka watched him melt into the crowd. His shoulders sagged. His next putt flew past the target hole and hopped onto the fringe.

Fisk smiled at me. He knew I recognized Hayagawa.

"Want an intro?" he said.

"I'll pass for now."

The sight of a grown man silently pleading for another man's attention disturbed me. I stared at Onizaka as he stabbed at putt after putt like a metronome gone haywire. He didn't sink one.

My caddie tugged at my sleeve. Time to tee off. I wiped the image of Onizaka from my mind, steadied myself over the ball, and clouted a long one. When I looked back at the practice green, Onizaka was gone.

Fisk shadowed me down the rolling fairway, half running to keep pace with my long strides.

"You're wondering why I haven't followed up my original column about the *Blitzklubs*, right?" he said.

"Do you think you're a mind reader?"

"You probably know why. I talked to Jack Miles. I'm not convinced he's ignorant of the *Blitzklubs*, but I don't believe he burglarized your shop."

"Dammit," I said with gusto. "And I was so sure."

"You still say the kid didn't steal them?"

"That's right."

"Who's your suspect now?"

I stopped short and Fisk barreled into me.

"God's honest truth, Randall. I don't have a clue," I said, and left him jabbering on the fairway.

Hordes of spectators swarmed out of the corporate promo tents. I had played before galleries in mini tour events, but never the sheer mass of humanity that followed the big names when the Tour swung into a large urban area. I wedged onto the green and two-putted for a par. No one in the crowd noticed. In fact, the thick ring around the green dissolved into a stampede of feet the moment the British Open champ sunk his putt.

Then it happened. Somewhere along the path to the next tee I walked into the zone. Athletes in every sport speak with reverence about "the zone"—a place where probability gives way to the surreal. Where skill, luck, and determination combine to synergistic effect. Where the speed of a baseball, the hum of a football, the arc of a basketball, the flight of a drive all seem guided by divine intervention. Where, in a word, the athlete feels possessed.

I noticed the first clue when I gripped my driver while waiting to hit off the eleventh tee. The corded rubber seemed to mold itself to my fingers, almost as if gripping back. I looked down the fairway. It was the tightest on the course. The rough pinched the landing area into a neck barely 30 yards wide. With spectators streaming down both sides, it should have seemed tighter still. But perception shifted in the zone. That narrow neck stretched wide as a football field.

I stood over the ball, waggled the driver, surveyed the hole. I visualized the ball scream down the barrel of the fairway, shuck off its spin with a single high bounce, then dribble in staccato to a stop.

I took back the club, paused for what seemed an eternity at the top of the backswing, then released. The ball exploded off the clubface. It roared high over the fairway, following the exact track and describing the same bounces I'd visualized. Without a doubt, I was in the zone.

I would have preferred stumbling into the zone during the tournament itself instead of a damn practice round. But you can't find the zone by force of will. You can't summon it by fervent prayer or coax it like a genie from a bottle. You prepare for it with gallons of sweat and long hours of plying your trade. In the end, it finds you when you least expect it, and evaporates just as mysteriously as it gathers. All you can do is hang in for the ride.

I'd felt the zone on several occasions, but never with such intensity. Maybe it echoed off the crowd. Maybe it drew strength from my two famous playing partners. Maybe the gods of golf were playing tricks. Whatever the reason, I stayed in the zone for the rest of the round. Every drive split the fairway. Every iron shot stuck close to the pin. Every putt ran on rails to a cup the size of a manhole. I carded a 30 on the back nine, four strokes better than the British Open champ and five shots better than the Tour's second leading money winner. The champ was particularly impressed.

"And you aren't on the Tour, mate?" he said as we shook hands. "A crime. A bloody crime."

True to my stated agenda, I parked myself on the practice range until dusk. Deep semi-circles of spectators crowded several of the big names, while my public consisted of the Judge and a nearsighted teenager who mistook me for Johnny Miller. Incredibly, the zone followed me to the practice tee. My swing felt so smooth I barely sensed the clubface striking the ball. My shots whistled in the thickening air. The dark ball dissolved into the gray sky, then materialized on the turf. For one giddy moment, I allowed myself to dream of walking up the eighteenth fairway in Sunday's dusk with a comfortable lead and a short putt to seal victory.

The Judge dropped me home shortly after ten. I didn't see the car deep in the shadows of the driveway until my knee banged into the bumper. Adrienne Miles lay behind the steering wheel, her seat reclined like an astronaut's. The window whispered down, and the seat shot upright.

"I haven't heard from you in several days," she said.

"I didn't know the script called for me to phone you," I said, not breaking stride for the stairs.

The car door opened and closed. Heels clipped on the driveway pavement. Fingers closed around my arm.

"It's important I talk to you," she said.

"Isn't it always?"

Adrienne followed me up the stairs. I considered slamming the door in her face, but decided that wouldn't prove anything except my capacity to be an asshole. We didn't say a word. She propped herself on a kitchen stool while I rummaged through the refrigerator for a couple of beers. Whatever I felt about Adrienne, I could think of worse things than looking at her in the light. A pink tank top stretched across her taut tummy. A tanned thigh curved out from a slit in her powder blue mini skirt. I leaned against the stove and tried to keep my eyes inside my head.

"Someone has been calling me on the phone," she said. "A man. He asks about the money."

"What money?"

"I don't know. It's exactly what he says—the money—as if I should know."

"When did the calls start?"

"This morning. He's called about six times. The last call came an hour ago. I was so scared. I didn't know what to do, so I—"

"Did you report this to the police?"

"At first I thought it was someone fooling around. But after the second one, I phoned Detective DiRienzo. He wasn't interested."

"Why should he be? You already delivered his prime suspect."

"You really think I killed Syl," she said.

"You could have told me about you and Jack Miles."

It should have stung like a slap across the face, but Adrienne didn't flinch.

"How did you find out?"

"I know the right people to ask. Did you think I would drop it so easily?"

"No, I knew you wouldn't. I just didn't want to be the one to tell you."

She took a pull on her beer, hiked herself better onto the stool, and pinned the bottle between her thighs.

"We certainly didn't love each other," she said. "We didn't even like each other very much. We both resented the way Syl controlled our lives. That's what drew us together in the first place. It never would have gone beyond a single act of private revenge, but Syl kept feeding us ammunition.

"We didn't meet very often. Not even once a month. I never knew the kind of mood I would find him in. Sometimes he was pleasant, charming, even cleverly witty. Those were the fun times. But lately he would be in a rage. About Syl, about money, about his life. He said nothing had turned out the way he planned. The world rewarded the charlatans, he said, the people like Syl, while those with honest talent suffered. I tried to break it off the night Syl died. But Jack was like a big balloon someone popped with a pin. The life ran right out of him, right in front of my eyes. He cried. And when he cried, he looked just like Syl, though I never saw Syl cry, never thought he had it in him. I couldn't leave him. He sounded so depressed he might have killed himself."

Her voice trailed off. She stared at the floor for a long moment.

"We stayed at a motel near the cottage," she said. "Jack fell asleep about midnight. I left him and drove home. DiRienzo questioned Jack. Checked the motel records, too."

"And the other night when I was looking for you?"

"I was tracking down Jack. I wanted to ask him pointblank about those *Blitzklubs*. Look him right in the eye when he answered. I thought maybe he could lie to you, and you wouldn't know. But he couldn't lie to me."

"Did he?"

"Lie? I don't think so. But I used the clubs as a pretext to end it. I wanted to clear the decks for someone else."

I didn't need to ask who. She hooked a leg around me and pulled me close. Her skirt slipped back to her tan line. No panties. I sampled her thigh with my hand. It felt as firm as it looked.

"Not tonight," I said, unhooking myself.

But Adrienne slid off the stool and slowly lowered to her knees in front of me. Her tongue licked her lips as she worked on my belt. We held that pose long enough for the apartment door to burst open.

"Kieran!"

Adrienne flew backwards, landing splay-legged on the floor. The front door slammed shut. Deirdre's footsteps pounded down the stairs. I hurdled Adrienne and ran outside, but Deirdre was already grinding her gears into reverse when I reached the landing.

Adrienne whisked past me and sailed her Mercedes out of the driveway with a screech of rubber that sounded dainty compared to Deirdre's clunker. My landlords peered through separate windows. I waved.

Deirdre buzzed me into the lobby, waited for me to climb four flights of stairs, and opened the door to my knock. None of this guaranteed entry to her apartment.

"You bastard," she said, and nearly severed my toe.

I knocked again. This time I deftly cupped my hand over her mouth and pushed her inside, carefully keeping my body turned so she couldn't kick me anywhere I'd regret. I didn't foresee her bite.

"Ow! Goddammit!"

"I suppose you and Adrienne Miles were trying to unlock the mystery of her husband's murder. Just be glad it's only your finger."

I went into the kitchen and stuck my hand under the faucet while Deirdre banged around her living room. She was relatively calm when I joined her. She tried to slap me only once, and not too fast for me to catch her wrist.

"What happened? Another new boyfriend treat you badly?"

"No, it's Pete." Deirdre wore sweatpants that bagged at the knees and a gray tee-shirt a few letters short of Fordham. She pulled away from me and flung herself onto the sofa.

"What about Pete?" I asked the question several times while Deirdre buried her face in the cushion. Finally, she lifted her head enough to talk.

"I went to visit him tonight and walked in on him, Tom, and Brendan Collins. I knew they were discussing something serious because I could read it in all their faces. But no one said anything. Tom and Brendan left, and I asked Pete what they were talking about. He said Collins thought he could work out a deal with the D.A. Both Collins and Tom were trying to convince Pete he should plead guilty if the D.A. went for it."

"What kind of deal?"

"I don't know. Pete was so confused by everything he could barely talk. He mentioned something about manslaughter and something about three to five years. The D.A. told Collins he'd need to clear a plea bargain with his superiors on this kind of case. If they went for it, he'd need Pete's answer right away. After that, no deal. He'd go for a murder conviction, nothing less."

"How soon is right away?"

"End of the week. Collins thinks the case against Pete is strong. And you know Tom. He's been thinking all along that Pete's bound to be convicted. He doesn't trust the system, especially since Miles was rich and we aren't. He thinks the plea is Pete's only chance. Pete likes to talk tough, but he's still a kid inside and he's still cowed by his father."

In theory, the deal made sense. The defendant buttoned down a certain three-to-five over a possible fifteen-to-life. No surprises, no vagaries of the jury system. But we weren't talking about any defendant; we were talking about Pete.

"You were right, Kieran. I was wrong," said Deirdre. "I never should have hired Brendan Collins to defend Pete. I thought I was helping him. All I did was screw it up."

No use gloating over her poor judgment. Even when I first warned her away from Collins, I had no idea he had butted into the case with the specific purpose of selling out Pete. And even hearing the conversation between Frank Gabriel and William St. Clare, I had no idea a fast end to the Sylvester Miles murder trial would be *this* fast. I should have known better. Seventy million dollars could grease a lot of wheels.

"Something's very wrong here," said Deirdre. "I'm being shut out after all I've done for Pete. He can't plead guilty, Kieran."

She moved enough to allow me room on the sofa.

"Kieran, you've got to do something. There is no one else I trust enough to help Pete."

"I know," I said. "I've been working this all along."

She nestled in the crook of my arm, all sniffles and trembling shoulders. We didn't speak, and soon her breathing smoothed into the long draughts of sleep.

I looked around a living room dotted with relics of our past: the portable television we had watched, the stereo we had listened to, the strangely shaped wicker baskets that had adorned our kitchen, the ceramic frame that once contained a photo of us but now held a shot of a rather unspectacular mountain.

I reached the lamp switch without disturbing her. A faint trapezoid of light from a car passing below scooted across the darkened ceiling.

Life reminded me of the view from a balloon drifting silently over the countryside. You could gaze at patchwork fields, tiny barns, motionless cattle, and ribbon highways running empty for miles. Then suddenly the highways would converge with five or six semis tangled at the intersection, and you would wonder how, in all that space, there could be such a mess.

Deirdre nuzzled my chest, and I knew I was headed for another major pile-up.

CHAPTER
14

I left Deirdre's apartment early the next morning and found Demo
Mike's note with I. W. Frippy's address stuck in my mailbox. Shady
Acres Rest Home. Not exactly around the corner.

A shave and a shower later, I trotted down to my car. First Pete,
then Frippy. Then practice shots on the Polo Field. But only if I didn't
blow my mind in the meantime.

A guard ushered Pete into the visitors' room. Physically, the boy hadn't
changed since our last meeting. But something seemed very different
about him. He looked shrunken, as if his teenage bravado had shed,
exposing a single raw nerve pulsating with fear.

"I heard about the offer," I said.

"Collins said he might be able to work something out with the
D.A. I'd have to tell the judge I killed Miles accidentally, then the
judge would sentence me to three to five years." Pete fixed his eyes on

the floor between us. "Collins thinks it's a good deal. So does Dad. If the D.A. goes with it, I might take it."

"Did you kill Miles?"

"No."

"Then it isn't a good deal."

"Hey, man, three years is a whole lot less than fifteen. I'll only be twenty by then."

"And you'll be an ex-con."

Pete smiled crookedly. "They said you'd tell me not to take it."

"Who are they?"

"Collins and Dad, mostly Collins. He said you don't have your head screwed on right, that it's somewhere up in the clouds always thinking about right and wrong instead of what's really happening."

"He said that?"

"Yeah. And he said it was none of your business to tell me I should go to trial. Because I'm the one who'll do the time, not you. And then Dad mentioned something about you and Aunt Dee once being together. Collins said you probably didn't care what happened to me as long as you looked good in front of her."

"That bastard," I said. "Do you believe any of this crap?"

Pete looked away.

"Pete, are you listening to me?"

He turned toward me, his eyes wild with fury.

"Goddammit, Kieran, I always listened to you. You taught me golf. You taught me how to fix golf clubs. You taught me lots of shit. But who should I listen to now? All Collins tells me is how shitty a case I have. All Dad tells me is take a plea. Aunt Dee tells me something else, but she's the one who hired Collins. You tell me not to take a plea. I can't remember a goddam thing about that night. Everyone's telling me shit, but I'm the one who's ass is on the line. Who the hell should I listen to?"

"That's your decision," I said. "But remember, of all the people you named, I'm the only one who doesn't have to be here."

"Yes, you do. Aunt Dee said you wouldn't walk away."

"So you'll listen to me?"

Pete shrugged. Good enough for now.

"When are you supposed to tell Collins you'll take a plea?"

"I don't know. Soon."

"Hold off for awhile."

"Kieran, if I let this slide . . ."

"Just awhile, Pete. I've been working on a few angles. Frank Gabriel wants to sell Milton Country Club to a Japanese company. Miles' vote was holding up the sale. I don't believe Gabriel borrowed a cart that evening to check some broken sprinkler heads. I think he met Miles on the golf course."

"Dr. Gabriel did it?" A wave of excitement shook Pete's skinny frame, then subsided. "Aw, who the hell's gonna believe my word against his?"

"You sound like your father."

"Yeah? Maybe Dad ain't that crazy."

"Tony La Salle is searching the inlet for a golf club. If he finds it, the police are going to look at this in a whole different light. I'm not talking about a long time. Twenty-four or forty-eight hours, tops. If nothing develops . . ."

"I take a plea."

"That's your decision. I won't try to talk you out of it."

Shady Acres Rest Home stood on the brow of a hill almost completely devoid of trees. The elms that once raised their boughs above the spires of the Victorian mansion had died, and the beech trees planted as replacements cast sparse shadows in the late morning sun.

A nurse behind the lobby desk assessed me with hooded eyes. The voice of a TV game show host carried thinly down a corridor. The smell of ammonia penetrated my sinuses.

"What is your relationship to the patient?" said the nurse.

"Friend."

"If Mr. Frippy is your friend, why have you never visited him before?"

"I meant friend as opposed to relative. Actually, we were once business associates. I practiced law with him."

"I see. Five minutes is all I'll allow. Not a second more." She pressed a button on her watch. "If my alarm rings before you pass this desk, I'll call the orderlies down on your head."

She meant it, too. I followed her directions to a tiny room where an attendant swirled a mop on the linoleum floor.

"Mr. Frippy?" I said.

The attendant shook his head and nodded at the bed. Had it not been for the dark eyes staring from a depression in the pillow, I would have thought the bed empty. The attendant fiddled with the blinds, and the sudden flood of light threw Frippy's gaunt frame into low relief. His nose bent sideways to a point. A toothless jaw stretched his parched lips into a tiny "O" that whistled with each breath. Wisps of white hair formed a corona on the pillowcase. A clawed hand slid toward a keypad attached by Velcro to the mattress. A motor hummed, and the bed lifted him to sitting position.

"You want to talk to him, he needs that," said the attendant, pointing to a table with a computer keyboard instead of a meal tray. I rolled it over Frippy's stomach and waited for something to happen.

"Can't do it hisself," said the attendant. "You got to help him."

I lifted Frippy's right hand by the wrist. His skin was dry as old newspaper. His bones were light as a bird's. Two fingers twitched across the keys. Gibberish words flashed on a monitor above the headboard.

"You got him all confused," said the attendant. "Fix his pointer finger on the letter A. That's right. Now tap his forearm."

Frippy cleared the screen, then waited with his finger poised over the keyboard.

"Tell him who you are. Talk loud. He hears bad as he sees. I'm surprised old Nursie let you up here. That other guy got him all riled up."

"What other guy?"

"Never you mind. You got five minutes from Nursie, you best use 'em quick. You don't want them orderlies after you. 'Bye, Mr. Frippy."

I moved over to Frippy's left ear. In a loud voice, introduced myself and said I hailed from Milton.

His fingers moved deliberately, clicking one key at a time. *i miss milton* appeared on the monitor.

"A wonderful community," I agreed. "Lots of changes lately. Buildings going up in places people never dreamed. You would be amazed."

i suppose i would.

We talked; rather, I talked and he responded by computer. He typed slowly and unerringly, as if his entire being resided in the thin corridor of nerves between his brain and his right hand. He never capitalized a name or punctuated a sentence. But the computer proved an effective means of communication for someone otherwise locked within a stroke-riddled brain. I mentioned several well-known citizens of Milton—lawyers, local politicians, sports stars—and he avidly asked questions the names suggested. A spark of life flickered in his eyes. His mouth flattened into a semblance of a smile.

I laced my stories with references to Sylvester Miles, William St. Clare, and Frank Gabriel. None of the names evoked any reaction. Three minutes remained. I cut to the point of my visit.

"You are the executor and trustee of Josiah Park's estate," I said.

His fingers froze. The pace of his whistling breath quickened.

go away appeared on the monitor. Each peck deliberate.

"You had certain duties to the estate. You didn't carry them out."

go away

"I'm not here to dig up old secrets. But a man's been murdered."

After a long pause, *who murdered*

"Sylvester Miles. A Japanese corporation offered to buy Milton Country Club. Miles was holding up the sale, probably because he discovered the problem."

what ive already said yesterday

"What did you say yesterday?"

already told you once

"I wasn't here before, Mr. Frippy. Who did you tell this to?"

go away i have nothing else the home has it all

"What did Gabriel and St. Clare do to you?"

nothing dont know them go away

"They forced you to cooperate, right?"

please

"How did they do it?"

Frippy lifted his head from the pillow. His lips trembled. His eyes seemed to search for me in the dim blur of his world. The keyboard clicked slowly.

savage

The cursor ran wild as Frippy's fingers collapsed on the space bar.

His eyes closed. Air whistled over his dried lips. I lifted his hand from the keyboard and lay it on the pad. A large tear rolled slowly down a wrinkle in his cheek.

I found the attendant changing sheets in a room down the corridor.

"Frippy said he had another visitor yesterday."

"Well, now I don't think that's right. These people don't get many, most get none. And the days all run into one and another. Gets them all addled. Now Mr. Frippy here, he sometimes thinks I'm the doctor."

"But he had another visitor recently. You said so yourself."

"Now I did say that. 'Bout a week, two weeks ago."

"The guy who riled him?"

"That's right. I didn't get his name, and I don't think anyone else did. We don't keep visitor records."

"What did he look like?"

"Older man. Older'n you, that is. Silver hair, nose like a bird's."

I named the day before Sylvester Miles' murder. The day Roger Twomby told me Miles left Milton to investigate that potentially embarrassing situation.

"Coulda been that day," said the attendant. "They talked a long time. Nursie sent the orderlies to throw the fella out. Mr. Frippy got all riled. Took him a few days to get right again. But when he's lucid he can tickle that ivory. Damn, he can tickle that ivory."

Spectators loved Westchester's seventh hole, a short dogleg around a thick stand of trees. From a small set of bleachers erected at the tip of the dogleg, you could track the flights of tee shots, feel the solid chunks of short approaches, and groan at putts sliding giddily across the triple level green.

The Pro-Am galleries swelled beyond anything mustered during the practice rounds. But the atmosphere was relaxed and festive, especially compared to tomorrow's bump and grind. I spotted Judge Inglisi from across the fairway. He sat in the middle of the bleachers, with windbreaker, towels, and umbrella strategically positioned so no one could cramp him. The group playing seven included a TV comedian who shanked a wedge shot into one of his partners' golf bags. He mugged for the crowd while the others finished the hole. The bleachers emptied, and I made my way toward the Judge.

"Can't learn much watching these clowns," he said. "That includes the pros."

"We have to talk about something."

"I can hardly wait."

A tee shot from the next playing group thumped in front of us. Another large gallery streamed along the ropes. New sets of feet shook the bleachers.

"Not here," I said.

The Judge sighed. We climbed down and followed a sloping cart path to a waste area screened by willows. I laid out my case quickly and surely: the meeting between Gabriel and St. Clare; the sketch made from the description of the estate deed; Sylvester Miles' visit with Frippy. By the time I reached my own conversation with the old lawyer, the Judge was firing salvoes of questions. Not out of annoyance or skepticism; he was genuinely interested.

"Did he capitalize the s in savage?"

"He doesn't capitalize anything. He types blindly with one hand."

"So maybe he would have if he could."

I shrugged.

"Figures." The Judge broke off a willow branch and picked its leaves one by one, either thinking or waiting for something to dawn on me.

"Savage means nothing to you?" he finally said.

"Not as a proper name."

"About twenty, thirty years ago, back when the divorce laws were different, Savage was the detective of choice among the shysters. He used all kinds of cameras and lenses and electrical equipment to get the job done. Sounds Mickey Mouse now, but he was the first. Stuff the

CIA couldn't find, Savage would dig up. He isn't around anymore. Disappeared tailing a woman one night." The Judge finished scaling the willow branch and whipped it into the grass. "You let this out, you'll blow Milton sky high."

"I know. I want to avoid that."

"And that's just one scenario, pal. You trip over the wrong set of feet, and you can end up with a broken arm. Not a good idea on the eve of the Classic."

"From Gabriel and St. Clare?"

"Dr. Lightbulb and the daffy Mayor didn't get where they are by being perfect gentlemen. No one does. And you forget that someone had to kill Miles."

"Don't worry."

"Why is it that every time I hear you utter those two words I reach for the tranquilizers?"

I bid the Judge good-bye, and walked against the flow of players and spectators until I found myself alone atop the fifth tee. Far below, the last group of the Pro-Am turned the dogleg out of sight. A greenskeeper pulled the flagstick out of the fourth green and tossed it onto his tractor.

I stretched out on a bench. The golf course was quiet except for the twitterings of birds and occasional eruptions of applause from beyond the wooded hills. A yellow maintenance barn in the hazy distance seemed painted rather than real.

I didn't know how far the conspiracy extended. Gabriel, St. Clare, and Collins certainly. Adrienne Miles and Jack Miles maybe. DiRienzo possibly. And who else? What other feet lay hidden beneath Milton's fine lace tablecloth, ready to boot me in the ass. Miko Onizaka? I had other ideas for him.

The plan came together slowly. I felt like a golfer whose ball had found a particularly nasty lie, with branches above and brambles below, a sliver of fairway and no shot to the green. I selected and discarded an entire golf bag of ideas as the shadows lengthened around me. Finally, I had it. Something that just might keep a lid on Milton, spring Pete from jail, and not jeopardize my toehold on the PGA Tour.

CHAPTER
15

My apartment's extra bedroom housed my share of the Inglisi &
Lenahan archives. Stacks of cardboard boxes rose from floor to
ceiling, with a network of narrow aisles in case I wanted to excavate the
detritus of my former career.

I dug through the piles until I struck a box labeled legal forms.
Deep within the musty file folders, I tapped into a vein of blank subpoenas. Most were folded, ink-stained, or just plain messy, but I found
enough neat ones to go around.

Demo Mike's front door was locked, and the doorbell didn't raise
an answer. I stepped out into the driveway. A handful of pebbles
brought him to an upstairs window. He tossed down a key, and I let
myself in.

Demo's room was a cross between a library and the control tower
at Kennedy Airport. He sat at a computer console displaying the lurid

graphics of a video game where a monster ten stories high terrorized a smal city.

"Typewriter," I said.

Demo pointed to a cluttered desk without taking his eyes off the game. I dislodged a pile of computer magazines, loaded the first subpoena form, and pecked away. Demo's game ended in a surprising string of obscenities. He rolled his chair beside me.

"That's a bogus subpoena," he said as I pulled out the first one.

I ignored him and started number two.

"So's that," he said.

I typed the third.

"Aw, come on. Who are you trying to fool? Even I know that's bogus."

"Demo, shut up and you might learn something. These aren't parts of a real lawsuit. I'm banking on curiosity and guilt to bring these people into court."

"That's abuse of process."

"You're right. But when I finish, no one will raise a stink."

I typed the last three, proofread the entire bunch, and handed them over to Demo.

"Serve them," I said.

"Now?"

"Unless you have a date with Godzilla."

"How much will you pay me?"

Quick study, that Demo. A week earlier he would have served these subpoenas for pure enjoyment. Now we haggled for ten minutes before arriving at a fee somewhat less than highway robbery.

The subpoenas all were local except one, for which I wrote out detailed directions and told Demo to save till last.

"Did one of these people actually kill Sylvester Miles?" he said.

"More than likely it was two of them. I'm just not sure which two."

Demo drove off to his appointed rounds. I went home and squir-reled myself into the darkness of the backyard to work my shoulders, back, and hips with an exercise bar. I didn't muse on the Classic. The merest thought of my tee time, now less than twelve hours away, un-leashed a torrent of stomach acid. Instead, I extrapolated the events I just set in motion. The plan was simple: throw everyone together like scorpions in a basket and watch the stingers fly. Best case scenario: a confession. Worst case? Well, even if the lid blew off the basket, the police and the D.A.'s office couldn't ignore the information I'd gath-ered. They might not drop the charges against Pete; too much circum-stantial evidence linked him to the scene if not to the crime. But they certainly would reopen the investigation, and Pete probably would make bail.

I went to bed around ten. One can only extrapolate so far, and my thoughts invariably strayed to the Classic. Forget about the zone. I kept projecting myself onto the first tee, hearing the murmur of the gallery, feeling the stares of my playing partners (two medium-big names recog-nizable in any golf household), and squeezing a club suddenly soft as a wet noodle in my hands. At least my pants stayed up.

I must have fallen asleep because the phone woke me close to mid-night. At first, I thought the silence was a prank, maybe Adrienne Miles' illusory caller. Then a harsh whisper resolved into the strained voice of Demo Mike.

"He's dead, Kieran. That last guy. Jack Miles."

I bolted upright.

"What?"

"You heard me."

"Where the hell are you?"

"A gas station. Pay phone. Can't talk. People around."

"Okay. Calm down. Just answer yes or no. You found him at the cottage."

"Yeah."

"Already dead?"

"Yeah."

"Violent?"

"Uh-huh."

"Gunshot?"

"No."

"Knife?"

"No."

"Bludgeoned?"

"Guess so."

"Report it to anyone?"

"Just you."

"Anyone see you at the cottage?"

"Don't know. Got out as fast as I could."

I told Demo to head for a roadside diner I remembered about ten miles from the cottage. He'd be less conspicuous waiting for me there than loitering at a gas station.

I burned it to the diner in thirty minutes flat. Demo looked as jangled as a speed freak. He sat in a booth with an untouched cup of coffee at his elbow and his fingers twisting a pile of chewing gum wrappers.

"We should call the cops," he said.

"Not yet. I want a look-see first."

"I'm not going back there. Cops have ways of finding things out. I don't need any more of my fingerprints and footprints at a murder scene. I'll tell you what I saw."

"I'll drive. Tell me on the way."

Demo was too spooked to hightail it back to Milton alone and too curious to wait for me in the diner. Once we got rolling, he explained how he served all the Milton subpoenas in three hours and decided to take a shot at Jack Miles. He saw the cottage lights from the highway, parked his car, and took the dirt road on foot. ("Do you think I left footprints?") The front door was ajar. He called hello, but heard no answer. The only sound from inside was the plunking of water into a sink. He pushed at the door, but it budged only a few inches. When he poked his head through the opening, he saw why: a body sprawled on the floor. ("He looked like he was doing the cha-cha.") Demo ran like hell—didn't even feel his limp, he said—and stopped at the gas station to call.

"Do you think anyone knows I saw something?" he said.

"Maybe a UFO," I assured him.

Except for one car obviously piloted by a drunk, the highway was empty. Good thing. Despite my bravado, I didn't want anyone spotting us near the cottage. I hid the car halfway down the dirt road.

"I'm not leaving," said Demo, and no amount of cajoling would change his mind.

I slipped through the shadows. The crickets fell silent. The breeze vanished from the trees. My softest footfall resounded like the crash of a cymbal. My heart thumped in my chest. The cottage turned slowly before me, lit like a jack-o'-lantern with its thin mouth frozen in a voiceless scream.

I barely managed to squeeze through the door. Demo's description had been accurate: stand Jack Miles up and he could have been dancing the cha-cha. One knee was bent, raising one foot slightly above the other. His arms spread out sideways, hands closed in loose fists as if snapping his fingers. His head looked like an overripe tomato dropped from a second story window. Blood oozed across the floor, filling the deep grooves between the planks, then engulfing a set of keys. Dry, turning to brown. And the stench. I was no coroner, but the guy had to be dead at least two days.

The cottage itself had been ransacked. Drawers spilled, closets rifled, boxes overturned. The neatly piled manuscripts and magazines now littered the floor. Some pages had been torn, others crushed into dirty snowballs. The computer keyboard dangled from the desk on a snippet of cable. The blackboard lay in shards.

Jack Miles must have surprised someone in the cottage. Burglar? That was the obvious conclusion. But two brothers meeting similar violent ends couldn't be coincidence. And the pulpy state of Jack's head spoke more of anger than fear.

I crouched beside the desk. Sylvester Miles' legacy to his brother fanned out beneath a broken drawer, the rubber bands that once bound four neat stacks snapped to hell. I gathered up the letters, stuffed them into a paper bag, and tucked the bag under my arm as Jack had done the afternoon of the will reading.

Demo and I drove back to the diner in silence. He didn't ask about the package, probably to preserve the last shreds of deniability remaining from this adventure.

I arrived home shortly after two. My starting time for the Classic was at 7:56, barely six hours away. The bats and butterflies didn't fill my stomach. Or if they did, I failed to notice. I had a long night of reading ahead of me.

As I reached the stairs, I heard a rustling like the wings of a giant bird over my shoulder. Instinctively, I raised my arms. The sky exploded. Searing heat scored the back of my neck. Then nothing.

I lay crossways on a horse, like a body in an old Western movie. My hands and feet dangled toward the ground. Far below in the velvet darkness, glass crunched and tin cans clattered. The heat had cooled to a warm throb.

I woke on a bed of newspapers, one arm twisted beneath my spine. A sickening pink sun balanced on a wooden fence. A crow picked at a lemon rind smeared on my foot. I'd be teeing off in the first round of the Classic soon. After a little more rest. A little more rest . . .

CHAPTER
16

Things tumbled into place like chips inside a kaleidoscope. Green paint peeling off a dumpster. Splintered wood of a fence. Gutted lemons. Sunlight glistening off broken glass.

I assembled myself slowly—sitting, kneeling, and finally standing. Dried blood striped each arm and caked in the palms of my hands. My head pounded, my neck burned, my back bristled like an archery target.

I spotted the familiar eaves of my landlord's house peeking through the treeline. My attacker or attackers had dumped me barely half a block from home. I limped down an alley, cut through a backyard, and squeezed past a fencepost into my driveway. The movement washed away most of the rockiness but none of the pain.

The letters were strewn across the driveway. Dimly, I wasn't surprised. I gathered them together and trudged up the stairs. My apartment was in order; no sign of entry. Again, no surprise.

I stood under the warm flow of the shower, slowly working the muscles of my back, neck, shoulders, and arms. The maroon shirt and eggshell pants I had pre-selected for the first round hung on a closet doorknob. The shirt perfectly matched the bruises on my forehead and jaw.

I managed the drive to the Westchester Country Club in under ten minutes. The guard at the contestant's parking lot blocked my path until I shoved my tournament badge under his puss. I left the letters in the car and stumbled from the parking lot to the locker room. Everything moved in fast motion. Spectators and staff darted across my path. Electric carts careened around hairpin curves. Voices in the locker room chirped like a nest of fledglings. I lowered myself onto the bench in front of my locker. Judge Inglisi spun out of the haze.

"What the hell happened?"

I bent to untie my sneakers.

"Kieran—"

"Never mind what happened."

"You look like you slept in a cement mixer."

"Dumpster," I corrected. "And I was outside it."

"I warned you," said the Judge. "I said you were playing a dangerous game with the Miles thing."

"Don't congratulate yourself yet." I lifted one foot out of its sneaker and pushed it gingerly into a golf shoe. "This hand was dealt before we talked yesterday."

"What's that supposed to mean?"

"Forget it. It's done. I'm here. I'll do what I have to do."

"You're going to play?"

"I didn't fight my way here to watch."

"You can't even walk eighteen holes, much less play golf."

I worked the other foot into its golf shoe. A stab of pain shot up my leg.

"Get over to the marshals' tent," I said, choking back a yelp. "Tell them I'm here. Tell them I'm ready to play."

The Judge left in a huff, probably more disturbed at my ordering him around than at the obvious insanity of my intentions. I tried to tie my golf shoes, but the laces kept slipping out of my fingers. Forget it, I decided. My feet were so swollen I'd need a blacksmith to unshoe me. I collected my caddie and walked—swam was a better description—to the first tee. The humid morning air clung to me like bath water.

A few dozen spectators lolled on the bleachers. A gent wearing an official Classic blue blazer announced the threesome preceding mine. Applause coursed through the gallery. I pulled an iron from my bag and shuffled to a grassy area beside the tee to warm up.

"You're going through with this?" said the Judge.

"Yep," I said, and lifted the club over my shoulder in a poor imitation of a swing. My hands released, and the club fell to the ground.

"You're nuts. You belong in a goddam hospital."

I picked up the club and waited for my head to clear. My second swing was a minor success; at least I didn't drop the club. Repeated motion gradually oiled me, and by the tenth swipe my muscles felt fluid enough to spank a golf ball somewhere near the green.

The threesome teed off. My two playing partners and their caddies emerged from the clubhouse, their reputations swelling the crowd in the bleachers. I waved jauntily to the Judge and bent myself under the gallery rope. The blazered gent announced our starting time.

The others hit, each shot landing comfortably on the green. I normally would have hit a five-iron, but I pulled out the three in deference to my rickety bones. The gent introduced me as the reigning Met PGA champ. A half dozen people clapped. The rest wondered aloud about my bruises.

I settled woozily over the ball, watching it separate into two ghostly images, then reform as a dimpled white orb. No way I could play eighteen holes. No way. But that wasn't the point. Not anymore.

I lifted the club, forcing my body to coil and uncoil. Impact felt like an open hand slapping sheet metal. I clung to the grip and let the force of the follow through spin my head toward the green. The ball flew back against the gray sky, dove to earth like a wounded bird, struck the pin, and stopped a foot from the cup.

The crowd hooted and cheered. I waited until the noise subsided.

"I withdraw," I announced, and limped toward the clubhouse.

The Tour officials were confused, but too polite to ask any questions. After some paperwork, I slumped on the bench in front of my locker. Several pros stared warily from different corners of the locker room.

I exchanged my shoes for infinitely more comfortable sneakers and started my painful march to the parking lot. The British Open champ was due to tee off, and the rush of spectators stood me up like a stiff winter gale. The Judge rescued me.

"What the hell was that all about?" he said, positioning himself like a windbreak. "Why hit one shot? So you can say you played on the Tour?"

"I found Jack Miles murdered last night," I said. I didn't want to tell him about the subpoenas, so I skipped over Demo and plunged right into the scene at the cottage.

"Jesus H. Christ," he said.

"I was jumped as I pulled into my driveway."

"Same people?"

"If so, why am I alive?" I said. "Look, everything I told you yesterday is true. I just don't believe it answers every question."

We reached my car. I opened the door and pointed to the letters spread over the passenger seat.

"What the hell are these?" said the Judge.

"Letters different army buddies wrote to Sylvester Miles after the war, and three from Syl to Jack. Syl left these to Jack in his will. Not a very funny joke between two brothers."

The Judge snatched one letter and pointed to Corny O'Meara's name on the return address.

"Old Corny was one of Syl's army buddies," I said. "Deirdre told me that the day Pete was arrested."

"Small son of a bitchin' world, huh? Why the hell did you grab these?"

"I think they'll tell us something."

I grouped the letters according to writer: Syl's three to Jack, then larger piles from Corny O'Meara, Marcel Velge, and Hank Press.

"Something's missing," I said. "When I saw these letters before, there were four different people who wrote to Syl."

"Maybe you left them in the mess."

"No. I'm sure I took them all. And I'm sure there should be another stack. Dammit, I can't remember the name of that fourth guy."

Corny O'Meara was dead. Marcel Velge was in Belgium, which did me the same amount of good. That left Hank Press.

"Feel like flying?" I said.

"I always feel like flying. Where to?"

"East Orange, New Jersey."

Traveling by private plane wasn't as simple as hopping into your car, explained the Judge as I slugged coffee in a pilots' lounge at Westchester County Airport. There was fueling to be done, mechanical checks to be made, flight plans to be filed, not to mention waiting your turn in the rotation at an airport jumping with corporate jet traffic. I spent the time poring over the letters, and occasionally limping across the lounge so my muscles wouldn't stiffen.

The moment we climbed into the Cessna, the Judge assumed his pilot's persona. Every movement carried a slight dramatic flourish. His eyes squinted behind aviator glasses. His stubby fingers flipped two and three switches at a time. His voice slowed to a mid-Southern drawl as he spoke in code with the controller. Very expert, very sober. Still, I was scared shitless about flying in a single engine plane piloted by a man who drove his Ferrari with maniacal glee. I didn't pull my knuckles from the seat cushion until the Cessna banked over the Hudson and the three mile ess of the Tappan Zee Bridge spun into view.

My ears cleared, and I picked up the last of the three stacks of letters. Neither Marcel Velge nor Hank Press had substantiated my new theory that Sylvester Miles' murder traced back to post-war Germany. Ultimately, Corny O'Meara didn't either. Of course, there was that fourth correspondent. The man whose name I couldn't remember.

Corny's last letter, postmarked July, 1946, and addressed to Sylvester in Apalachicola, Florida, said: "Hey, buddy, bring your bride to Milton, the greatest little town on God's green earth."

I showed the letter to the Judge.

"Bet Syl regrets taking that advice," he said.

Teterboro was the closest airport to East Orange, but a southwest wind put it smack in the landing pattern of airliners coming into Newark. The Judge opted for a dinky field called Hanover in the middle of something called Hatfield Swamp. The tiny quonset hut had a phone, and our taxi showed up without too much delay.

The nurse at the VA Hospital's reception desk assumed I was a patient returning from furlough. The Judge answered that worse problems lurked beneath the bruises, principally in the gray matter area. The nurse, amused by the clever repartee, cut through half the normal red tape and told us to wait in a tiny lounge decorated in several shades of yellow. A few minutes later, an orderly wheeled Hank Press into the room. Despite the summer heat, Press wore a thick terrycloth bathrobe, flannel pajama pants, and battered slippers. A growth as large as my fist bulged beneath a scarf knotted around his neck.

I introduced the Judge and myself as friends of Sylvester Miles. Would he mind talking about his old army buddy?

Press raised a trembling, wrinkled hand to the spot where his trachea once had been.

"Do I look busy?" he croaked.

The Judge and I laughed indulgently. Then I broke the news about the murder.

"Shame," said Press. "Guy survives gunshot wounds and gets killed on a golf course. They catch the guy?"

"The police think Corny O'Meara's grandson did it," I said.

"You're kidding, right?" said Press.

"I wish I were."

"Ain't that a kick in the ass," said Press. "You know, Corny was the reason Syl moved to that little town."

"I know," I said. "The Judge and I don't believe the kid killed Syl. I think something that happened during the war might have come back to him."

Press narrowed his eyes. "Like what?"

I told him about the *Blitzklubs*, Sylvester Miles' will, and the burglary of my pro shop.

"*Blitzklubs*, eh?" Press smirked over his scarf. "Son of a bitch."

"What?" said the Judge.

"Let the man talk," I said.

"Miles and I were stationed together in Nuremburg not quite a year," said Press. "He transferred to our unit from combat infantry after the surrender. We knew about his history. The wounds, the mortar nest in Anzio. None of us seen much action, and we expected him to be some kind of crazy cowboy. He wasn't. Walked with a bad limp, used a cane when nobody was looking. Coulda gone home, but he wanted to stay. Softest spoken guy of the bunch."

Press let his hand fall to his lap. He took several quick breaths before resuming.

"One day, Miles came to me and said he needed a jeep. I had connections in the battalion motor pool, so a jeep was no sweat. Miles couldn't drive. With that bad leg he couldn't pump a clutch. So I went with him. We drove way out into the countryside, with him squinting against the wind and not saying much of anything. I figured he had a *fraulein* stashed out there somewhere. Maybe one for me, too, I hoped.

"We came to a small village. The people hadn't seen much of the war, they were so tucked away in the middle of nowhere. Stared at us like we were a couple of Martians. Followed us through the streets until we came to something that looked like a small factory built into the side of a hill. They started shouting at us, but Miles whipped out a Luger and they got pretty quiet.

"He shot the lock off the door, and we went inside. Turned out the factory was one of those places, like a steel mill but not exactly."

"A forge?" I said.

"That's it. Except it was pretty empty, see, like maybe the owner couldn't get enough materials with the war. But on one wall there were all these metal tubes like gun barrels. Miles started gathering them up, and when I got closer I saw these gun barrels had funny little heads. Like golf clubs. I asked Miles what he wanted this crap for. And he said he was gonna make these clubs the most famous in the world. He wrapped them in burlap, and we loaded them in the back of the jeep and drove back to Nuremburg."

Press stopped to catch his breath.

"I don't know what happened to the clubs. Normally if you wanted to send stuff home you needed to ask the supply sergeant. If you had a lot of stuff, like those clubs woulda been, you needed to grease some palms. I can't say if Miles ever bothered. Last I saw those clubs, he was showing them to this Belgian interpreter we had with us. I never saw the clubs again."

"Was that Marcel Velge?" I said.

"How do you know about him?"

"Syl kept all the letters you fellas wrote to him. Letters from you, Corny, Marcel Velge."

"And Eddie Z, too, probably."

I caught the Judge's eye and nodded. Eddie. That was the name on the missing letters.

"Syl kept all those letters," said Press. He smiled, pleased that Miles held the old days in such high regard. "Syl showed you, eh?"

"Not exactly," I said. "He left them to his brother Jack when he died. That's how I saw them."

"The brother, huh?" said Press.

"Know him?" I said.

"He called me on the phone once or twice. Talked about some big idea he had for writing a book about the war. Wanted to know if he could interview me. I said hell, what do you want to interview an old soldier like me for. I never saw any combat, just a lot of railroad tracks. But he said he was interested in all the things Syl's buddies did in the army. He talked to Eddie Z, but Eddie said he'd only be interviewed for money. I wasn't looking to make a buck. Hell, I'd talk to anyone for free. But I guess this Jack Miles never bothered with his idea. I sure never heard from him again."

"When did you last speak?"

"Over a year ago."

"Did he ever interview Eddie?"

"Not that I know," said Press. "Eddie sat right where you're sitting not two, three months ago. Came all the way from Pittsburgh. Hadn't seen him in years and years. Had a bug up his ass about the money. Some loony idea that Miles got it out when we didn't."

"What money?" said the Judge. "I thought we were talking about golf clubs."

"Those clubs were small potatoes," said Press. "I don't care what they're worth."

"What money?" I said.

"Our Swiss bank accounts."

The Judge and I glanced at each other. Press grimaced as he sucked air around his tongue.

"I told you we were stationed at the district transportation center in Nuremburg," he said. "Nuremburg had the biggest railyards in Europe at the time. Big as a city itself. Acres of land, miles of track, all kinds of sidings into old warehouses.

"Now our company knew exactly what was coming in on the trains before they even got there. That was our job. We'd route it down the right track, check the freight to make sure what it was, offload it, and send the empties back. But the yards were so big you could lose a car or two on a siding, no problem.

"There were five of us—me, Miles, O'Meara, Eddie Z, whose real name was Zelinsky, and Marcel Velge. In other words, we had a record keeper, a dispatcher, two freight checkers, and a guy who spoke most any language we'd need. Miles came up with the idea. We'd sidetrack a car into an abandoned warehouse, offload it at night with some German nationals Velge hired, and sell the goods ourselves. Cigarettes were the best, and Old Golds the best of them. You could get five bucks a pack, something like two hundred fifty *deutschmarks* at the time. But we'd spread it around. Sometimes it'd be sugar. Other times it might be liquor, the real stuff reserved for officers. We made a mint, the five of us. But we couldn't take the money out."

"That would have been too goddam easy," said the Judge.

"Don't know much about army pay, eh?" Press gulped more air. "Army pays you in the currency of the country you're in at the time. Pounds in England, *francs* in France, *lira* in Italy, *marks* in Germany. After the war, the Army knew that most guys had something shady going on over there. They'd treat it with a wink and a nod as long as the money you made stayed put. To send money home, you needed to buy a money order. And to buy a money order you needed to show your currency control book. That allowed you to send home twice your monthly pay each month. No one was going to get rich on that.

"We were making ten times our monthly pay in a day. So Miles and Velge, they came up with this idea of opening Swiss bank accounts. See, the Swiss *franc* was the stablest currency around, so it was a good place to keep it. The trick was to get it home, because the Army knew that, too. But Velge, he thought maybe there was a way. He knew something about finances. He traded diamonds in the Congo before the war, and he was an accountant. So we dumped our money into these accounts. Velge never figured how to get at it, at least not without landing us in a shitload of trouble. So we left it. We didn't care. Hell, there was so much money around it looked like it'd never stop. Besides, we were tired of being away from home. That was more important to us.

"Eddie Z visited two, maybe three months ago. He was on his way to see Miles because of some lamebrained notion Miles got our money out of Switzerland and was living high off the hog. I told him the last I seen Miles was back in the fifties after his wife died. She left him pretty well off. But Eddie said no. That's our money he's living off. Asked me if I wanted to go with him. Said we'd get Corny and talk to Miles and get him to own up to double-crossing us. I said, 'Eddie, Corny's been dead for years. And who gives a damn about the money? It was a lark, those days.' But he didn't want to hear nothing about Corny. He kept harping about the money, and I said, 'What the hell good is that money going to do us now? We're old men.' But he didn't give a damn. That money was his, even if he got it the day before he died. If I wasn't coming, he'd go alone."

"Why did Eddie think Miles double-crossed you guys?" I said.

"Eddie was down on his luck," said Press. "Got laid off when big steel went down and never quite went back to work. Wife died, kids moved far away. Guess he just got it into his head the money could help him. He hired a lawyer in Pittsburgh to look into the accounts, something we all were afraid to do because we figured the Army'd still be watching. It took the lawyer eight, nine months to get an answer. I guess Eddie didn't have much to pay him, so he took his sweet time. Turns out, his account was closed out long ago, before 1950. Mine, too. Eddie showed me the lawyer's letter. He still wanted me to go, but I told him it wasn't such a big deal. I'm past the point of wanting that money now. And the truth is, I didn't see anything in that letter saying Miles was the guy who emptied those accounts. Sure, it was odd the money was gone, but I still thought Eddie was dreaming. But then, he never did like Miles very much."

"Why not?"

"On account of Velge. Eddie didn't like the idea of a foreigner horning in on the dough. Especially since Miles gave Velge so much authority over the operation. Corny and I'd tell him he was crazy. Miles treated us square, and Marcel was an okay guy. We needed his languages to make the operation work. Guess Eddie never quite got those suspicions out of his head."

"When exactly was Eddie here?"

"Easter Sunday. Hospital served a ham that day. That's how I remember."

"What does Eddie look like?" I said.

"Lost most of his hair. Has some red welts on his scalp. I thought they were skin cancer, but he said they were just welts. He's scrawny.

Not very tall, with bowed legs. Looks sorta like a chimp if you use your imagination. Always was wiry tough. One guy in our company started calling him Eddie Monkey. Eddie thrashed the shit out of him bare-handed. That's when we started calling him Eddie Z."

CHAPTER
17

A line of squalls grounded us at Hanover for two hours. The Judge fumed; I slept. Once airborne, we chewed on what Hank Press had told us. We agreed all roads led to Eddie Z, but the Judge doubted I could find him.

"You think he's waiting around to get caught?" he said.

"He came here looking for money he's been owed for fifty years. He won't fold his tent so quickly."

The sky was full dark by the time I rolled into my driveway. Light shined in my living room window. Deirdre sat Indian-style on the sofa. She wore one of my golf shirts and not much else. Just like old times.

"Where the hell have you been?" she said.

Yep, just like old times. I stepped into the light.

"God, Kieran, what happened to you?" She jumped off the sofa and began a professional examination of my bruises. "I went to the tournament after my shift. Hmmm, these don't look so bad. No one knew anything about you, so I called the Judge. Couldn't find him, either. You should put something on this one. Then I read the newspapers, so I knew you didn't play."

I brushed her hand away from my forehead. "How's Pete?"

Deirdre frowned. "Same old story. He said you spoke to him about the plea. Collins and Tom went at him again for an answer. He held them off, for now anyway."

I guided Deirdre to the sofa, sat her beside me, and leaned forward so she could massage the knots in my back. Two sweaty but empty beer bottles stood on the coffee table. Wet circles dotted the evening edition of the local newspaper.

"Any more live ones?" I said.

Deirdre slid off the sofa. I grabbed for the paper, clumsily toppling the empties onto the carpet. The local news section carried no mention of Jack Miles' murder. Days could pass before anyone missed him. I turned to sports, and immediately caught a blurb in a Randall Fisk column entitled "Classic Moments":

Local pro Kieran Lenahan treated a tiny gallery to one of the strangest scenes in the Classic, or in any other Tour event for that matter. Looking as if he spent the night in a gin mill, Lenahan staggered to the tee and slapped a weak two-iron greenward. The ball glanced off the pin and stopped two feet from the cup. After basking in applause, Lenahan raised his arms and withdrew from the tournament, claiming golf was too easy a game.

Deirdre returned with two fresh bottles. Alternating sips with pressing the frigid glass against my bruises, I outlined my Milton Country Club sale theory in the vaguest terms. No names, no dates, hardly any details. If Deirdre caught a whiff of another suspect, she'd run to the

D.A. or DiRienzo and demand Pete's release. I didn't want that, not just yet.

I gave her a full blown version of Jack Miles' murder. Gory details never fazed Deirdre. She gently patted one of my bruises.

"And this is to stop you from snooping?" she said.

"The Judge thinks so. I'm not so sure."

"Why don't you tell all this to DiRienzo?"

"The time isn't right yet."

"That's a crock, Kieran. You don't have that much time. You haven't told me everything."

No sense denying the obvious. Deirdre knew me too well.

"I need to be damn sure of what I'm doing before I make my move."

"Don't brush me off like that, Kieran."

"There is much more going on in this town than a murder. It's better if I'm the only person who knows."

I jumped into Hank Press' story partly to deflect her anger, partly because I needed answers. She grunted whenever I mentioned Corny's name, and snickered at my estimate of the black market operation's take.

"What do you know about your father's army career?"

"It was bullshit, like everything else he did."

"Without the bile, okay?"

"I don't know much. Tom's better on that."

The O'Meara house was dark except for a bare bulb glowing in an attic window and the blue light of the television shimmering within the enclosed porch. Tom lay asleep on the recliner while the harsh snow of a blank video cassette tape swirled on the TV screen. I leaned against the wall. My legs had stiffened during the flight from Jersey, and the two block walk from my apartment hadn't loosened them. I noticed Tom's cane hooked on the armrest of the recliner, and wondered how I'd handle the pain everyday.

Deirdre softly called her brother's name. Tom snorted himself into grogginess, then jumped awake, his hands quickly gripping the cane like a baseball bat.

"Pete!" he shouted.

"It's us, Tom," said Deirdre. "Kieran and me."

"What is it? I don't like being startled. You know I don't like being startled."

"I'm sorry, Tom," said Deirdre. "Kieran wants to ask you some questions."

Tom grumbled and aimed the remote control at the TV. The porch darkened. His silhouette turned toward me until one eye caught a shaft of streetlight slanting through the window.

"It's about your father," I said, speaking slowly while my mind scrambled to compose delicate phrases. "And an old army buddy of his named Eddie Zelinsky, or Eddie Z."

"Yeah?" said Tom.

"Do you know him?" I said.

"I know something about him," said Tom. "He and my father were together in Nuremburg after the war. Yeah, Dad mentioned Eddie a lot. There was Eddie, Sylvester Miles, my father, and another guy."

"Hank Press?"

"That's him. They were all good buddies. How do you know about Eddie?"

"Press told me about him. I traced Press through Miles' brother."

"Why are you bothering with these guys?"

"Seems like Eddie Z had a motive for killing Miles."

The recliner creaked as Tom readjusted himself. He held the cane upright, bouncing the rubber plug on the armrest.

"I'm listening," he said.

"Press told me about a black market operation Miles ran with your father and three other guys in a transportation company stationed at the railyards in Nuremburg. Pretty ingenious, really. There was only one minor drawback. Army currency control prevented them from sending the money back home. So Miles and a Belgian named Velge encouraged the men to open Swiss bank accounts where they would stash the money until someone figured out a way to get it home. But no one ever did, and the guys let the money sit because they were afraid of being caught if they tried to withdraw it."

Tom's head remained motionless while the cane bounced rhythmically.

"About three months ago," I continued, "at Easter, Eddie visited Hank Press in a VA hospital in Jersey. He finally checked on the money and discovered the account had been closed years ago. He was convinced Miles looted it."

"What convinced him?" said Tom.

"Doesn't matter. The point is that Eddie was coming to Milton to confront Miles. He wanted Press to join him, but Press refused. He also wanted to take your father along with him."

"He's a little late," Tom said with a forced laugh.

I sensed something behind me, padding through the darkness. Before I could focus, Tom whumped his cane against the side of the recliner.

"The hell you sneaking in here!"

Gina scurried off the porch and cowered in the hallway. A sliver of cheek and a corner of one eye edged past the doorjamb.

"Goddammit, Gina, make me a sandwich and an iced tea. Do it! Damn lazy bitch." Tom stared her away from the door. "You people don't want nothin', right?"

"Not if you talk like that," said Deirdre.

"Talk any way I damn please. This is my house, sister dear. You moved out long ago. All right, Kieran. Where the hell were you?"

I cleared my throat. "Press said Eddie thought your father was still alive. It was part of the reason Press refused to go along, other than he couldn't travel anyway. Eddie visited Press at Easter, so he must have come to Milton soon after."

"If he did, he didn't come to see me," said Tom. "He musta come to his senses."

"Maybe he called when you were out and spoke to Gina."

"If he did, Gina woulda told me and I woulda just told you. He didn't, okay?" Tom lay the cane across the armrests and hitched himself upright in the chair. "And let me tell you something else. You may be fooling around with my sister again. That's your own damn business. But don't come sneaking into this house with wild stories some old soldier told you about my father. My father wasn't involved in no black market operation. He was an honest man. He worked for every dollar he ever had, not that he ever had much. Nobody gave him anything he didn't deserve."

Tom fired up the TV, flashing through the cable channels until he found a documentary about Montgomery and the North Africa campaign. Deirdre pulled me into the hallway.

"Let's get out of here," she said. "He's behaved relatively well lately. We stir him up any more, and Gina will pay the price."

We crossed the street to Toner's, the neighborhood pub. The few regulars either stared blankly at a baseball game on the tube or communed silently with the fish lazing in the aquarium behind the bar. No one paid us any mind as I ordered our beers.

"I've seen the O'Meara men in too many tough spots," said Deirdre, as we slid into a booth. "I know exactly how they'll act. If Tom ever believed Pete is innocent, he's given up completely now. I can hear it in his voice. Life's been bad to Tom. He can't take swimming against the tide."

"I didn't expect the spirited defense of your father."

"That's something new. Last couple of years, anyway. He never wanted to believe the bad stuff about dear old Corny. And once he couldn't deny it anymore, he couldn't stomach him. That's Tom. Things are black or white. No fine shades of gray like us sophisticated people see. He feels guilty as hell for not reconciling himself with Dad before he died. Why the hell do you think he watches all those damn war shows? He's no more interested in those battles than I am. Ask him a basic question sometime. He'll look at you like you have three heads. He's not learning. He's doing penance."

The second thing I planned for the next morning was to begin my search for Eddie Z. The pounding on the door came so early it preempted the first thing as well. I untangled myself from Deirdre and headed toward the door, pausing only to inspect myself in the hall mirror. My muscles and bones felt surprisingly good, but the bruises had darkened to the ugly purple of Sylvester Miles' dead fingers.

Tony La Salle waved a crooked golf club at me.

"It was in the inlet, all right. How the hell'dya know to look there?" Tony squinted. "And what the hell happened to your face?"

I was too interested in the *Blitzklub* to answer. The shaft was bent but not broken, with the grip twisted like a barbershop pole.

"Would you testify to where you found this club?" I finally said.

"Pay me for finding it, and I'll tell anyone whatever the hell you want."

I wrote Tony a check and brought the *Blitzklub* into the bedroom just as Deirdre swung her long legs off the bed. She was already late for the day shift, and the sight of a bent golf club didn't impress her.

"This club belonged to Sylvester Miles," I said. "Tony La Salle just dredged it out of the inlet. It means Sylvester was killed while practicing, which also means he was killed hours before Pete was anywhere near the linksland."

"Good. Let's tell DiRienzo."

"We can't. Not yet."

"We know about Eddie Z, we know he had a motive to kill Miles, and we know he was coming to Milton. You have this club. How much more proof do you want?"

"I need to deliver Eddie Z. If I don't, all this evidence means nothing."

"Then I'll tell DiRienzo."

"You do that, Deirdre, and Pete will be in even more trouble."

"Because of what you haven't told me."

"Because of something no one else should know."

"Okay." Deirdre plucked the phone off the nightstand. "I'll call in sick, and we'll spend the day looking for Eddie Z."

"Wait," I said. "Pete needs to know what's going on."

"We'll call him, too."

"No. It can take hours to get through to an inmate. Better if you run up there and tell him exactly what I learned. Tell him not to do anything stupid."

Deirdre cocked her head and looked at me with one eye, trying to decide why I wanted her out of my hair.

"Where will I meet you?" she finally said.

"Forget about me. Go to the hospital. When I figure out how to trace Eddie, I'll know exactly where to find you."

Deirdre fussed as she pulled on her whites. Hospital duties accustomed her to taking charge, and she didn't appreciate being relegated to messenger duty. Lucky for me she understood the need to contact Pete immediately. Otherwise, I'd have been in for a long morning of bristly temper.

After Deirdre left I sat down with the *Blitzklub* pitching wedge. Golfers knew hundreds of ways to bend a shaft. Across the knee, around a tree, against a golf cart, into hardpan. And now, apparently, against collarbone and skull. The twist in the grip intrigued me. I removed thousands of grips each year. If I didn't plan to re-use the grip, I simply sliced it off with a razor. Otherwise, I would inject a syringe full of gasoline into the rubber to break the adhesive. Even then I needed every ounce of my considerable hand strength to pull the grip off the shaft. The *Blitzklub* grip curved more than ninety degrees off line. Someone very strong, or very desperate, had twisted it to hell. I envisioned two elderly warriors locked in a struggle on the barren, deserted plain of the linksland. One fighting for the life he might have had, the other for a life spun out of whole cloth.

My only leads on Eddie were Hank Press' description and the logical assumption that Eddie arrived in Milton shortly after Easter. If so, he had waited nearly three months to kill Miles. How did Eddie spend that time? Did he contact Miles? Or did he observe him from afar, calculating the time and place of the murder? A lonely stretch of links on a misty evening. Perfect. And with the job done, he didn't flee back to Pittsburgh. He lingered, plotting another way of collecting his due.

He must have been living somewhere. Motels were out. Even a fleabag would be too expensive for someone on Eddie's thin budget. Rooming houses? There had to be thousands.

Suddenly I realized where I had seen Eddie.

Then the phone rang.

"He's gone to court!" cried Deirdre. "He's pleading guilty!"

I reached the courthouse before anything happened. Collins and Fowler stood at the bench and conferred with the judge, a flinty, crewcut former prosecutor named Miller. Pete slouched at the defense table. His head was shaved to the skin except for two fuzzy crosses above the left ear.

Deirdre rose from a seat near the rail.

"I've already spoken to Pete," she said. "I told him everything."

"Did he understand?"

Deirdre raised her hands. Her fingers were crossed.

"What about him?" I nodded toward the front row of the gallery, where Tom and Gina sat with two yards of bench between them. Gina actually seemed to be kneeling, and at twenty feet I heard the low drone of prayer. Despite the heat in the poorly air-conditioned courtroom, a long-sleeved cardigan stretched tightly across her bony shoulders. Tom glanced at her and scowled.

"There isn't any talking to him now," said Deirdre. "He's resigned to see Pete in prison. It's another tragedy for him to bitch about."

The lawyers stepped away from the bench, and the court clerk called the case. Deirdre and I took seats.

"I understand we have a disposition," said Judge Miller. "Let's get on with it."

Pete didn't move during the entire allocution. He stood with his head bowed and his hands clasped behind his back. Judge Miller read the involuntary manslaughter count of the indictment, which Collins and Fowler had agreed to be the substance of the plea. In essence, Pete was to admit that he beat Sylvester Miles with a blunt instrument and without any regard for the consequences.

"Do you so admit?" Judge Miller wound up.

Pete mumbled an answer.

"Hold on, Pete, hold on," whispered Deirdre.

"I did not hear you, Mr. O'Meara," said the judge.

"Yeah. I said yeah. Whatever you say."

Deirdre sank against me. Tom stalked out of the courtroom with the look of a man who had just dusted his hands of a problem. Gina wailed until the guards hustled Pete into the holding pens. When she hurried out, both hands rubbing the tears from her cheeks, I noticed the wool socks pulled high above the hemline of her cotton shift.

Deirdre leaned on my shoulder all the way to the parking lot. Half the time she cried, the other half she cursed the day she hired Brendan Collins. I let her talk, let her moan. Promises sounded hollow, so I didn't make any.

I found Gloria in her usual diner booth and her usual lunchtime mood.

"Get a load of this," she said, looking at my bruises. "Someone finally brain you?"

"I ran into a doorknob."

"Says you. Hey, aren't you supposed to be playing in some golf tournament?"

"I gave it up. Too dangerous." I lowered myself onto the seat. Most of my soreness was gone, but I still felt twinges if I moved too quickly. "I need to see a parking ticket."

"At twelve-fifteen?"

"This ticket is connected to the Miles' murder."

"What are you trying to pull, Kieran? The whole town knows Pete O'Meara pleaded guilty this morning."

"Already? I came here directly from White Plains."

"News travels faster than you drive, obviously."

Gloria asked the waiter for another glass of iced tea, which was her way of digging in her heels. I didn't say a word, dared not even drum my fingers, while Gloria leafed through stories of UFO abductions and Hollywood affairs. Eventually, she dabbed her chin with a napkin, and we walked around the corner to the town court.

I didn't want to bump into DiRienzo, so Gloria used her key to open the side entrance. Sunlight leaked around the drawn window shades, giving the courtroom a drowsy air.

"When was the ticket given?"

"The night of Miles' memorial service."

Gloria unlocked a file cabinet and plunged into a confusion of paper. After stirring up a half year's worth of tickets, she pulled out a pile clipped by a bobby pin. Only one car with Pennsylvania plates in the batch. Before I could copy the info onto a piece of paper, Gloria snatched the ticket from my hands.

"Oh boy, I remember this joker," she said. "He was so mad about that ticket he didn't even wait for his court date. He strutted in the very next day and said the police should be ashamed of themselves for giving a ticket to a war veteran during a service for another war veteran. Well, did I start making eyes at the judge, as if to say who let this guy out of the booby hatch. But the judge let him talk, and after the guy simmered down, he paid. You should have seen the bills he plunked down on my desk. They should have been fumigated. What the moths didn't eat, the town got."

I took back the ticket. "Damn, the only address listed here is in Pittsburgh."

"What else did you expect if that's where he's from?"

"I assumed he stayed in the area for a few months."

"You know what they say when you assume," said Gloria. "Wait a second."

She dove into another drawer.

"This wing nut wanted a receipt," she said, bits of paper whizzing past her ears like feathers at a cockfight. "I told him I couldn't write him one until after his official court date. Really, I could have. I was just busting chops. He gave me his address and asked me to mail it." She put a finger to her chin and gazed up at the ceiling. "I don't think I did. Anyway—" She snatched up a piece of paper. "Here it is."

Eddie listed a White Plains address.

"Thank you, Gloria." I left her reeling with a kiss on the forehead.

In another time, the rooming house would have been a mansion; in another place, a fraternity house. The roof sloped like a ski jump, and the wraparound porch jutted over a prominence with a sterling view of downtown White Plains. At least when the leaves fell.

I rang the doorbell. A crooked finger peeled back the lace curtain of an adjacent window, and an old woman with tight blue curls gave me the once over. Apparently I passed muster because the latch clicked and the door opened.

"What is it?" she said, clutching a shawl around her neck. She was stoop shouldered and wore black canvas sneakers, one of which she planted firmly behind the edge of the door.

"I need to talk to one of your boarders."

"Who are you?"

I told her. Without moving her foot, she reached for a black marbleback notebook on a metal bookcase.

"Nope, you're not listed," she said.

"I don't live here."

"I know that, but my boarders can't have a parade of strange visitors tramping through my door. They give me a list everyday of people likely to visit. Only those people get past this door. I'm not running a social club."

"What if the boarder doesn't expect the visitor?"

"Then it's too bad. There's phones."

"The boarder's name is Eddie Zelinsky."

She closed an eye I suddenly realized was glass and bored into me with her good one.

"He's in trouble, ain't he?" she said.

I nodded.

"So are you by the looks of that face."

I nodded again.

"Come with me."

She led me down a hallway decorated with faded floral wallpaper to a bedroom where a television blared. A half-eaten lunch lay on a snack table set in front of a chair strewn with pillows. She lifted a skeleton key off a picture hook, and ordered me to stay close behind her.

"You never know," she said.

We climbed a steep, narrow stairway. She moved easily for her age, her sneakers thumping on the bare wood steps. I kept pace, though the climb reactivated all the pain receptors a good night's sleep had calmed.

The stairway turned twice before reaching a tiny bedroom wedged beneath an angled ceiling. The bed was neatly made with the sheet folded down over an olive green blanket. A tiny valise sat on a wicker chair. A shaving cup, razor, toothbrush, and tube of toothpaste were carefully arranged on a small wash basin. A powder blue leisure suit hung over a chair. The air carried the faint odor of camphor.

"He acted awfully strange," she said. "Always getting calls. Running out in the middle of the night. Why he once got up from the dinner table to answer a call and never came back. My best roast beef, too. I didn't know he wasn't here today till he didn't come down for breakfast this morning. You're welcome to look around."

I already had started with the valise, which was empty. I moved on to the dresser drawers, even lifted the limp mattress of the bed. She prattled about Eddie's habits, which didn't seem particularly strange for an old man in pursuit of the fortune that eluded his youth. Anyway, I found nothing but clothes and toiletries.

"What did he do with himself when he wasn't running out or talking on the phone?"

"Most days he just stayed in his room. Sometimes he'd wander into my room, and we'd watch game shows. He always said how he thought those game shows were fixed, and the people didn't really get the money.

"Then usually around late afternoon he'd go out. He claimed he had a friend with a fishing boat somewhere. Over on the Hudson River, I think. He brought back fish a few times. Sorriest looking things I ever saw. Stuck them in the deep freeze like I was supposed to cook them."

"Who was this friend?"

"Eddie never said."

"Did Eddie ever tell you he expected visitors?"

"I'll have to check." She sat on the corner of the bed and flipped through the notebook. The pages were thick and gray with age. A date headed each, followed by a list of names written in blue fountain pen flourishes.

"There," she said. Her thin finger pointed to the name Sylvester Miles. The date was April 12.

"Eddie's first full day here," she said.

"Did Miles ever visit?"

"If he did, I would have put a pencil mark next to his name. There's no mark, so he didn't visit."

"And this line through the name means what?"

"Means Eddie didn't want to see the man even if he came calling. He told me that the second day he was here."

"Could Miles have visited without you knowing?"

"There's nothing happens here that I don't know."

I parted the window shades. Far below, Eddie's car baked on a weed-choked patch of asphalt.

"Mind if I take a look out back?"

"If you want."

The car was a drab Chevy eaten through with rust holes. A long dead air freshener shaped like a Christmas tree dangled from the rear-view mirror. Maps lay on the front seat. The ashtray overflowed with butts of filterless cigarettes. Fast food detritus littered the back seat and floorboards. I sifted through the mess while the old woman aimed her one good eye through the windshield. Eddie left nothing behind—no notes, no addresses, no phone numbers, just markings on a map showing the route from Pittsburgh to East Orange to Milton. Nothing I hadn't already surmised.

"He's in big trouble, isn't he?" she said as I closed the door. "That Miles fella, he's the guy that was killed a couple weeks back, right?"

"That's right," I said and closed the car door. "What time did Eddie go out last night?"

She spoke of time in terms of television shows. Translating her chronology into hours on a clock, Eddie had received a call around eleven. He talked briefly in sharp tones (she had turned up the juice on her hearing aid) and immediately left the rooming house. She looked out the window at one point. The weather report hadn't started, so it must have been about 11:20. He paced the sidewalk as if waiting for someone. When she looked again (the weather report ended), he had gone. She thought she remembered hearing a car, but she couldn't be certain.

"What about early this week?" I said, referring to Jack Miles' murder.

The old woman chewed her tongue, thinking.

"He was out late those nights, too," she said. "That's the thing. Ever since he stopped fishing, he kept staying out later and later. Guess he just went round the clock this time."

"When did he stop fishing?"

She flipped through the notebook but couldn't find the answer.

"I don't know exactly. Couple of weeks ago, maybe."

Close enough to Sylvester's death, I decided.

"Did you say those fish Eddie caught are in your freezer?"

"Last I looked."

"Can I see them?"

She kicked open a basement door and told me to keep my head

low. The freezer was vintage fifties, massive and white with rounded edges and a latch handle. She lifted the lid and rooted through frozen slabs of meat.

"Here's one of them," she said.

I wiped the frost off the plastic wrap. The scales glistened like gun metal. A tiny dull eye stared into mine.

"What kind is it? Eddie never told me."

"A bergall. Long Island Sound is full of them." I tossed the fish back into the freezer.

"I should call the police, right?" she said.

"Not yet. I'll leave you my name and phone number. If he comes back, call me."

"Oh, he will," she said. "I'm sure of it. He's already paid for next week."

CHAPTER
18

"**Y**ou're not coming and that's final," I said, shrugging into a black turtleneck. Pain from the beating screamed across my shoulders and back as I fought through the sleeves and collar. When I popped out the other side, Deirdre looked no happier than when I went in.

"You have a car. I have a car," she said. "I'll tail your butt wherever you go."

"Deirdre—"

"You know I will. You drive so damn slow you'll never shake me."

I stretched a navy blue woolen cap onto my head. I don't know how I thought I could leave my apartment dressed like a cat burglar and not arouse her suspicion.

"You look dumb," she said.

"All right. You can come come along. But you're staying in the car."

Deirdre grinned triumphantly. "We'll see."

Milton Marina was a squarish harbor dug out of a swamp where Poningo Point joined the mainland. A narrow channel ran to the Sound past the golf course, the Marshlands Conservancy, and a dozen Poningo Point estates.

I stopped the car half a block from the entrance. A single vapor lamp splashed light on a ten-foot chain link fence. The rest of the marina was dark except for the window of the watchman's shack and the running lights of a party boat.

Deirdre immediately guessed what I was after.

"Ridiculous," she said.

"According to Pete, Tom went fishing almost everyday for two months before the murder. The lady at the rooming house said Eddie Z went fishing every evening too, right up until Sylvester Miles was murdered."

I added that Pete told me Tom brought home lots of bergalls from his fishing trip, the same fish Eddie presented to his landlady.

"Great evidence," said Deirdre. "Any idiot who drops a line in the Sound catches bergalls."

She folded her arms and tucked back her chin to ward off any further explication.

"Maybe it is a coincidence, but Tom lied to us about Eddie. You saw Gina in court this morning. You know damn well she dressed herself to hide a new crop of body bruises. She heard our conversation with Tom the other night. She knows Eddie hooked up with Tom. She knows somehow that will help Pete. She knew Tom lied to us. And Tom knew she knew. He banged her around so she wouldn't tell us the truth."

I went on about the keel mark I'd seen in the sand and the puddle Pete slipped through on the hallway floor right beneath Tom's hipboots. Weak evidence, maybe. But I weaved it all together like a trial summation. That's the evidence, lady of the jury; draw your own conclusion.

Deirdre wasn't buying.

"You're saying my brother killed Sylvester Miles and now wants his son to go to jail for it. God knows Tom's capable of some nasty things, but not that."

"I didn't say Tom murdered Miles. But he knows a lot more about it than he's let on. And Tom has some strange ideas, especially about Pete. He wanted to pack Pete off to the youth farm two years ago, before you and the Judge stepped in."

"That was different."

I grinned tightly.

"I'm not coming with you," she said.

"I didn't think you would."

The chain link fence ended about half a foot from the ivy-covered brick wall of the Poningo Point fire station. I worked myself sideways through the gap. Being slim has its advantages.

Four docks stretched into the dark waters of the harbor. I padded through the shadows and crouched at the ramp leading down to the last dock. Deirdre's silhouette hung motionless in the gray light filtering through my car. The watchman nodded in the window of his shack. Music and laughter drifted across from the party boat, moored completely across the marina from the slip where Tom tied his motorboat.

A sudden breeze set the boat bells clanging. A searchlight snapped on in the watchman's shack. I flattened myself on the ramp. The beam passed, then winked out.

I moved quickly, half-running, half-crawling, my sneakers slapping on the bobbing dock. Distant lights danced on the black water. Across the marina, laughing voices shouted encouragement. Then came a splash and a cheer. People were swimming. In the harbor. At night. The thought sent a chill down my spine.

Tom's boat thudded against heavy rubber fenders hanging over the slip. From the dry land of the golf course, the boat always seemed too flimsy, even for the gentle chop of the Sound. Up close, it hardly looked any sturdier. I'd seen eggbeaters larger than the upraised outboard motor, and pup tents roomier than the foredeck's cabin. At least a thorough search wouldn't take more than a few minutes.

I steadied myself with the boat's railing and worked along the gunwale to the cockpit. I didn't know what I expected to find—filterless cigarette butts, a treasure map, a note from Eddie Z. The only loose objects my penlight revealed were two empty buckets and a scrub brush.

Another party-goer hit the water. Cheers and laughter rolled across the marina. I shuffled aft, the deck heaving beneath me. Nothing there but an empty ice chest, a neatly coiled rope, a tackle box stayed with bungee cords.

A car horn tapped lightly. Through the masts and spars of the intervening boats, headlights flashed several times. A figure wavered in the darkness. The party noise ebbed, and I heard the distinct plunking of a cane on the dock.

The clever move would have been to slip into the water and cling to a pontoon until Tom finished his business. The clever move, that is, for someone not petrified of any body of water deeper than a bathtub. Given half a second to decide, I chose the second clever option. I dove into the cabin.

Tom's feet landed heavily above me. The boat bobbed like crazy, spanking waves against the pontoons. Something slapped onto the deck. I peeked beyond the edge of the door in time to see Tom haul in a mooring line.

The engine sputtered and quickly died. Tom cursed. The engine coughed again, but this time he hit the gas and she steadied. I felt the propeller engage, heard the water thrash. The boat eased away from the dock. The bow swung around. The engine idled down, then throttled forward.

The sounds of the party boat, thin beneath the rumble of the engine, faded completely away. I ventured another peek. The running lights were out. Tom's workshoes formed vague humps in the darkness. I squirmed deeper into the cabin, flat against something spiny, like a piece of driftwood wrapped tightly in plastic.

I had no conception of speed, no sense of time. Consequently, I had no idea where we were in relation to the land. The beat of the engine slowed to a chug. The boat veered to port, then to starboard, then to port again as if Tom were looking for something. Probably a special fishing spot. I hoped he didn't mind the company. Actually, I hoped he never found out he had any.

The driftwood dug into my shoulders and backside in several places. I suddenly realized it felt less like driftwood than a statue. The point nudging my spine felt like a shoulder. The knob pressing my kidney felt like a knee. As Tom tooled in a slow circle, I carefully rolled over and flashed the penlight.

Tom wasn't out for the fishing.

The plastic hugged Eddie Z's rigid body. Duct tape sealed his mouth and bound his hands together as if in prayer. Blood from a head wound smudged the inside of the plastic. His knees were drawn up around an anchor lashed to his midsection. I doused the penlight. At the same time, Tom cut the engine.

The water lapped ominously against the hull. I silently rolled myself over. I heard noises—metal on metal, metal on wood, wood on wood. I couldn't imagine what any of it meant. Then the night fell strangely quiet. The boat rocked gently in counterpoint to the lapping water. From a distance, the faint buzz of an engine rose and faded.

Feet scraped. The cane tapped the deck, probing in the darkness. I tensed my muscles as I waited for him to duck into the cabin.

My foot caught him solidly on his bad leg. He toppled like a bowling pin just outside the cabin door. I flung myself toward him, but something crashed against my skull. The night exploded into sparkles and quickly collapsed into blackness.

A fuzzy gray circle floated far away. A disembodied voice spoke thickly in my head. *Catch the circle before it fades. Miss it, lose it, let it slip through your fingers and you die.* I lunged forward. My chin grated on broken glass. A vise tightened around my head. The circle darted away. *No no,* I tried to scream. But my tongue swelled behind my teeth and my lips stung, unable to part.

The circle danced back into view, smaller and fainter than before. I could catch it, I knew, if I could free my wrists, if I could unbow my spine, if I could crawl across the broken glass rasping my chest.

Ha, haa, haaaaa . . . The laughter in my head stretched and stretched into a single drone. The circle shrank to a pinpoint. I tried to flail my arms, tried to kick my legs. But my wrists and ankles gathered into a ball behind my back. Frantic, I sucked for breath, but my mouth was sealed. The pinpoint flitted like a crazy firefly. I turned my head, snorted air through my nose. The pinpoint brightened, then ballooned into a large fuzzy circle.

The world shuddered with a loud splash. Water sprayed over me. The vise twisted my head. The fuzzy circle widened into a purple expanse powdered with many bright pinpoints swimming through wispy orange tendrils.

The broken glass, beneath my back now, cut into my wrists and ankles. A dark head blotted out the orange wisps.

"No anchor for you," said the head. "Tide's going out. You'll be way out the Sound before anyone finds you."

I suddenly pitched forward. Something thin and round and metallic, like the shaft of a golf club, sliced across my stomach. A tongue of cold water licked my face. Realization hit me like a thunderbolt. I was on a boat, gagged and trussed and staring down at the deep water somewhere beyond the harbor inlet. Tom had dumped Eddie's body, and I was poised to follow.

The drone in my ears strengthened. It sounded like an engine. Even so, it was too far away. Just too damn far away.

Tom pushed me overboard.

I hit fairly flat, otherwise I would have plunged straight to the bottom. I thrashed and squirmed, trying like hell to stay near the surface. But the oily waters closed around me, pitch dark and ice cold. I stopped struggling, conserving my last precious molecules of air like a man in a gas chamber. Everything became still. I drifted slowly downward, feeling the pressure squeeze my chest. Somewhere beyond the blackness, that engine thundered. Too late, too late.

Suddenly, the water flashed bright gray. An angel with a swirling tangle of hair breast-stroked toward me. This is death, I thought, and blew air through my nose.

CHAPTER
19

Judge Inglisi ballooned in my field of vision, staring at a small TV high on the wall. The picture tube shined bright green, and a familiar voice announced golf scores.

"Am I dead?" The words sounded like mine, but seemed to come from somewhere else. The TV, maybe. Judge Inglisi swiveled his head toward me.

"That's the third time you've asked," he said.

"What was your answer?"

"No, you're in the hospital."

My head ached like hell, but I forced myself back over bumpy patches of memory: hitting my one shot in the Classic, interviewing Hank Press, tracking Eddie Z to his rooming house. After that, Tom's rocking boat, darkness, bone-chilling cold, an angel swimming through a dream.

The next time I looked, the TV screen was blank. Judge Inglisi had changed into a nurse, which definitely was an improvement. I bucked up onto my elbows, and my head reeled.

"Easy." The nurse patted the IV attached to my arm and plumped a pillow behind my head.

The room tumbled into perspective. The drawn blinds, the accordion screen running alongside the bed, the plastic water pitcher. Judge Inglisi, wedged into a chair, stirred out of sleep.

"What happened?" The voice was recognizably mine.

"Tomorrow," said the Judge, and nodded off.

"What's tomorrow?"

"Sunday," said the nurse.

Next morning, a different nurse removed the IV. An orderly served me a tray of warm orange juice, tea, and pudding. My head still ached, and taking a deep breath launched me on a painful coughing jag. The Judge popped in shortly after lunch.

"You had a concussion, and you swallowed a lot of water, but the doctor doesn't think you're brain damaged. I wonder how the hell he knows."

"Same flattering Judge. My close brush with death didn't chasten you?"

"Nah. One of these days you'll kill yourself. I promise to speak well of you in strange company." He squeezed himself into a chair and adjusted my bed so he'd be comfortable talking to me.

"Okay, you want to know what happened," he said. "Deirdre saw brother Tom pull out of the marina. She couldn't imagine why he would go sailing at night, especially since he didn't turn on his running lights. When you didn't come off the dock, she called the cops and reported a problem in the harbor. They sent a launch, and she jumped in with them. They caught up with Tom out past Poningo Point just as you hit the water. Deirdre dove in after you."

"Deirdre saved me?"

"Not exactly. She found you and a cop hauled you up."

"What about Eddie Z?"

"I'll get to him," he said. "The police arrested Tom for attempted murder because that's all it looked like at the time. You were *incommunicado*, and Tom clammed up tight under questioning. Come yesterday morning, DiRienzo had the bright idea to find out exactly why Tom was out on the water at night. He scrambled a diver, who found Eddie hugging an anchor at the mouth of the inlet. The cops have been hammering away at Tom ever since about both the Miles boys. They've run all kinds of checks on Eddie, Jack, and Syl, looking for connections."

"Did you tell DiRienzo about Hank Press?"

"I don't volunteer anything," the Judge said tartly. Then he shrugged. "They already knew about Press."

"Is Pete still in jail?"

"Why would they release him? He's pled guilty, and the jail isn't too small for him and Tom. Deirdre's up in arms about everything, nephew and brother in jail. She's spitting bullets." The Judge rolled his eyes. "She excoriates the hell out of the guy, with good reason, and now she's mad at the cops."

"For arresting Tom because he tried to kill me?"

"Hell no, for sullying the good O'Meara name."

He punched on the TV button and ran through the channels until he found the telecast of the Classic's final round. As the camera cut from hole to hole and the afternoon winds played havoc with the leader board, I tried to crawl into DiRienzo's head. I knew where his investigation pointed, and I needed to reach the destination first. Pete's future depended on it.

But I couldn't muster any concentration. Thoughts trailed off into a mental white noise. The voices of the sportscasters nipped at my ears. The slightest head movement, and my brain rattled around inside my skull. I finally surrendered and stared numbly at the screen. The paunchy veteran birdied three out of the final four holes to tie the British Open champ, then won a sudden death playoff that lasted five holes.

"Knew that old coot had something," said the Judge. "You beat the both of them, so that makes you unofficial Classic champ in my mind."

"What a consolation," I said.

The Judge stretched until the chair nearly split, then shut off the TV. "Back to work for me tomorrow. See you."

"Sure will," I said without irony.

I dozed off for about an hour and woke up with a clear head and lungs I could fill without coughing. Dinner, even the hospital variety, restored my powers of concentration. A half hour of brain work opened large holes in DiRienzo's obvious theory. I knew my next move; I just needed the signal to begin.

It came in the form of Deirdre. She sailed into the room and yanked the accordion screen closed around the bed.

"Damn cops charged Tom with all three murders." She paced alongside me and whumped the mattress with her fist on every pass. I didn't say anything. Pull Deirdre in two directions, and she became irritable. Pull her in five or six, like now, and she snapped at anything that moved.

"They're saying all kinds of things about Tom and Eddie being in cahoots."

"Isn't that what we thought when we went after Eddie?"

"It's what *you* thought. I might say some nasty things about Tom, but he's still my brother. Besides, I was trying to help Pete. Now they're both in the stew."

"Forget about Tom," I said. "He dumped Eddie's body, and he surer than hell tried to kill me."

"Okay, so he goes to jail for that. Throwing in the Miles murders makes us sound like a family of homicidal maniacs."

"If it makes you feel any better, I don't believe Tom killed Sylvester any more than I believe Pete did."

"You and your damn ideas. You were so sure Pete's innocent you let him plead guilty without talking to the cops."

"The time wasn't right."

"When will it be? When the last O'Meara gets dragged through the mud?"

"Look," I said. "We all agreed Eddie Z was after Sylvester's money and convinced Tom to join his crusade."

Deirdre grunted.

"If they were after his money, why kill him?" I said.

"Maybe Eddie lost his temper. Maybe Tom did. I don't know. I can't think like these people."

"Tom has a temper with Pete and Gina, but he can be cool, like he's been with the cops. We don't know Eddie, but he was in the area for three months before Syl was killed. He had something more sophisticated than murder in mind, probably blackmail or extortion."

"Kieran, I don't see how any of this matters."

"I think I know who killed Sylvester. It won't help Tom, but it will help Pete."

Deirdre grinned ruefully. "You thought you knew before."

"Twice, to be exact. First Jack Miles got killed, and that changed my mind. Then I found Eddie on Tom's boat, and that changed it again. This time I've worked it all the way through. Besides, I've run out of permutations." I folded my arms across my chest.

"You're not telling me, right?"

"Not until we can do something about it, which isn't now."

"But you'll want me out of the way, like last time."

"And get myself killed? Uh-uh. This time we work together, start to finish."

Deirdre lifted the chart from the foot of the bed and deciphered the scribble.

"Says here you'll be in another twenty-four to thirty-six hours for observation."

"No matter. Pete's pled and Tom's been charged. Another day or so isn't critical."

Deirdre told me about the lawyer she hired for Tom and how Gina was bearing up under the stress. Then she climbed onto the bed and lay with her head on my chest.

"Thanks for saving me," I said, crooking an arm around her shoulder.

"I didn't actually . . . I only . . ." She shuddered, and all the fight drained out of her. "Kieran, if Tom had . . . if anything . . ." And then she cried.

"I know," I said, at my philosophical best. "Crazy stuff happens."

I finally persuaded her to leave at midnight. She yawned heartily and shuffled out of the room. When I was certain she wouldn't return, I phoned Demo Mike with detailed instructions.

Demo Mike slipped into the room at the stroke of three. Four hours remained in the night shift, and the hospital hummed as softly as a refrigerator.

"Did you find everything?" I said.

"It's all in the duffle bag."

I changed into the clothes Demo brought me. No one spotted us in the corridors, on the emergency stairway, or in the parking lot.

"Why the early start?" said Demo. "Court doesn't open for six hours."

"This may take that long."

"No more dead bodies, I hope."

"I plan on taking this one alive."

Riding shotgun in Demo's crate, I directed him up the turnpike to Stamford. My assumption was that someone with nowhere to go would return to his most familiar haunts. But we spent an hour tooling through Stamford in ever widening circles. Boring work, especially when fruitless.

"Screw it, Demo," I said with sudden inspiration. "Head back to Milton."

The car wasn't parked in front of Andy Anderson's shop. We spotted it on the other side of the industrial park, hidden in the shadows of an abandoned loading dock. I rooted through the duffle bag until I found the loose rubber golf grip Demo brought from my pro shop. A few lead fishing sinkers instantly changed it into a blackjack. I tossed Demo the clothesline and nodded grimly. Time to go.

We crept quietly toward the car, keeping to the shadows as best we could. The driver side window was open a crack. Fog coated the inside of the windshield. I motioned Demo to the back of the car and crouched beside the door with my fingers lightly on the handle. I signaled a count of three, then flung open the door.

I didn't need the blackjack. Miko Onizaka tumbled out like a sack of fish. He grunted when he hit the ground, rolled onto his back, and snorted. He reeked of Scotch and sweat.

"Tie him up," I said.

"Kieran—"

"Do it! Fast."

While Demo bound Onizaka's rubbery wrists, I poked through heaps of moldy clothes, sticky Scotch bottles, and slimy fast food containers. Nothing surfaced. I popped the trunk lever and lifted the lid. The trunk light was only fifteen watts, but bouncing off the *Blitzklubs* it shined like the sun.

"What are they?" said Demo. He stood at my shoulder, his eyes darting between the clubs and Onizaka's inert form.

"Nothing you want to know anything about. Let's get him in your car."

"Kieran, this is crazier than the dead body. This is kidnapping."

"I take full responsibility."

We piled Onizaka into the back seat. I loaded the *Blitzklubs* in Demo's trunk, then climbed in beside Onizaka with the blackjack in hand. Never can be too ready.

"Where to?" said Demo, as if he expected I'd say Mexico.

"My place."

For two straight hours, we plied Onizaka with hot coffee, cold towels, and questions. First he tried to play drunk, then he tried to play dumb. Finally, he broke down. Once Onizaka started talking, I was glad for Demo's presence. I might have used the blackjack.

At eight-thirty, we tied Onizaka's hands and covered them with a windbreaker. We needed no other precautions. Miko Onizaka was a totally defeated man. Before we left for the courthouse, I took the *Blitzklubs* from Demo's car and buried them behind half a ton of files in the archives.

Fortunately, the Judge already had taken the bench for his morning calendar, and I double-talked his law clerk into letting us stash Miko in the Judge's chambers.

"A very important witness we need sequestered," I said, pushing Miko into a chair while Demo quickly fashioned more bonds out of clothesline.

"I don't know anything about any witness," said the clerk.

"Neither does the Judge."

Demo and I left the clerk with a bad case of the stutters and circled through the public corridor to Judge Inglisi's courtroom. The people I subpoenaed sat among the lawyers and litigants who jammed the gallery benches. Each was obviously irate, but courtroom decorum jacketed them in a thin veneer of civility. Only DiRienzo was boorish enough to launch a frontal assault. He accosted me as I walked down the center aisle. His hands worked into fists, and his breath seethed like a runaway steam engine.

"This subpoena is a damn fraud," he said, his voice losing control. "Tom O'Meara and the kid killed Miles. Can't you leave well enough alone?"

"No, I can't."

Up at the bench, two lawyers not connected with my ruse huddled with the Judge. DiRienzo's shouting had silenced the entire courtroom, and the Judge stared down at me. His brow furrowed like a cornfield, and his jut jaw stretched the folds of his jowls. Not at all happy. He told the two lawyers to scram, and crooked a single stubby forefinger at me. Get your ass up here, right now.

"You damned well better have a good reason for this," he said.

I explained how, before Jack Miles turned up dead, dragging all these people into court seemed the quickest way to smoke out the killer.

"That's old news now, Kieran," he growled. "Why didn't you call this off?"

I told him why. The flesh returned to his jaw, and then his jaw dropped.

"You have Miko Onizaka tied up in my chambers!"

I quickly sketched what Onizaka had told Demo and me.

"Do you believe him?" said the Judge.

"It makes as much sense as anything else."

The Judge drummed his fingers on the bench.

"Who did you subpoena?" he said.

I recited the names, and he jotted them onto a legal pad.

"All right," he said. "But this is your show. If you get into trouble, I'm not bailing you out."

"Someone from the D.A.'s office should be here," I said. "Preferably Fowler."

Heaving a sigh, the Judge ordered his court officer to clear the courtroom of everyone but the people on the list. Once that was done, he instructed the officer to call the D.A.'s office.

"I oughtta kick your ass," he said to me, "except it's already been done. Twice."

I pushed the two counsel tables together and invited everyone to be seated. No one moved until the Judge banged his gavel. He tried his damnedest to suppress a sardonic smile.

Demo and I stood at the head of the table while the real players in this game lined up on opposite sides. William St. Clare, plainly embarrassed by Adrienne's presence, slumped so low in his chair his sideburns grazed the table. Frank Gabriel folded and unfolded his arms, pursed and unpursed his lips. Angry splotches of red ran from the tip of his chin to the top of his dome. Brendan Collins looked like an unmade bed.

Across the table, DiRienzo fumed. Adrienne, peppermint cool in pastel pink and blue, gazed serenely at the ceiling while one hand worked the curls behind her ear.

"We have a problem," I said, "and I thought we should sit down and iron it out before it gets too big."

Collins piped up first.

"My client and I have attended this . . . this . . . whatever this is under protest and without waiving any rights to contest the jurisdiction of this court. We plan to file suit for abuse of process and malicious prosecution."

"Cork it, Brendan. No one's suing anyone," I said. "Especially since Milton Country Club does not hold title to all of its eighteen holes."

Demo Mike whipped the deed out of the duffle bag.

"You can't prove that!" said Gabriel.

"I don't need to. Someone else in this room can tell the whole story. Especially when he realizes the fragility of his prized reputation."

St. Clare nearly crawled under the table. DiRienzo, grinned like a cartoon cat.

"What the hell are you laughing at, Chicky? You said you arrested Pete O'Meara because you know Milton better than anyone. You don't know crap."

DiRienzo swallowed his grin. I continued:

"We all know how Dr. Gabriel, Mr. St. Clare and Sylvester Miles organized MCC. The project floundered for years because the golf course needed land for six more holes. The obvious move was to buy the neighboring property, but Josie Park spurned every offer. Then fate intervened. Josie Park died and willed his property to the Town of Milton for the sole purpose of creating a nature conservancy. Any other use was grounds for a complete reversion to the estate.

"At the time of Park's death, Dr. Gabriel was a councilman, and Mr. St. Clare was the mayor. They knew they could slice off forty acres from the conservancy without anyone noticing, not even Sylvester Miles. There was only one drawback—Josie Park's lawyer, best friend, and trustee, I. W. Frippy. The trust charged him with the duty of overseeing the use of the land. If he didn't protest, Gabriel and St. Clare could treat the land as their own. So they hired a private investigator named Savage to dig up some dirt about Frippy and blackmailed him into submission."

"You can't prove this!" said Gabriel. Veins crackled across his skull like lightning bolts.

St. Clare hung his head in his hands. "He doesn't need to," he muttered.

"Shut up, Billy!" said Gabriel.

The Judge banged his gavel.

"Savage did his job," I said, "and I.W. Frippy conveniently forgot about his fiduciary duty to the estate. All the documents remained on file in the courthouse, open to public view. But the public wasn't interested. Milton Country Club built six holes and used the land as its own. Then, all these years later, a certain founding partner whose highly leveraged financial empire needed an infusion of cash, secretly negotiated the sale of the club to Tomiro Enterprises.

"The Board split, with Sylvester Miles abstaining. Miles, you see, regretted his marriage to Adrienne and wanted to leave her as little as possible if and when he died. He could tie up his business assets and tie up his shares in the club. But he couldn't tie up the cash if the club sold beforehand. He wanted to find a legal way around this, so he abstained. Then he stumbled across the problem with the land. He visited Frippy at his nursing home the day before he was murdered in order to confirm his suspicions. By all accounts, their conversation terribly upset the old lawyer."

Gabriel pounded his fist. "This is all very interesting, Lenahan, but I still don't see the point."

"Simple," I said. "You and the Mayor are here to rescind the sale to Tomiro Enterprises."

"The hell we will," said Gabriel. "I'll never change my vote. And neither will Billy. Right, Billy?"

St. Clare's answer never left his throat. Collins started to argue an obscure point of real estate law. I told him to shut up and stared straight at Gabriel.

"You broke Frippy, but you won't break me. The Town of Milton can haul your asses into court and fight you for title. Even if you win, Tomiro Enterprises will be long gone."

Gabriel slumped in his chair, the reality of the situation sinking in.

"But none of that will happen because you're voting to rescind the sale, and everyone in this room is promising to keep the title defect a secret."

The courtroom door opened with a loud creak. Fowler stopped short, assessing the strange scene below the bench. The Judge motioned for him to sit, and he slid into the last row of the gallery.

Gabriel and Collins whispered furiously to each other. I held up my watch.

"My offer closes in five minutes."

More furious whispers before Collins opened his briefcase. As he scribbled a resolution on a legal pad, I sent Demo to prep Onizaka. Collins finished his hasty draft, Gabriel and St. Clare signed their names, then Collins notarized the signatures. The entire transaction took four minutes. A general rustling coursed around the table.

"One more minor detail," I said.

"What is it now, Lenahan?" said Gabriel.

I folded the resolution into my pocket for safekeeping, then opened the chambers door. Onizaka clomped wearily up the steps to the witness stand.

"Some of you know this man," I said, "but for the benefit of those who don't, he is Miko Onizaka, a golf pro and former employee of Ichi-Ni-San Golf World, a subsidiary of Tomiro Enterprises." I waved Fowler to move closer. "Miko, tell everyone what you told me earlier this morning."

"I am from small village near Osaka, Japan." Onizaka rubbed the raw skin of his wrists as he spoke. "I wanted very badly to live in America. Tomiro Hayagawa took interest in me and brought me to America as staff pro at Ichi-Ni-San. He promise many things if I play good golf. He promise to make me head pro at the American country clubs he plan to buy. But I brought dishonor on him and his company, and fell out of his favor. My time as staff pro in America grew short.

"Dr. Gabriel know my problem. In spring, he tell me he need help putting together deal between his club and Mr. Hayagawa. He said he write me to be pro in contract of sale if I help. I ask how he want my help, since I fall out of favor with Mr. Hayagawa. He told me he have trouble with partners over sale. One not want to sell, other try to decide. He want someone to persuade other to vote for sale. He want someone he could trust and reward.

"Dr. Gabriel did not speak to me for many days. I lose my apartment. Sleep in my car. Practice hard for Met because win help me find new sponsor.

"Day of Met, bad weather. During second round, Dr. Gabriel wait for me on Wykagyl course. He said vote set and conditions perfect for me to meet Mr. Miles. I must go to Milton Country Club before sundown. Mr. Miles practice alone.

"At end of Met second round, I lead by six shots. Mr. Hayagawa congratulate me. Wish me luck in final round. Then I remember Dr. Gabriel. I drive very fast to Milton Country Club and find hole near water. I recognize Miles with golf club, but he is not alone. Two men with him, one very old, other a cripple with cane. I hide in reeds and listen. Old man and cripple demand money. Miles promise to give them soon. Old man and cripple walk to water and get in boat. Miles resume practice. He is old man, too. I do not want to persuade him. I feel bad to do it, and I feel I do not need Dr. Gabriel's deal anymore. I believe I will win Met and Mr. Hayagawa will take me back. I start to leave when I see someone else on links."

Onizaka bowed his head and began to rub his wrists again. He'd paused at the exact same point earlier in my apartment. I glanced at the table. Collins and Gabriel huddled close, eyes riveted on Onizaka. St. Clare chewed his tongue. DiRienzo lifted the pen from his notebook. Adrienne still twirled her curls while her other hand clutched a corner of the table.

"Go on, Miko," I said. "Who came onto the links?"

"Dr. Gabriel," said Onizaka.

"That's a goddam lie!" shouted Gabriel. Collins clamped a hand across his client's mouth.

"Go on," I told Miko.

"Dr. Gabriel talk to Miles. They argue about sale. Gabriel rip club from Miles' hand. Hit him hard beside neck. Miles fall down, lay still. Gabriel swing at head like it big golf ball." Onizaka swallowed hard. "He drag body to pond, pull stones from bank and sink body in water. Then he throw murder club into harbor."

Gabriel broke out of Collins' grasp. "Lies!" he screamed.

St. Clare dove at Gabriel, pressing his stubby thumbs into the dentist's throat. DiRienzo rounded the table with amazing speed and swatted St. Clare to the floor.

"You killed Syl," the ex-Mayor blubbered.

Gabriel sneered at St. Clare, then at the rest of us. He fixed his collar and assembled his last shreds of arrogance.

"Tom O'Meara did it," he said. "He killed Syl with his cane. We all know that."

"Makes no sense," I said. "Syl promised money to Tom and Eddie. You know how Syl operated. Promise people the world and hope they don't return to collect." Demo handed me the broken *Blitzklub* from the duffle bag. I waved it in Gabriel's face. "Forensics will prove this is the murder weapon. You threw it into the inlet so it wouldn't be found. But you sunk Syl in the pond for other reasons. Sure, you wanted to screw up the time of death estimate. But you also wanted the body discovered quickly. You wanted to convince St. Clare he'd meet the same end if he didn't vote for the sale."

"You're crazy," said Gabriel. He looked around the table, but no one met his eye. "You're all crazy. You're going to take the word of this drunken Japanese bum. I never saw Syl that night. I never had any deal with this drunkard."

But the Judge already had summoned a detail of court officers. They formed a tight semi-circle behind Gabriel's chair.

"After that," said Onizaka. "I lost Met and needed new way to restore self with Mr. Hayagawa."

"That's enough, Miko," I said.

CHAPTER
20

A subdued Pete O'Meara returned to work by the middle of the following week. He holed up in the bag room, silently cleaning clubs and emerging only to wolf down lunch. His sole comment on his ordeal was a mumbled thanks for all I'd done. Adolescent pride undoubtedly told him he would have extricated himself from the mess given enough time. I composed a speech on hubris for better days, like when those crosses faded in his thickening hair.

One morning in early September, I swung by Adrienne's house. A limousine was parked in the driveway and two suitcases sat on the front steps. Adrienne stood alone in the parlor. The sharp creases of a glen plaid suit and the tight bun of her straw-colored hair added severity to her beauty.

"Vacation?" I said.

She shook her head. "Home."

"Traveling awfully light."

"I have an older sister outside Cleveland," she said. "Married, two teenaged children. I used to think she was a boring fool. Now she's invited me to live with them until I'm on my feet again. It's the best offer I've had."

We stared at our shoes. Despite the profusion of house plants, the parlor suddenly seemed barren.

"I want to apologize for suspecting you."

"Forget it," she said.

"I can't. I should have known better."

"It doesn't matter. You treated me fairly, which is more than most people have done."

We walked outside. The limo driver had loaded Adrienne's bags and watched us from behind the steering wheel. I lifted a long cardboard box from the trunk of my car. Adrienne knew immediately what was inside.

"If I let Miko talk that day in court, he would have admitted to stealing these. After he lost the Met, he was desperate to restore himself to Hayagawa's good graces. Among other things, Hayagawa is a high-powered collector of golf memorabilia. But he wasn't interested in an incomplete set of *Blitzklubs*. Maybe you will be."

"But—"

"No buts. I've thought about this from every conceivable angle. No one will know you have them, and an anonymous auction is easy to arrange."

I carried the box to the limo and asked the driver to open the trunk. He looked nervously toward Adrienne. She bit her lip, then nodded. The trunk popped open. Eleven long cardboard boxes—identical to the one in my hands—were stacked neatly inside.

"I found them behind a false wall in the attic," she said. "I knew if Syl had one set, he would have them all."

We smiled, each accepting the secrets that would bind us forever.

I watched the limo curve out of sight on Harbor Terrace Drive. Sometimes you mesh with another person, but like teeth on two celestial gears you spin away, left with thoughts of an alternate future. I'd remember Adrienne a damn long time. Not the desperate scene in my kitchen. Not the sharpie who cried poverty and spirited a fortune out of Milton in the trunk of a limo. I would remember the promise of that first fetching glance from across her parlor. How quickly it seemed another world ago.

People all over town stopped perceiving me as a golf pro. I was the man who solved Sylvester Miles' murder, and nearly got killed doing it. I testified at two preliminary hearings, and even cooperated with DiRienzo in tying up several loose ends.

"Hey, I came pretty close," he blurted one day in sudden defiance. "The kid wasn't involved, but his old man was."

Crime detection as horseshoes.

As the summer waned, I slid back into my club pro persona. The question I heard most often was, why hit the one shot in the Classic? My stock answer—so I could say I played on the PGA Tour—wasn't the complete truth.

No one ever admitted to jumping me the night before the Classic. The Judge still suspects Gabriel, warning me off his turf. I'm partial to Miko because he was the only person to profit from knocking me out of the tournament. Which brings me back to that one shot. If I'd simply withdrawn, or not appeared at all, Miko would have replaced me as an alternate. But as soon as I banged that three-iron I became an official contestant, and no one could take my place.

Late in September, Deirdre plopped a large suitcase on my bedroom floor.

"Have to jump into this with both feet," she said, tossing her clothes into an empty dresser drawer.

I'm comfortable living with Deirdre again. We're a few years older now, and don't take the same crazy things for granted. But I won't make any predictions. Two feet can run doubly fast once their owner catches a whiff of commitment.

Tom O'Meara pleaded insanity, but Judge Edward Miller, the same judge who accepted Pete's guilty plea, ruled him sane enough to stand trial for the murders of Jack Miles and Eddie Z. Fowler built his case in workmanlike fashion. Tom and Eddie had tried to blackmail Sylvester Miles, and his murder threw them into desperate confusion. Tom believed any hope of grabbing the money died with Sylvester, but Eddie convinced him Jack had access to the loot. They broke into Jack's cabin, and when Jack surprised them they broke his head. After that, their only chance was Adrienne. Eddie tried the funny phone calls, but nothing ever developed. When I questioned Tom about Eddie, Tom decided to bail out. He could scare Gina into silence, but he couldn't trust the old codger.

The jury convicted on both counts, and Judge Miller sentenced Tom to consecutive sentences of twenty-five to life. In his sentencing colloquy, the judge noted it took a particularly calculating—and rational—person to hide behind his son's plight while pursuing his own agenda. Gina O'Meara, surrounded by reporters after the sentencing, insisted Tom was a good husband and father.

A grand jury indicted Brendan Collins for obstruction of justice for his part in railroading Pete's guilty plea. He roundly protested his innocence but, on the advice of his own attorney, copped a plea for two-to-four.

———

William St. Clare signed over a power of attorney to Roger Twomby and left Milton for an extended vacation. A conspiracy indictment died in the grand jury, and St. Clare ultimately avoided all criminal charges. The Dutchman's assessment of the ex-Mayor didn't go far enough. Any fool could make a fortune; only a perfect fool could maintain his innocence.

The D.A.'s office treated Miko Onizaka as a material witness and never prosecuted the obvious charges of conspiracy or obstruction of justice. I never revealed him as the person who burglarized my shop in order to steal the *Blitzklubs*. When the last criminal trial of this whole affair ended, the Immigration Department deported Miko to Japan and the triple-decker driving range he struggled so hard to escape.

Frank Gabriel fought his conviction to the bitter end, but the jury convicted him after forty-five minutes of deliberation (with half of that time devoted to lunch). His lawyer argued Gabriel's relatively advanced age and long years of public service in a desperate plea for leniency.

"Public service?" noted Judge Miller, by then intimately familiar with every actor in this series of crimes. "Long years of self-service is closer to the truth."

He maxed Dr. Gabriel at twenty-five-to-life.

The feds investigated Sylvester Miles' finances and learned Eddie Z hit the final shot of his sorry life dead on line. Marcel Velge had found a way to withdraw the money from those Swiss bank accounts, and he and Syl split a fortune. Hannah Miles, née Hannah McGriff, was a prostitute suffering from terminal cancer when Syl plucked her out of a Florida swamp to play the role of his wealthy, dying spouse. He planned to invent a new life in small-town Milton, and needed Hannah's "family money" to conceal the true source of his cash from Corny O'Meara and the others.

Andy Anderson mailed me a blurb from an antiques magazine. The International Foundation for Art Research, which traces art works and other treasures looted from postwar Germany, decided against pursuing the missing *Blitzklubs*. Despite their value, the clubs were neither works of art nor national treasures.

Two weeks after Gabriel's trial ended, Fowler sent me the *Blitzklub* pitching wedge. "Yours by default," he wrote in the accompanying note. I initially planned to repair the club, maybe pack it off to Adrienne to complete the set. But ultimately, I couldn't bring myself to inject gasoline into that twisted, tortured rubber grip. I cleared a special place for it in the Inglisi & Lenahan archives.

CHAPTER

1

Demo Mike tapped the forefinger of his good hand against the computer screen. Dark lines appeared in the powder blue field, whirling out of an imaginary distance and assembling themselves into a roof, walls, windows, doors, even gutters and a patio awning. Every detail accurately drawn by a globe of lasers atop the cab of the Milton Fire Department's spanking new pumper.

Behind me, another fire engine squealed around the clubhouse circle and killed its siren as it banged down the slope of the parking lot. Demo didn't react. He hiked the heavy black slicker higher on his badly sloping shoulders, pushed the oily black firefighter's helmet to the back of his head, squinted hard at the screen.

"Demo, I don't see any smoke or flames," I said, scanning the real windows and roof. "Maybe it's a false alarm."

"We'll find out, Kieran," he said. "This machine doesn't lie."

The din mounted around us. Firemen shouted as they laced the parking lot with hoses, tied in to hydrants that suddenly sprang from the azalea bush beside the sixteenth tee and the pine shrubs lining the practice range. Another truck angled into position, two powerful flood-lights bathing the building in instant daylight. A cherry-picker lowered its anchoring struts and raised its arm while the fireman in the bucket fiddled with a water cannon.

The building in the fire department's crosshairs actually was a con-glomeration of three separate units. Most obvious, and dearest to my palpitating heart, was the pro shop where for four years I had plied my trade as golf professional at the Milton Country Club. A large garage abutting the shop housed the club's fleet of fifty electric golf carts. The club's Hispanic restaurant workers lived in a warren of rooms above the garage. In the good old days before political correctness, everyone at the club called these rooms the monkey house. Now you heard it only from unreconstructed bigots or from people, like myself, who doubted vapid vocabulary engendered kinder souls.

Demo tapped a little box on the screen labeled INFRARED. The building image immediately darkened to black. Slowly, tiny digitalized boxes of color appeared: blues, greens, purples.

"Bingo," he said as a splotch of purple lightened to a pulsating red blob.

"That's a fire?"

"That's combustion."

"Oh," I said. Having practiced law before becoming a golf pro, I understood fine distinctions. This one escaped me completely.

"It could be a flaming gas, or it could be a glowing solid. Very eso-teric stuff to the layman."

Demo tapped his finger again. The image rotated slowly through 360 degrees. The red blob oscillated like a wobbling toy top. I looked at the building again. Still no visible combustion. Maybe the machine can lie, I hoped.

"Damn. Can't get a good depth fix with this friggin' thing."

This was a hell of an admission from Demo, a kid with a genius IQ who would have made Harvard or Yale if a stroke hadn't felled him during his junior year of high school. He didn't fit the normal volunteer fireman profile, but the chief pressed him to join because no one could work the new pumper's computerized fire detection system. Demo, one of those twenty-somethings born with 46 chromosomes and a computer chip in his genes, jumped at the chance to practice applied wizardry. I'm not anti-tech. I just believed the new pumper needed a track record longer than a month before I yielded my underying faith.

"You have any idea where that might be?" he said.

Demo's combustion glowed somewhere behind my shop. Maybe in the bag room, where the membership stored its golf clubs; maybe in the cart garage.

"The bag room has a closet about there," I said. "The cart garage has one directly on the other side of the inside wall."

"The garage has battery chargers, right?" said Demo. "Hmm. The heat source isn't super hot yet. Could be a short in one of those chargers. Could be a smoldering wire touched something off. Anything flammable in those closets?"

My stomach sank. "Lots of things."

Demo killed the screen and shoved off toward the chief. Limping fast, his entire body rose and fell like a piston.

"What's going on?" I said.

"Everything's fine, Kieran. Whatever's burning in there, we'll take care of it. You just back away for now."

I didn't like being dismissed by a twenty year old, especially one who admitted to looking up to me as a role model. But Demo now numbered firefighting among his many bailiwicks, so I stumbled over some hoses to the edge of the practice range where the restaurant workers huddled at the base of a pine tree. Half still wore their dirty kitchen linens, the rest gripped blankets around their shoulders. They were squat, grim men with flat faces and thick black hair who suddenly materialized at your elbow to clear away dinner plates or refill a salt shaker. They seemed even more grim than usual in the stark wash of the floodlights. Worried, as if they knew something Demo's laser-guided infrared homing system didn't show.

Demo spoke to the chief, who waved a few other firemen into a tight circle. After a minute of nodding and shaking and pointing, they broke away. The restaurant workers sensed something afoot and started jabbering something harsher than the Spanish I usually recognized.

A crowd gathered behind me. Neighbors, college kids cruising a summer's night, people attracted off the Post Road by the bright lights and grinding engines. I remembered a fire at a dry cleaners in Milton village on a winter's night many years ago. Only a boy, I'd stood in a crowd, hooting at firemen, wondering when the flames would flash, waiting for something to happen because this was a show and the dry cleaners didn't belong to me. Then I saw a classmate, a pretty Italian girl with dark curly hair, crying as she picked her way through the crowd. Her father owned the adjoining barber shop, and she feared the fire would spread. Right at that moment, I stopped hooting and laughing, stopped wishing for something spectacular to happen.

I glanced again at the restaurant workers. As badly as the fire would affect me, it would devastate them. My insurance was paid up. My summer inventory was mostly gone; my huge investment in fall merchandise luckily hadn't arrived. The workers lived in the monkey house, probably minus insurance. If the fire spread, they'd have their blankets and linens. Nothing else.

The first plume of smoke curled out from under the eaves of the monkey house roof just as the water started arcing up from the ground hoses and funneling down from the water cannon. The college kids applauded. A fireman opened the door to the monkey house staircase.

Thick black smoke billowed out, and almost immediately a red glow appeared in the windows above. One worker screamed, and suddenly I didn't feel as sanguine as Demo.

Glass shattered somewhere. Several more smoke plumes eddied from under the eaves. A flaming curtain flapped in a window. One of the college kids narrated the action sportscaster style while his buddies howled. The fireman in the cherry-picker worked the levers, steering for a better angle at flames rushing along the gutter line.

That's when the building blew.

A tremendous fireball tore upward through the roof. Flaming timbers shot skyward, spinning wildly. Shingles peeled back, fluttering like bats. The cherry-picker's arm rocked, then suddenly buckled, dumping the fireman to the wet pavement with a sickening thud.

Time stopped for a single elongated second. The flames froze; the hiss of the water, the shouts of the firemen, the last echoes of the blast receded into silence. And then everything returned in a crashing rush. Several smaller explosions shook the building in quick succession. An EMS crew surrounded the injured fireman, frantically clapping an oxygen mask onto his face and lifting him onto a gurney.

The flames raged out of control, licking at the sky. Blasts of heat pushed us back into the practice range. The college kids, suddenly humbled, gaped in silence as whole sections of plywood wall cracked and splintered, layers opening like the pages of a book. Through gaping holes in the cart garage, fiberglass shells bubbled and bulged grotesquely. Batteries popped, shooting their cell caps through the air like sparklers.

Some time later, Demo pulled up wearily beside me, wiping the length of his good arm across his brow.

"I never expected . . . the readouts said . . . Maybe we opened it up wrong, created a draft. We're just gonna let it burn itself out now. Can't spread anywhere, you know?"

"What about the guy in the bucket?" I said.

"Mickey? Pretty bad, I heard," Demo said, and dragged himself back to the pumper.

Another section of wall crumbled with hissing, crackling, snapping sounds. My suddenly visible pro shop looked like hell. Literally. Club displays and clothing racks collapsed in flaming heaps. A huge golf bag dangling from a rafter ignited like a mini-Hindenburg. Yes, I had my insurance paid up. But the thought comforted me as much as being flattened by a drunken driver and knowing I could sue from my hospital bed.

Watching soon turned pointless, so I headed for my car. That's when I remembered three items no amount of insurance money could compensate: a framed photograph and the first two golf trophies I ever won. I'd carted these mementoes around with me for over twenty years. College dorm, law school rooming house, my office at Inglisi & Lenahan, a Florida apartment during my professional golf apprenticeship, and finally a glass shelf above the pro shop's cash register. Almost certainly, the fire had reduced them to curled ashes and dollops of metal.

Now I understood why my pretty Italian classmate had cried that night so many years ago. Fire consumes. It doesn't matter that you have insurance. It doesn't matter if tomorrow you'll report it to your agent and he'll cut you a check for emergency cash. Fire consumes, and more than the walls and the carpets and the furniture. It consumes the spirit, the opera that echoed while the barber cut your hair, the sudden putting contests you enjoyed with members on rainy afternoons. The Lares and Penates of the modern world.

I swallowed hard, and slammed shut the car door.

A thunderous pounding rousted me from a nightmarish sleep. In fifteen seconds of staggering down my hallway, my mind replayed the fire in super-fast motion, then plunged forward into a future haunted by insurance forms and irate members who conveniently forgot they stored their golf clubs at their own risk.

A second tremblor shook my seismograph.

"Coming, goddammit!" I opened the door and caught Det. Charles "Chicky" DiRienzo in mid-wallop. He snapped to attention and straightened his tie, which I'd have wagered was a clip-on.

"Your shop burned down last night," he said. One cheek peeled back slightly.

"What did you say?"

"Your shop. A fire. Last night." The other cheek trembled, stifling a grin. The bastard thought he bore me the bad news and relished it.

"That's what I thought you said." I stroked my chin, eyeing him, anger rising in my gut. "Haven't you learned doorstep manner?"

"What?" DiRienzo's big eyes flattened to a matte finish. He passed his wadded sport jacket from one hand to the other.

"You know, like a doctor's bedside manner. You ring the doorbell. You ask to come inside. You suggest I sit down. You tell me you have some bad news. And then . . ."

"You already knew," he blurted.

"Demo Mike phoned me. I saw most of it."

"Yeah, well, that's good because the fire marshall wants to talk to you."

"Does he suspect arson?"

"The fire marshall assumes arson in any structural fire unless and until he proves otherwise," said DiRienzo. He unfurled his jacket and punched his arms into the sleeves, narrowly missing me. "And whoever torched that place is in trouble. Big trouble. Mickey Byrne died an hour ago. So let's cut the wiseass remarks and don't say another word until you're asked a specific question."

Common decency in the face of death cried out for me to apologize for my immature harangue. But DiRienzo didn't deserve common decency, and besides, he wasn't Mickey Byrne's keeper. I dressed quickly and followed DiRienzo down the apartment stairs and into his unmarked Plymouth.

I quit the practice of law when my partner, Big Jim Inglisi, became Judge Inglisi. I could have continued the firm under my own name and waited until the county's voters tossed the Judge off the bench at the end of his term. But I needed a break for many reasons, and one of them was a growing distaste for the job. Even in a small town like Milton, the practice of law deteriorated into idiotic posturing on behalf of unreasonable clients. Simple real estate closings became adversarial pissing contests. Routine business deals detonated into lawsuits.

"You can't be introspective," Big Jim told me. "You must divorce the kernel of your being from what you do during the workday."

I didn't buy it. First of all, "kernel of being" was not in Big Jim's parlance, so he obviously ripped that advice out of a lawyer's self-help manual. Second, with every firm victory, we planted another time bomb in a minefield of enemies.

Case in point: Chicky DiRienzo. When I was a green young attorney and DiRienzo was a rookie patrolman, the cops arrested a teenager for a string of burglaries on Poningo Point. The kid lived on the Point himself—the son of some stock market muckamuck—and Big Jim, who continuously trolled Milton's toniest neighborhood for business, landed the defense. At the trial, Big Jim tossed me the job of cross-examining the prosecution's main witness, Patrolman DiRienzo. Even then, Chicky's childish understanding of the Constitution and the wide gaps in his deductive reasoning presaged the type of detective he'd become. The cross-examination was short, brutal, and effective. The kid got off, and I added my first enemy to the firm's list.

Ironically, none of Big Jim's enemies held grudges. He injected just enough buffoonery into his style that people he outright screwed would laugh as if to say, "There he goes again." I was too sullen and serious in my execution; nobody laughed.

Exiting Milton for my golf apprenticeship and returning as a golf pro defused some of the time bombs. Not Chicky's. And after I solved the Sylvester Miles murder while he sniffed up all the wrong trees, he even added a few sticks of dynamite.

DiRienzo squelched the radio chatter and deadfooted the Plymouth to MCC in silence. Despite myself, I noticed some refinements to his bovine image. He'd shaved his squiggle mustache and let his buzzcut grow out, which brought his head into approximate proportion with his bulk. He also traded his sharkskin suit for a professorial look of corduroy pants and tweed jacket. Not the most practical fibers for early August, but then DiRienzo could crack a sweat in a meat locker. I imagined opera lessons couldn't be far behind.

We rounded the clubhouse circle. Several of the restaurant workers sat Indian-style on the grass, staring down at the charred, dripping shell. The white stucco of the pro shop walls had blackened. Most of the monkey house roof had blown, then burned away. Jagged holes gaped in the plywood walls of the cart garage.

DiRienzo eased in between the last remaining fire truck and a Chevy with a county official sticker on the rear window and a brass badge on the bumper. A group of firemen, bareheaded but still wearing boots and slickers, nodded at DiRienzo but pointedly ignored me.

"Surchuck around?" said DiRienzo.

"Still inside," said one of the firemen.

DiRienzo told me to stay put. He ducked under a line of fluorescent orange tape and disappeared into the rubble.

I leaned against the hood of the Plymouth and stared at the building I'd known so well for so many years. The pro shop had been built back in the early 1960s, a small, square building with a steeply peaked roof like a Swiss chalet. No basement, no fancy accoutrements, just a place where the pro could sell balls and tees and the occasional set of golf clubs. Shortly afterward, the club tacked on the bag room, a storage area twice the size of the shop where members could park their golf clubs in between rounds. Again, nothing fancy. Plywood walls, minimal insulation, bare bulb lighting, and no heat.

In the late 1960s, after electric carts became the rage, the club added a garage along the entire length of the shop. Above the garage, the club built six rooms, each outfitted with a full bath. Originally envisioned as a penthouse, the club hoped to accommodate guests and prospective members of substance in convenient luxury. But the grand idea never materialized, and the rooms lay empty until the late 1970s when the club's restaurant manager, Eduardo Rojas, installed his immigrant workers.

Faces came and went; sometimes as many as thirty workers crowded into those six rooms. Immigration agents raided yearly, hauling away the illegals. In my four years as golf pro, the monkey house population stabilized at twelve. Immigration paid it no mind.

Someone shouted from inside, and the four firemen waded into the building. They emerged a few minutes later, carrying large mayonnaise jars filled with charred rubble to the trunk of the Chevy. On their next trip inside, the firemen lugged out a bunch of metal containers. My varnishes, turpentines, thinners, paints, and a jug of gasoline. All were deformed, blackened, bulged, split along their seams. The firemen lined up the containers on a clear patch of macadam. Each was tagged, but I couldn't read the writing. A skinny kid balancing a minicam on his shoulder climbed out of the pro shop and taped the containers with a slow sweep of the lens.

DiRienzo poked out of the shop next, like a movie dinosaur cracking out of its eggshell. A short, red-faced man followed carrying a small satchel. He barked orders to the skinny kid, then focused on me.

"You Lenahan?" he said. I nodded. "Paul Surchuck, county fire marshall."

He shook my hand firmly. Navy blue epaulets decorated his denim work shirt. A gut the size of a basketball cantilevered over the waist of his hipboots.

"Any idea what started the fire?" I said.

"Some, what about you?"

I shook my head, surprised by the quickness of his response more than anything else.

"Doesn't matter. You're here to help me find out. The detective tells me you witnessed the fire last night." Surchuck's voice disintegrated into a wheeze. He reached through the Chevy's open window and plucked a pack of cigarettes from the dash.

"I saw most of it," I said.

"How'd you get to the scene so fast?" Surchuck whacked the Chevy's lighter with the palm of his hand, waited about two seconds, and yanked it out. The cigarette caught slowly.

"A friend in the fire department phoned me when he recognized the call involved the shop. His name is Demosthenes Michaelides, but he goes by Demo Mike."

Surchuck looked at DiRienzo, who grunted in corroboration.

"Okay, you got here. What did you see?" Surchuck slipped a tiny tape recorder out of his shirt pocket, telling me I didn't mind being taped rather than asking if I did. DiRienzo opened a notebook.

I explained finding Demo at the new pumper's computer monitor and watching him work the infrared sensor, which showed something hot at approximately the center of the first floor.

"Near a closet?" said Surchuck.

"That's what I thought," I said, and went on to say I saw the first plume of smoke under the monkey house eaves a few minutes later.

"What color was the smoke?"

"Dark gray, maybe black. Hard to tell because the floodlights were so bright. Then one of the firemen opened a door."

"Which door?" said Surchuck.

I pointed to a dark cavity in the bag room's outer wall.

"It opens into a stairway leading directly up to the monkey house."

"What the hell's the monkey house?" said Surchuck.

"Sorry. The six rooms above the cart garage. The restaurant workers live there."

"Monkey house, huh? If that don't beat all." He scanned the broken windows and cratered roof. "Smoke came out of the door?"

"Lots of it. Thick and black."

Surchuck ushered me to the containers. He eased into a crouch and lifted a gallon tin by sticking a pencil through its bent handle.

"You recognize this?"

"That's a polyurethane," I said.

"Not just any poly. This is Imron, right?"

I nodded. DiRienzo scribbled diligently.

"What do you use that for?" said Surchuck.

"Refinishing wood clubheads," I said.

Surchuck slid the tin from the pencil, scuttled past a bloated turpentine jug, and tapped the pen on the rim of a lopsided can.

"What about this?"

"Lacquer thinner," I said. "I use it to clean the spray guns and brushes."

"Do you know storing these two flammables in that building violates the local fire code? Were you ever cited for it?"

I said nothing. I knew storing this stuff was a violation, just as Surchuck knew I probably stashed it whenever the town fire inspector made one of his unsurprising calls.

"Did you store anything else in there that might have caused a large explosion?" he said.

"Like what?"

"Like a large quantity of gasoline. Or propane."

"You see the only gas I kept there," I said. "Why would I use propane?"

"Well, for one thing, I didn't see any fixed heating system in the garage, or in that other area—" He turned to DiRienzo and snapped his fingers.

"The golf club storage room," DiRienzo read from his pad.

"Bag room," I said. "That's because there isn't any heating system. I use a kerosene heater near my workbench in the winter."

DiRienzo stopped scribbling. "You said kerosene?"

"Right. It's a small unit, made of white porcelain. I drain it every spring and store it on a shelf under the workbench. It should still be there, if the workbench is."

"I'll make a note to look," said Surchuck.

He asked about the cart garage. I explained the club leased a fleet of fifty electric carts from the Boland Brothers Cart Company. Under the contract, my staff performed the routine daily maintenance, like cleaning the shells, watering the battery cells, and recharging the batteries each night. If anything complicated needed repairs, Boland sent a mechanic.

"Who is on your staff?" said Surchuck.

"My shop assistant, Pete O'Meara, and myself."

DiRienzo sucked air, but I shot him a challenging glance. He hated Pete, and firmly believed the kid's checkered criminal history would be an unbroken black line if interlopers like Judge Inglisi and myself hadn't meddled with decent police work. He could tell Surchuck whatever he wanted in private; he wasn't going to accuse Pete of torching the place in front of me.

"You both have access to the building?" said Surchuck.

"We each have a set of four keys. Pro shop, garage, the door between the garage and the bag room, the door between the bag room and the shop."

"Anyone else have keys?"

"No one."

"What about the restaurant workers?"

"Keys to the stairway door, I suppose. No copies of ours, that's for sure."

"And no internal access between their area and yours?"

"None that I ever saw."

"Who closed up last night?" said Surchuck.

"I did. The last carts came in about eight-fifteen. It's getting dark earlier now."

"And nothing was amiss?"

"Not a thing."

"All right." Surchuck snapped off the tape recorder. "Just one more thing to show you."

He and DiRienzo led me around the front of the shop and through the caddie yard. The pro shop's air conditioner had tumbled out of the wall and crushed one of the wooden caddie benches. A small oak in the corner of the yard stood with its trunk blackened and its leaves shrivelled.

Far out in the ninth fairway, a good hundred fifty yards from the shop, two slickered firemen stood in a sand bunker. A fairway sprinkler chucked, spraying them with water. As we neared the bunker, I saw a large metal cylinder embedded at an angle in the sand like a dud artillery shell. Its visible end, once a flat circle of metal, bulged into a jagged, blackened gash.

"Know what this is?" said Surchuck. The spray swept past, pelting us with cold drops we all ignored.

"Never saw it," I said.

"You've never seen this before?" Surchuck said incredulously.

"No."

"That cylinder," said Surchuck, "killed a damn good fireman."

CHAPTER
2

I ducked into the caddymaster's shack and watched Surchuck and Di-Rienzo climb the hill toward the restaurant workers. Surchuck could tape the interview, but I wondered how DiRienzo's note-taking would wrestle with whatever Spanish dialect those guys spoke. On a day like today, you take your humor where you find it.

Despite the early hour, I reached my insurance agent by phone. After a brief stab at commiseration, he reminded me that the policy he shoved under my puss four years ago paid twenty percent of the estimated loss as emergency cash. He'd scramble a claims rep as soon as the main office opened. Committed to at least a few hours of waiting, I phoned the Village Coffee Shoppe and asked for Jackie Mack.

When I quit law to become a golf pro, I aimed for the PGA Tour. Six years after earning my card as a bona fide member of the Professional Golfers Association, my attempts at playing on the Tour were the stuff of myth: Sisyphus rolling his stone; Tantalus dipping his chin in the lake; Ixion lashed to his wheel.

I blew my best chance right after my apprenticeship ended in Florida. The PGA Tour officials "lost" my application for the Qualifying School, an annual tournament to fill Tour exemption spots vacated by last season's money-list bottom-dwellers. They had their reasons, and the reasons don't much matter now. Sometimes, in my more charitable moments, the reasons even make sense.

So I've spent my professional golf career as the pro at the Milton Country Club, the same club where I caddied as a boy and where I competed as a high school golfer. And I've tried to insinuate myself onto the Tour. I usually grab sponsor's exemptions for a couple of tournaments when the Tour swings through the Northeast every summer. Under a complicated set of rules, anyone who finishes in the top ten of a tournament automatically receives a berth in the next week's event. I still have visions of cracking the top ten and leaving Milton forever, like a comet breaking the gravitational bonds of the sun and spinning off into interstellar space. But that's not happened yet.

Last October, I finished fifth in the national Club Professional Championship. I picked up a nice paycheck and even landed a few advertising endorsements in golf magazines. But the most important prize was an automatic berth in the PGA Championship, one of professional golf's four grand slam events. By happy coincidence, the nearby Winged Foot Golf Club hosted this year's PGA, which meant I could compete with golf's finest players and still crawl home to my own bed each night.

For ten months, the idea of playing in a "major" floated in the warm realm of fantasy. Fuzzy images of myself paired with Greg Norman or Nick Price or Fred Couples filled my idle moments. Come August, icy reality chilled my nerves. I needed to prepare. Not on the Milton Country Club fairways, not on the practice tee, not in the backyard. I needed to see my shots fly down Winged Foot's fairways, across Winged

Foot's skies. I needed to putt Winged Foot's greens. So with the tournament one week away, I finagled a practice round at Winged Foot. I would hit about 200 shots while Jackie Mack, my special tournament caddie, annotated a yardage booklet like a copy of *Ulysses*.

Ian MacEwan, alias Jackie Mack, was the best caddie this side of those Tour regulars who earned single nicknames like Brazilian soccer stars. He thoroughly understood every strategic and mechanical aspect of the game. He read greens with a surveyor's accuracy. Nothing escaped his senses, not the subtlest nuance of a golf course's condition, not the slightest puff of wind, not even the minutest change in barometric pressure. More importantly, he tailored his personality, his demeanor, and his tone of voice to fit his golfer's temperament. Jackie saw himself and his golfer as a team, not two egos crashing into each other.

"The game and I just mesh," he once told me. "It's like I walk on a golf course and my senses expand. I hand my golfer a club, and I can feel from the way he grabs it exactly how his shot will fly."

His skills kept him in constant demand. The top players at Milton Country Club wanted Jackie Mack whispering his sage advice into their ears. Successful businessmen, who appreciated talent in any field, beamed with pride when Jackie toted their bags. A few, who saw a glint of promise through Jackie's unpolished exterior, tried to fix him with gainful employment.

"Everyone's disappointed in my life except me," Jackie said after refusing yet another job offer.

Jackie brought unpredictability to a high art. He might disappear for weeks, sometimes during the heart of the summer. Rumors would fly in the caddie yard, with reports of Jackie Mack sightings in unsavory places. Then he'd turn up without warning, sleeping on the caddie bench, stinking and unshaven, his curls matted. Once he even disappeared to pee while his foursome putted on the ninth green and didn't return until November.

The golfers tossed these antics off to typical caddie quirkiness. The caddies revered Jackie as a mad genius. I suspected a shiftless, opportunistic side, which showed itself after a golf ball conked Jackie on the head as he stood over a hill crest on one of MCC's blind holes. He hired a lawyer to sue the country club, the golf course architect (long dead), and every golfer who happened to be within four fairways of the accident. Members shunned him. For two straight months, the fabled Jackie Mack couldn't buy a loop. Caddie yard scuttlebutt said Jackie planned on winning a million dollar verdict and retiring to Florida or Switzerland. A sober-minded county judge dashed Jackie's dreams. He called the lawsuit "completely frivolous," and threw Jackie and his lawyer out of court.

Curiously, Jackie stabilized after this debacle. Caddie yard wags theorized the golf ball knocked some sense into his head. The members, particularly the defendants in the lawsuit, tsk-tsked about hubris. More likely, Jackie's newly discovered sense of responsibility emanated from Melvin Tucker. Tucker was not the club's best golfer and, if the caddies were to be believed, not the best tipper. But he hired Jackie as his steady caddie, and demanded Jackie's services every day. I practically had to kiss Tucker's ring to pry Jackie away for the PGA.

Apparently, I'd kissed Tucker's ring in vain because Jackie hadn't shown up at the Coffee Shoppe, and our appointed meeting time passed a half hour ago.

"If he does show," I told the owner, "tell him the practice round is cancelled."

News travels fast in a small town like Milton, faster still in the working-class neighborhood of Limerick where Mickey Byrne and I lived a few blocks apart. A huge crowd soon ringed the burned-out building. Caddies, club members, Limerick denizens unaccustomed to the fancy trappings inside country club walls but who felt entitled to see where one of their own had died. A police van descended, and two cops erected a barricade with blue sawhorses and fluorescent orange tape.

At 8:00, Pete O'Meara pushed his mountain bike up the tenth fairway. He dropped the bike in the caddie yard, wiped his brow with the sleeve of his hockey jersey, and screwed his baseball cap tight on his head.

"Holy shit, what happened?"

"Fire marshall's investigating," I said.

Out on the ninth fairway, two firemen dragged the metal cylinder on a hand truck.

"What the hell's that?" said Pete.

"That's what killed Mickey Byrne. No one's told me exactly, but I think it ignited and rocketed through the roof. You mean you've never seen it?"

"No way, man."

Pete's face combined the tall forehead and sweeping chin of clan O'Meara with the deep summer tan and dark eyes from his Bolivian mother. Those eyes narrowed as he caught sight of DiRienzo towering above the restaurant workers at the top of the clubhouse hill.

"Bet that bastard wants to talk to me," he said.

"He will. Answer politely, okay?"

"Hey, I'm always polite. But when he starts acting like I'm lying, I go ballistic."

"Keep cool this time," I said. The two firemen pushed the hand truck past us, huffing with effort. "And don't use the word ballistic. It won't sit well today."

Surchuck and DiRienzo came down to the yard while the firemen lifted the cylinder into the back of the fire truck. Their questions to Pete covered the same ground as mine. Pete answered with none of his teenage surliness, and DiRienzo said nothing to provoke him. Maybe, I thought, these two antagonists had turned a corner toward a more mature adversarial relationship. It never struck me as odd that DiRienzo didn't chum Pete's waters with the usual bait. But then again, I'm an optimist.

People piled in all morning. I holed up in the caddymaster's shack, basically hiding from anyone I recognized from the club or from Limerick, and keeping an eye out for someone resembling an insurance man. Surchuck and DiRienzo both left about noon, the last fire truck shortly afterward. Some golfers arrived to play, at least those few who didn't store their clubs in the bag room.

A splotch of red flashed around the clubhouse circle, and a few seconds later the caddymaster's shack vibrated with the hum of a turbo-charged engine. The engine idled down, then cut out. I found Judge Inglisi in the midst of his exiting procedure. The Ferrari's door thrown open, the Judge's stubby legs reaching toward the ground, his girth wedged between the steering wheel and the leather seat.

Judge Inglisi and I had practiced law together for eight years, but our history went back to my days as a caddie and his as one of the sorriest golfers ever to line up a putt. He gave up golf years ago, but still followed the game as a spectator and my career, he said, out of morbid curiosity.

The Judge squirmed, finally getting enough purchase to pop himself out of the car.

"Hell of a goddam thing," he said, shaking loose his linen suit as he waddled around the shack. "Paul Surchuck on this?"

"Left a little while ago with DiRienzo."

The Judge snorted. "At least they have one brain between them. Surchuck's a good man. He's testified before me on numerous occasions. He'll turn this thing upside down and inside out."

He leaned on a sawhorse, testing its strength. Being high summer, the nimbus of white hair mid-latitude on his head was shaved as slick as a green at Augusta. But his eyebrows were as dark as the day I'd met him, and they knit together as he surveyed the damage.

"How'd you fare?"

"Total loss."

"I'm sure you have insurance up the ass."

"Not for everything, and the PGA is next week. This doesn't help the psyche."

"That's why I'm here," said the Judge.

It figured. My shop burns to the ground, and the Judge dusts off his version of a Knute Rockne pep talk. Who can fathom the judicial mind, especially Judge Inglisi's. A group of caddies stood nearby, bantering in pidgin English. The Judge cocked an ear and frowned. I expected one of his usual comments about the imminent downfall of civilization, but he motioned me toward the lilac bush.

"Jackie Mack fell in front of a train this morning," he said.

I groped for a lilac branch. In the sudden silence, the Ferrari's engine clicked and hissed as it cooled.

"When?" I said.

"About 8:45."

Despite the shock, my mind immediately constructed a narrative. 8:45. More than an hour after we should have met at the Coffee Shoppe.

"Don't go blabbing this because no one knows. Naturally I found out because Deirdre called." The Judge paused dramatically, partly because he reveled in his self-importance, mostly because he thought me a lunkhead for not marrying Deirdre the moment I met her. And, being a judge, no amount of subsequent history or appeals to reason would dissuade him. "She was waiting for a train when Jackie went down. The engineer slammed on the brakes, but too late. Deirdre jumped onto the tracks to see if she could help. But there wasn't much left of him in one piece."

"Jesus Christ," I said.

"Took EMS and the police an hour to scrape him up. That's when Deirdre called. She was pretty upset because she was the only person who recognized Jackie, but police told her not to say a goddam word because informing next of kin is their job, and they weren't going to do that until they had positive I.D."

"No one else noticed him?" I said. Jackie stood out in most crowds with his huge mane of curly blond hair, skin burned bright red from hours in the summer sun, and a permanent squint that drew the corners of his mouth into a perpetual smile.

"I didn't say no one noticed him. I said no one recognized him." The Judge opened the Ferrari's door and burrowed in behind the wheel. "You know Milton Station. Once the stockbrokers clear out in the early A.M., you might as well be in South America."

"What the hell do I do now?" I said.

"Get yourself another caddie," said the Judge. "Sure as hell is easier than getting yourself a new pro shop."

Not long after the Judge zoomed away, my insurance agent reached me on the caddyshack phone to tell me the claims rep was delayed.

"Any problem?" I said.

"Not at all. Are your business records intact?"

"Doubt it. The shop's pretty well gutted."

"Try to reconstruct them as best you can. Supplier lists, bank records. The rep will be along. His name is Frank Platt."

I had only half my suppliers listed on the back of a scorecard when a club worker delivered a message. Georgina Newland wanted to discuss plans for a temporary shop ASAP. I handed the scorecard to Pete with instructions to finish the list and to interrupt me the moment Platt arrived.

———

MCC's clubhouse was a neo-gothic stone castle built in the late 1860s by a New York City socialite and Civil War draft dodger named Sheldon Whitby. In the 1890s, a man named Tilford bought the castle and routed the original twelve golf holes through the surrounding land. Seventy years later, three wealthy Miltonians bought the estate, expanded the seedy course to a regulation eighteen holes, and created Milton Country Club. The club converted the castle's basement into a locker room, the main floor into a restaurant, bar, and ballroom, and the second floor into administrative offices. The restaurant was leased to an outside concessionaire, who was free to solicit business from the general public in return for a percentage of the profits. Smart business move, since Whitby, as the castle was called, was listed in the National Registry and was a popular site for weddings because of stunning harbor views from the terrace.

Recently, the administrative offices outgrew the cramped second floor and relocated in the north wing of the main level. I rarely visited the offices and had little direct contact with the executive committee except for the yearly formality of re-upping my contract. The past October, the committee took the odd step of inviting me to answer questions at the regular monthly meeting. The topic: renovating the pro shop/cart garage complex. I sat at the end of a long oaken table while the committee, six men and Georgina Newland, peppered me with questions. I felt less like a witness than a mouse in a basket of vipers. The renovation project sounded like a sweetheart deal for a local contractor, and I couldn't gauge which member of the committee played what angle. All I knew was that the plan threatened to disrupt my life for a year. My considered suggestion, a kind of reverse *reductio ad absurdum*, was to raze the entire building and start from scratch. They dismissed me summarily, and that was the last I heard of renovation plans.

The door to the admin suite was ajar. Georgina Newland stood at the window, staring down at the shell of the pro shop. She wore a pink blouse and a white golf skirt that was wrinkled and creased from sitting, but otherwise perfect. Real perfect.

I cleared my throat, and she greeted me.

"I came here at nine to play," she said, as if stealing my thought that her outfit seemed out of context today. "I had no idea what happened. I haven't left this office since."

She sat wearily in a swivel chair and crossed her legs. One thigh curved just right over the edge of the desktop.

Club opinion on Georgina Newland varied widely. The caddies salivated whenever she sallied into the yard, her golf skirt riding mid-thigh on her ex-Rockette legs. The MCC executive committee, less awash in testosterone, resented the first female member of their previously all-male bastion. To them, her sweeping plans to "reimagine" Milton Country Club smacked of hysteria. In the psychiatric sense.

Like the caddies, I felt a tug from Georgina's classy features, long auburn hair, and figure that walked off the pediment of a Greek temple. And being older than the caddies, I also understood the true magnificence of a beautiful woman who topped forty. Yet, like the executive committee, I resisted her plans for general club improvement as annoyances without any real upside.

Between these extremes, my personal interaction with Georgina had been ambiguous. Her first year as an MCC member coincided with mine as pro. A rank beginner, she signed up for a whole slate of lessons. The first installment went well, I thought. Her grip was a mess, her swing stiff and awkward. But with a few weeks of intense work, I foresaw that long body whipping into the ball with power. I even sensed an attraction the way she lowered her eyes when I addressed her directly, and discreetly scoped me when I demonstrated various aspects of the golf swing.

She cancelled the remaining lessons the next day. She never explained why; I never asked. And our encounters in the meantime were cordial but unenlightening.

"The fire marshall interviewed me this morning," I said. "Has he spoken to anyone else?"

"Not to me," said Georgina. Her eyes swept me, like a laser guidance system that illuminates a jet fighter just before the SAM missiles fly. "I suppose he'll find faulty wiring or an overloaded circuit in the monkey house. I suspected something like this could happen. Those rooms didn't meet the fire code, you know."

I didn't, but nothing surprised me.

She spread a survey map on the desk and pinned down the curling edges with books and an empty ashtray.

"One thing I've kept in mind is that the club is the golf course, and the golf course didn't burn. So I've concentrated on getting us up and running as quickly as possible." Her voice carried an unusually sharp tone. Not quite defiance, not quite challenging. More like she wanted to remind me it was the *female* member of the executive committee carrying the ball for the old boys.

"Without a garage," she said, "electric carts are useless because we can't expose the battery chargers to rain. The only other option is gasoline carts."

"We do have caddies," I said.

Georgina scowled. "The membership wants carts. But Boland doesn't lease gas carts, so I lined up Tartan Golf Cart Company to deliver a fleet of fifty."

She waved a pencil over a section of the map. In real life, that was a grassy area behind the starter shack where members practiced chipping in a minefield laid by the greenskeeper's collie.

"A contractor will build a chain-link pen here," she said. "We'll lock the carts inside at night."

"Better think about barbed wire along the top of the fence."

"I'll note that," she said. "I've ordered a large trailer for your shop. It will have heat, air conditioning, phones, merchandise racks. No storage facility, but I don't think you mind."

"When can I expect it?" I said.

"Tomorrow," Georgina said with a proud smile blooming on her face. "I couldn't have my pro inconvenienced for too long, especially before the PGA."

She lifted the book and ashtray. The map rolled up by itself. I felt her radar again as I left the office. Sometimes I wonder if I emit signals when Deirdre and I are on the outs. Or maybe women just know my history and set their watches.

CHAPTER

3

By five P.M., the gawkers disappeared, the caddies mounted their bikes, the caddymaster threatened me with eviction. I made one more call to my insurance agent, who curtly told me Platt was on his way. Soon, Pete and I stood alone in the depressingly quiet yard. I almost blabbed about Jackie Mack. But word hadn't yet leaked out, and a promise is a promise. Between Jackie Mack and Mickey Byrne, there would be little joy in Limerick tonight.

Bored by the wait and intrigued by what might remain in the shop, I ducked under the barricade. The inside smelled like the world's dirtiest ashtray, with traces of rubber and plastic thrown in for the sake of nausea. Sunlight slanted through holes in the roof, highlighting scenes of chaos. Sweaters and slacks lay in twisted, blackened heaps. A pile of golf shoes cascaded from a shelf, their boxes burned away. Golf clubs stood singed and gripless on their display racks. The wire skeleton of a golf bag dangled from a rafter. A sludge of wet ash and fallen ceiling tiles coated the floor. Somewhere water dripped a rhythmic ping on metal.

As my eyes adjusted to the dimness, I saw just how whimsical a fire could be. Parts of some walls had burned through, others stood untouched. One side of a rafter was charred, the other side pristine. But the area I most wanted to search was pretty well destroyed. A rafter had collapsed, crushing the cash register and shattering the glass of the sales counter. Behind that, three feet of charcoal clogged my tiny office.

I started clawing at a spot in front of the counter. The ceiling tiles hadn't burned. But they were damp and heavy with hose water, and split like soggy crackers as I peeled them up. I dug through strata of tiles, finding lodes of tees, balls, gloves, all the minor odds and ends that exploded out of the counter when the rafter hit. I sorted them in separate piles, for no reason other than I didn't want to dig them up a second time. I'd cleared a three by three patch of remarkably green carpeting when Pete crouched beside me.

"What are you looking for?" he said.

"Remember the things I kept on the shelf behind the counter?"

"That old junk?"

"Those mementoes are older than you, and sometimes more relevant to my existence."

"Take it easy, huh? I'm just busting chops."

"Stop busting and start sifting."

"But, Kieran, you won't—"

A bright light snapped on, freezing us.

"What the hell's going on here?" growled a voice.

I scrambled to my feet. The light bounced closer, blinding me.

"I said, what are you doing here?"

I blocked the light with my hand, but couldn't make him out.

"Looking for some things," I said.

The light descended, slowly circling the piles I'd made.

"This place is off limits."

"I know. Sorry. I just wanted to look for the stuff because anyone else would toss it as junk."

"You must be Lenahan, huh? We need to talk. Make sure you trace the same path you came in on. You too, kid."

"Kid," Pete snorted beside me.

"Shut up and follow me," I said.

The man waiting outside looked like a racetrack tout clinging to the rail near the finish line. Gum rubber shoes, plaid pants, green Banlon shirt, matching nylon snap-brim fedora. Pete, catching up, choked back a laugh. We had stocked that exact hat for months and never sold one.

"Frank Platt, from the claims office," he said.

"Mr. Platt, am I happy to see you," I said.

If Platt shared my sentiments, he contained his enthusiasm. He tucked a thick file folder under one arm and waved the flashlight with his free hand.

"Is there someplace we can talk?"

"My car," I said.

We cut across the yard. Platt spread his file folder on the hood, humming tunelessly as he flipped through forms, sheets of handwritten notes, photos of the shop at the inception of my insurance policy.

"Your agent told you I'd need business records," he said. He had blunt features and pockmarks on his leathery cheeks. "Let's have them."

"Everything in the shop was destroyed," I said, handing over the scorecard.

"What's this?" said Platt.

"A list of my suppliers. My agent told me to put it together because all my inventory records were destroyed. I keep my bank records at home, and I've been here all day. But basically, I deposit my inventory receipts, cart rental receipts, and lesson fees into separate accounts. You should be able to reconstruct my sales from that."

"I won't. One of our accounting jocks will." Platt ran a stubby finger down the list, then slipped the scorecard into its proper spot in the folder. "I've got to tell you, there is a lot that bothers me."

"Like what?" I said.

"Like every year you lower your coverage on August one. This year, you increased it by forty, fifty grand."

"Usually my inventory tails off this time of year, and I don't restock until spring," I said. "That's why my agent offered sliding coverage. But this year I decided to stock up with closeouts."

"What the hell are closeouts?" said Platt.

"New but out-of-date merchandise. I wanted to expand my shop business, so I ordered a few hundred sets of golf clubs, a load of last spring's fashions, and a hundred dozen cashmere sweaters from an inventory liquidator in Illinois. Pete here agreed to work right up through Christmas."

Pete broke out in a dopey grin.

"Selling closeouts?" said Platt.

"Lots of pros do it," chimed Pete.

"The clubs are last year's models by now," I said. "I can buy them cheap, sell them cheap, and still turn a profit. Same with the spring apparel, which goes as cruisewear for people taking warm weather vacations. The cashmere, well, everyone likes cashmere."

"You had all this stuff in your shop?" said Platt.

"No, it never arrived," I said.

"Yeah, and we can't get the liquidator on the phone," said Pete.

Platt flipped to the list of suppliers.

"You have a Peoria Liquidating Company listed here. You just said the closeouts never arrived."

"That's a mistake," I said, glaring at Pete. "I'm not making a claim for that."

"Okay," said Platt. He scratched Peoria Liquidating. "You guys want to tell me what you were doing in the shop just now?"

"Looking for some mementoes," I said. "Nothing I'd include in a claim."

"Kieran," said Pete. "I told you—"

I shot Pete a milk-curdling glance.

"What?" said Platt.

"Nothing, man," said Pete. "Mementoes, like Kieran said. I know what that shit means to him."

"What were these mementoes?" said Platt.

"A couple of tacky trophies and an autographed photo of Arnold Palmer."

Platt grunted and made some illegible notes on the inside flap of his folder.

"Mr. Lenahan, is your shop business incorporated?" he said.

"No. I run it as a sole proprietorship."

Platt thumbed through his file, humming again, but louder than before. I got the feeling he was like a wind-up toy that hits a wall, spins around, and starts rolling again.

"I'll need your credit records," he said. "Personal credit. Card accounts, auto loans, whatever."

"What for?" I said.

"Never mind. Do you own your own home?"

"I rent."

"I'll need the name of your landlord."

"Wait a second. My agent told me I should speak to you about emergency money. What about that?"

"Emergency money?" Platt laughed. "I've already spoken to the fire marshall. His preliminary report finds arson."

"Targeted at my shop?"

"That's all I'm at liberty to say," said Platt. "Once the company hears the word arson, it won't make any payments of emergency funds."

"You think I burned my own goddam shop?"

"Hey look, pal, don't get nasty with me. The fire marshall tells me about flammables you stored in your workshop. You tell me about a liquidating company you can't raise on the phone. Ever take a lie detector test, Mr. Lenahan?" Platt gathered his file, set the hat on his head, and walked away with the jaunty step of someone who just hit a trifecta.

"Man, does he suck or what?" said Pete.

"You know what sucks, Pete, is you trying to help."

"Hey, like I'm supposed to know not to list Peoria Liquidating because we didn't get the stuff yet."

"I'm talking about you piping up when he asked why we were snooping around the shop. Don't you see he's trying to catch us in a lie?"

"Yeah, well, I just wanted you to know you wouldn't find those mementoes because they weren't there the day of the fire."

"They weren't?"

"That's what I was trying to tell you. I saw they were gone over the weekend. I figured you finally got embarrassed and took them home."

"I didn't touch them," I said.

"Must have been a real asshole to swipe them," said Pete.

The clubhouse lounge was bleak as February. Chilly gusts of air poured out of the ceiling vents. Dark panelled walls sucked up light from the Tiffany chandeliers. A Spanish language news broadcast blared from a TV perched above the top shelf liquors. Jose Rojas leaned against the cash register, the phone against one ear, his finger in the other.

I swirled the last cottage fry through a drop of ketchup and shot another glance at the three busboys sitting on a bench near the kitchen door. They held the exact pose as when my dinner arrived, their arms folded across their chests, their heads tilted as if cocking their ears toward a distant sound. Or watching me. I couldn't read their eyes in the shadows.

Jose hung up the phone and came back to my spot, hard against a pillar at a turn in the bar. Unlike the other workers, Jose enjoyed exercising his English with customers. I sensed more in his small talk than the idle chatter calculated to elicit tips. Jose yearned to assimilate, and to find work in the United States on a par with the engineering degree he said he earned at a university in Bolivia.

Jose was normally a jovial sort, something a medieval doctor or a modern psychiatric quack would predict from his endomorphic physique. He wore his jet black hair in one of those trendy cuts, shaved around the ears and long on top, with two pincer shaped locks curving to his cheekbones. His looks and his demeanor set him apart from the other workers, and from his older brother, the dour Eduardo, who managed the restaurant. Melancholy gripped Jose's mood tonight, understandable since he'd just been burned out of his home. But he remembered the strand of conversation the phone call had interrupted, and he picked it up immediately.

"I lock up about twelve, twelve-thirty last night," he said. "Eduardo stayed to do the books. I went down the hill. The monkey house was quiet. We had three weddings in three nights, and everyone was tired. A few guys who worked the last shift sat in one room drinking beer."

I turned quickly toward the three workers. One was gone; the other two hadn't moved.

"I went to bed," said Jose. He lifted my empty platter and wiped the counter with short, jabbing strokes of a towel. "Pepe woke me up a little later, after one. Said he smelled smoke. I jumped out of bed. The guys ran from room to room, but couldn't find nothing burning. You ever been up in the monkey house?"

I shook my head.

"Very drafty. You spray cologne in one room, you smell in all the others. Impossible to tell where the smoke coming from. I told everyone to run outside, then I call the fire department. The trucks come right away. Faster than I thought."

"So you reported the fire," I said. "You smelled smoke. But you didn't see any flames, right?"

"That's right."

I remembered the expressions on their faces in the glow of the fire. Something bothered me, and I wasn't sure what.

"Why the panic?"

Jose rubbed his forehead with the heel of his hand as if considering a careful answer. He started to speak, but the words gurgled in his throat. I knew why. I hadn't seen anyone, heard anyone, felt anyone's presence for that matter. But I knew Jose fell silent because Eduardo stood right behind me.

"Jose," said the voice over my shoulder, drawing out the second syllable as if in warning.

I shifted around on the barstool, gave Eduardo the low-beam grin I reserved for casual acquaintances I'd just as soon ignore.

"I need the book," Eduardo said to Jose, then nodded at me as an afterthought. He was a wisp of a man with a bandito mustache and a face as flat and impassive as a pre-Columbian statue.

How Eduardo Rojas remained as restaurant manager was a mystery that rivalled the death of the dinosaurs. It certainly wasn't his personality, which ranged between the suspicious and the outright paranoid. It certainly wasn't his charm, which surfaced as often as the Loch Ness monster. And it certainly wasn't his warm heart, not with his autocratic and imperious handling of his underlings. It could only be because he turned a profit, which, for the executive committee, forgave a host of sins.

My interaction with Eduardo was tepid at best. I'd say hello, he'd respond in a tone that made me promise myself to buy my next burger at McDonalds. The caddies whispered that Eduardo carried a switchblade under his tuxedo jacket. For once, those knuckleheads could be right.

Jose handed a thick binder across the bar. At the same time, a look passed from Eduardo to Jose. I knew our discussion about the fire had ended.

Eduardo took the book to a grinning pair of prospective newlyweds in a private dining room off the lounge.

"Where are you guys staying now?" I said to Jose.

"My brother set up cots in the locker room for us. He told us we could stay there until someone complained."

"And then?"

"He will turn a deaf ear to the complainers."

I nursed a beer and thought about how my life had changed in the last twenty-four hours. We tend to conceptualize our lives as a series of tiny stretches. Point A to Point B, Point B to Point C. Intervals of time and space too short and too close to admit danger. Last night, I locked up the pro shop door, hopped into my car, drove my accustomed route of Post Road to Beach Avenue to Poningo Point Road to Limerick and home. I fashioned a meal from leftovers, drank a beer, and turned in early. My only concern was waking up to play a practice round at Winged Foot. Point A to Point B. What could possibly happen in the interim?

Tonight I sat in the clubhouse lounge, my pro shop in ruins and my tournament caddie dead. Quite a wide gulf between Point A and Point B.

I squared my tab with Jose and stood beneath the clubhouse's *porte-cochere*. Only a thin band of pink remained where the sun had set. Mist boiled off the club's swimming pool. Crickets chirped. An onshore breeze carried the salty smell of the Sound up from the harbor. The tower floodlights suddenly dimmed, Eduardo Rojas closing up about four seconds after I left the bar.

I didn't mind my car being at home. Contemplative walks soothed me, and contemplative walks across the darkened fairways of Milton Country Club bordered on the mystical. I couldn't explain why my psyche melded so perfectly with this amalgam of rolling woodlands and flat coastline. I felt only the throb of some internal homing device luring me back whenever I felt troubled.

As I started down the slope of the parking lot, a dark limousine circled the drive. I thought for a moment of *The Great Gatsby*, and the final guest Nick Carroway saw drive up to Gatsby's front steps long after the last party ended. But the limo didn't stop at the clubhouse. It passed me on the slope and stopped broadside just outside the police barricades. The rear passenger window slid down, then up. And then the limo glided away.

The town of Milton rides the northern coast of the Long Island Sound close to where the state line juts west to claim Greenwich for Connecticut. People with the usual dim understanding of history trace the town's name either to John Milton, of *Paradise Lost* fame, or to a family of Miltons who, by pure coincidence, dominated the seat of Lord Mayor during the 1700s. In fact, Milton is a corruption of Mill Town, the early name for a settlement that sprung up around a gristmill standing where a wide, grass-choked stream called Blind Brook empties into what is now Milton Harbor.

Milton conjures images of understated wealth, inaccessible waterfront houses, ancient estates tucked in enclaves even the locals forget exist. Merchant Street, tree-lined and quaint, runs barely four blocks from the town square to the train station. The city's original telephone exchange gathered such prestige over the years that the addition of a new exchange brought protests from realtors. Yet there are neighborhoods those same realtors will avoid when showing off Milton's charms to prospective buyers. One of these is Limerick, a decidedly downscale neighborhood about a mile up the creek from that same gristmill (now a restaurant) that gave Milton its name.

I grew up in Limerick and sometimes wondered if I'd ever leave. I lived in the current species of Limerick chic: the garage apartment. Most of the pre-World War II Limerick homes had some sort of outbuilding, a garage, a barn, sometimes a toolshed. My landlord's had been a plumbing shop, which he converted in the late 1970s, when the building codes were lax and you didn't need to bribe half of City Hall for a variance.

I found my landlord fuming in the floodlit driveway.

"Look at this shit." He stabbed a hoe at a flowerbed littered with petals. "Goddam cable company. They come to replace a wire and trample my daughter's garden to hell. You talk to them, and they don't even understand English. What the hell is it with this country anymore? You try to speak your own language, and nobody understands a goddam word. Can I sue them?"

Amazing how people's perceptions of you differ from the self-image you carry around in your head. I could live in Limerick another fifty years, win fifty golf tournaments, and people would still ask me for legal advice.

I broke down a full semester of tort law into twenty-five words, stressing that damage to a flower garden wouldn't win him a major monetary judgment.

"Goddam," he said. "Everybody can sue but me."

Up in my apartment, I listened to my answering machine. I thought Deirdre might have called, if not to offer condolences for the shop at least to tell me about Jackie. But the lone message wasn't from her.

"Can't make it, Kieran," said Jackie with static crackling in the background. "But I guess you won't, either. I'll be there at the PGA for you, one way or another."

I reversed the tape and sat for a long time in silence.